I0739244

giRL
a novel

THIS BOOK HAS
A SOUNDTRACK

SCAN HERE FOR A
PLAYLIST OF EVERY
SONG MENTIONED

GIRL

Marky Watson

Gorilla Farm Press

Inquiries:
GORILLA FARM PRESS
255 N Rosemont Blvd Unit 16011
Tucson, AZ 85732-5202

gorillafarm@gmail.com

The characters and events portrayed in this book are
fictitious. Any similarity to real persons, living or dead, is
coincidental and not intended by the author.

ISBN: 979-8-9926979-1-9 (paperback)

First GORILLA FARM paperback printing: March 2025

Printed in the United States of America

Electronic edition: ISBN: 979-8-9926979-0-2 (ebook)

Library of Congress Control Number pending

Cover design by: Marco Malvado, Jr.

For Karla

CHAPTER 1

"**A**n orgasm will totally help my cramps! And anyway, period blood makes the best lube!"

That's how quickly Girl convinced me to have sex the night we met even though it was her time of month. It's no wonder she had such an easy time talking me into committing murder.

Let me be clear about something right up front, though. I think murder is stupid. I don't care how much you hate somebody. If you examine the situation and come to the conclusion that you should *kill* them? Well, sorry, but you're an idiot. For one thing, it's going to mess you up in the head for the rest of your life. On top of that, you probably won't get away with it. Hardly anybody ever does. They end up eating crappy food and wearing ugly clothes and getting diddled by their cellmate for the next fifty years.

Trust me. Murder creates far more problems than it solves. You've got to be completely, hopelessly stupid to kill another person. And I don't mean just *teenage* stupid. Or, like, *nineteen-eighty-something* stupid. I was certainly both of those. I'm talking *throw-your-life-away* stupid. *Do-anything-for-love* stupid.

Girl stupid.

Girl... I loved that name. It was like she was some sort of mythical creature.

And just to really put a head on things, my name's Guy. Guy Larsen. Seriously, what was I supposed to do? Girl and Guy? It's like we were destined to be together! Or at least that's what she told me that first night, lying next to me on my bare, unframed, flat-on-the-floor mattress, which now looked like a Jackson Pollock painting thanks to our messy menstrual mating.

I shared rent on a three-bedroom apartment with a handful of other young alt scenesters whose number fluctuated near-monthly. When I met Girl, I was paying a little extra to have my own room while other people paid less, sharing the two remaining bedrooms in combinations that frankly I didn't want to know the details of. One waifish stray was buying weed for the house and chipping in on utilities while they nested in a corner of the living room.

The apartment took up half of the top floor of a four-story building on a side street in West Hollywood, California. It was only a few blocks from Hollywood Boulevard in one direction and Sunset in the other.

I'm sure that during Hollywood's golden age, thirty or forty years earlier, the little studio-plus flats downstairs were full of would-be starlets trying to be discovered at the counter of Canter's Deli a couple of streets away. Now they mostly housed aging call girls and hopeful screenwriters.

The sun was just coming up. Girl and I had been talking all night. Well, okay, not just talking. But all of the sex and drinking and pot and food and more sex were only accessories. Like if that night was an outfit you put on to go out clubbing, those things were chains or dog collars or lip piercings. But the conversation? That was an expensive leather jacket. Or maybe a tight dress that turned heads. It was the thing you remembered. The bloody sex and everything else? Well, it was all amazing. The best ever. But still not as incredible as the words that came out of Girl's mouth.

"The rest of the world can just go die screaming. You and me, we're the only two things in the universe that matter. It's like we're the first two people... No, fuck that! We're like, you know, the first two molecules floating in nothing, just waiting to smash together and start *everything!* And we actually *found* each other so now the universe can be created! I mean—Girl and Guy? *As if!* We were so totally meant to be together! Everything that's ever happened ever ever to *anybody* was just so that you and me could find each other last night! Now we can finally stop dickin' around and actually start *living!*"

She was pretty stoned, but I didn't care. I couldn't stop listening to her talk! I wanted to find out everything about her.

"I know why I was named Guy. It was my grandfather's name. But why are you Girl?"

"My actual, like, *real* name's stupid," she said, wrinkling her nose in adorable disgust. "Abigail. Abigail Zamora. You're *soooo* lucky to have a name that has, like, meaning and history or whatever. My fucking fuck of a father hated having a last name that was at the end of the alphabet so much he decided he'd give me a name that was at the *beginning* of the alphabet. How bogus is that? Like it matters that of all the kids with Z names I'm first in the lunch line for tater tots!

"He went into a book store, found one of those 'name your baby' books, opened it up to the girl names and picked the first one. He didn't even *buy* the stupid book! Just—Abigail. There. I mean, what if the first name in that book had been, like, *Aachmedilia* or something? That's the kind of thing I was talking about when I said he hated me."

"Okay… But why *Girl?*"

"Oh. Yeah. Well, see, I went to this wrestling thing and there was this wrestler's girlfriend manager sidekick chick who called herself 'Woman.' Just… 'Woman.' I thought that was so *excellent!*"

Girl stood up on the bed and grabbed an empty Mickey's Big Mouth bottle from a row of them on the windowsill. Holding it in front of her mouth like a microphone, she raised her voice to wrestling announcer volume; *"Now coming to the ring accompanied by WOMAN!!"*

She tossed the bottle onto a pile of laundry in the corner of the room and lowered her voice back to normal, "She was totally righteous. I wanted to be just like her. So I decided I'd be *Girl!* That's *way* sexier than Woman! Woman sounds old. Girl sounds little and cute! Like me!"

She grinned and pointed to herself with both thumbs. That made me laugh, which got her laughing. Then suddenly she hitched into a higher gear and exploded with the *insane* laugh that had been my introduction to her the previous evening.

I'd been standing to one side of the stage in LoLo, the basement below Lola Lounge where bands played. The vast club—underground in both ways—was a converted utility cellar which formerly served a not-quite-downtown LA business block. A decommissioned boiler sat in the middle of the cavernous space like a steam-powered Buddha, complete with a spray-painted smiling face.

As I stepped from the narrow stairwell and made

my way through the punk rock netherworld of LoLo in my thick-soled Doc Martens, the ceiling was low enough that I could feel the tips of my eight-inch Liberty spikes playing across the hanging fluorescent fixtures fitted with blacklight tubes. Under their ultraviolet gaze, expensive porcelain tooth caps glowed beneath safety pin nose rings.

I rounded the boiler, letting my fingers dance along the globular belly for luck. My friends Recreational Surgery were performing. The bass player and guitarist were having a contest to see who could knock more acoustic tiles out of the suspended ceiling with their heads. Some people in the audience started jumping up and down to see if they could hit the panels too, but with the band members a foot or so higher because of the plywood stage, all of this fruitless bouncing just riled up tempers in the crowded mosh pit.

Two crustypunks with broad denim shoulders started pounding their fists on a smaller guy in a pink polo shirt who had innocently pogoed into them with collar-popped abandon. The poor preppy looked like he'd have been more at home in a UCLA frat bar in Westwood than in the darkest bowels of Hollywood's eastern fringe surrounded by sweaty mohawks.

Combat boots and deck shoes collided with the edge of the low stage as the three young men stumbled into the performers. There was an earsplitting *shrieeeeeeek* from the amps as microphones and guitars were jostled. Without losing the drummer's rhythm, the guys in the band shouldered the grapplers back into the flailing tumult of the audience and kept playing. At this point everyone in the vicinity had set aside any facade of disaffected rock and roll swagger in favor of an entertaining brawl—either participating or loudly spectating.

Above the drums, above the guitars, above the shouts of encouragement coming from the edges of the human pile and their counterparts of "Break it up!" I heard it: *The Ghastly Giggle*.

"KEEEE-HICK-HEE-KEE-GHEE-HICK-EE-H-H-HEE!!!!"

An absolutely crazy, creepy chipmunk chittering stabbed into my left ear. I jumped like I'd touched electricity and turned to see *what the fuck made that psychotic noise?!*

In the chaotic push and crush of the crowded dance floor, I found myself inches away from the sexiest profile I'd ever seen. She was so totally engrossed in watching the fight that I could just stand there and study her as long as I wanted; she saw nothing but the bloodshed in front of the stage. Her shoulders were pulled up and her fists were clenched under her chin. Her dark brown eyes were wide and unblinking under thick, natural brows which were almost obscene in their unsculpted, pubic fullness. She had a little smile on her matte red, pressed-together lips. Her glassy stare and body language made it clear that she was rapturously laser-focused on the scene before her.

As I was observing this blissful beauty, she bared her teeth—lipstick-mottled with a sexy gap between the front two—and made that noise again:

"HICK-KEE-HEE-GHEE-EE-H-KEE-GH-HEE-HICK-KEE!!"

It was half inhale and half exhale, like she was gasping for breath while being tickled. It sounded like something you'd do on purpose to get on somebody's nerves. I would come to learn, though, that there was absolutely nothing forced about this fake-sounding, bone-raking cackle. On the contrary; her normal, everyday, polite, *on-purpose* laugh was sweet and girlish and demure. *The Ghastly Giggle* was her unselfconscious, involuntary laugh—like when some people accidentally snort or hee-haw.

And still she didn't notice me looking at her. I said a silent prayer that the tangle of fists and mic stands and flying spittle would keep her entertained so I'd be allowed to watch her all night.

Actually *speaking* to this goddess, though, seemed beyond my capacity; despite my defensive gritty exterior, I was fundamentally shy. I'd been that way my whole life. I'd always had a hard time getting girls to think of me in *that way.* Oh, sure, I had plenty of female friends, but most of the time that's all they were—friends. One time in high school I told a girl for whom I had strong romantic feelings that I liked her. Her response? "I really like you, too, Guy. You're like a brother to me."

I was safe. Comforting. The stand-up fellow a girl could talk to about the bad boy she had a crush on. In my social circles, people started calling me "Nice Guy" and "Good Guy". It was a reputation I couldn't shake no matter how aggro I looked. Still, I guess it was better than what the school bullies used to call me: "Gay Larsen." Sometimes I thought maybe life would have been easier if they were right.

Now here I was, faced once again with a girl I really wanted to say something to. I wanted to win her over with my wit. I wanted to seduce her with my charm and cleverness. Instead I just stared.

She was so tightly fixated upon the carnage that to interrupt her nearly religious concentration seemed downright blasphemous. I simply stood there appreciating her perfection like I was contemplating an exquisite work of art.

She had hair that was bleached white and clippered short except for a long magenta shock in the front that was held out of her eyes by a plastic barrette with Smokey Bear's face on it. She was short but not petite. Her figure was soft in a baby-fat kind of way. She wore a sky blue T-shirt with an iron-on of that old Farrah Fawcett poster with her nipples showing through a red one-piece bathing suit. Her bottom half was wrapped in a sort of kilt made from a Mexican blanket which, I noticed, was a nearly perfect match for the one in the background of the Farrah photo on her shirt. It was a little detail, but like the tip of an iceberg it suggested hidden depths I was dying to explore.

I made up my mind. I was actually going to say something. I had no idea what. Anything. Maybe *This is crazy, right?* or some sort of compliment like *Cool shirt!*

I drew breath, ready to let my mouth produce whatever drivel might come out, when she suddenly leaned in close and spoke to *me!*

"THIS FUCKING ROCKS!!" she shouted over the band, who had only started playing faster and louder when their audience began headbutting each other.

Her face was covered with tiny beads of sweat. Everyone in the muggy basement club was drenched, but on her it looked like something a stylist had done for a photo shoot. She was looking right up into my eyes and I had to resist a silly urge to pucker out my lips and kiss the tip of her nose. I could feel her breath on my chin. It sent a chill from my ankles to my belly.

Then, just like that, the moment was gone. She turned her attention back to the mob. The fight was petering out and everybody was going back to war-dancing around imaginary bonfires. I saw the college boy crawling to the relative safety of the stairs that led up to the bar.

There was a tooth on the edge of the stage.

The relaxing of aggressive fists and elbows caused a re-shuffling of the crowd as brave souls from the fringes mingle-danced closer to the band and as quickly as she had appeared, the girl was gone, swept away in a tsunami of leather and lace.

The whole encounter had probably lasted no more than fifteen seconds, but in the time it took my heart to beat a couple dozen times, it had become hers. I was smitten.

CHAPTER 2

An unremarkable green awning reaches toward the sidewalk from above a forgettable door. There is formerly golden script on the sides of the awning and on the glass of the door: Lola Lounge.

Opening the door, you walk into a bar and (nearly vestigial) grill. It's a weekday; maybe afternoon, maybe midnight. You see barflies staring at ice cubes and shiny, gray burgers. Maybe there's a sports game on the TV up in the corner or maybe Lawrence Welk. Looking around, you see empty tables, a pay phone, restrooms. The smell of tobacco smoke and yesterday's beer have turned the air thick and strangely seductive. It's quiet here. Like a church or a cave.

But...

Walk into Lola Lounge on a Friday, Saturday, or (randomly) Wednesday night, and you sense a subtle difference. A hint of clove in the air. A deep thrumming through your feet.

Way over in the right-hand corner there's a door you didn't notice before. On the door, a faded metal sign declares *NO ACCESS*. On a loveseat beside the door are two young women dressed to match in pastel thrift store prom dresses and black leather jackets. A round cocktail table in front of them holds a gray metal money box, an ink pad, a rubber stamp, and two matching drinks in tall, fluted glasses. Pineapple chunks on plastic swords.

Pay them.

Get your hand stamped.

Open the door.

As you descend narrow concrete stairs, music envelops you—earsplitting. Thick smoke throws everything into soft focus. The smells of human sweat and piss and breath and farts are woven together with the reek of cigarettes and joints to form a complex olfactory tapestry.

You've entered LoLo.

So many dark corners. So many people. I had to find her. I couldn't go home that night without at least learning who she was. I approached everybody I knew both downstairs and up in the Lounge, but nobody recognized my description. I was on my way down the stairs for one last sweep before giving up. The Spider Veins were onstage, using a shopping cart full of pots and pans as percussion. Over their deafening blast and rattle I heard my name.

"GUY! I HURT WHEN I LOOGY AND HURL!"

It was Todd, the bass player for Recreational Surgery. He was perched in a small alcove in the wall where the stairs made a ninety degree turn halfway down. He still had white powder from the ceiling tiles in his hair and on the lenses of his thick-rimmed glasses. He was sitting cross-legged, perfectly still, reading *The Prince* by Machiavelli as people stumbled drunkenly past him. He was always doing shit like that. Chicks ate it up.

Now for some reason he was shouting gibberish at me.

"WHAT?" I leaned closer.

"I SAID I HEARD YOU WERE LOOKING FOR GIRL!"

And now he was talking like Tarzan. An unpredictable fellow, that Todd.

"YES! ME LOOK FOR GIRL! MUCH PRETTY!" I shouted, playing along.

"SHE'S BACKSTAGE WITH BILLY!"

Okay, this was sort of a good news/bad news kind of situation. Yes, I'd found her, but apparently she was with "Big" Billy Biggs, the lead singer of Recreational Surgery. Nice guy. Friendly acquaintance of mine. Not exactly the kind of dude you wanted to try to separate from a woman, though. Like his name says: *Big.*

"IS SHE *WITH HIM* WITH HIM OR JUST WITH HIM?"

I yelled, feeling like I was on a fifth grade playground.

"I'M NOT SURE! I THINK THEY MIGHT BE FUCK BUDDIES OR SOMETHING!"

I thanked him for the tip and made my way down the remaining steps.

I shouldered my way through the forest of lurching bodies to a pair of swinging doors that led to a storage room, which served as backstage. Pushing them open, I assessed the situation: I was infatuated at first sight with a strange little girl who I knew nothing about. She may or may not be romantically involved/having sex/all of the above with a six foot five, three hundred pound Samoan guy with *Fuck Around and Find Out* tattooed on his neck. She apparently had a thirst for violence and her laugh could scare away the hounds of Hell. So why were my palms wet and my mouth dry at the thought of seeing her again?

The heavy old doors swung closed behind me, reducing the volume of the music to merely thunderous. I was in an access tunnel. In front of me at the end of the passageway was another door. Like the walls that framed it, that door was covered with graffiti and photocopied stickers with the names of bands, a few of whom would become rich when Punk's little brother Grunge hit the mainstream a few years later. None of us could predict the Seattle Invasion then, though. These were just anonymous bands leaving their mark on an anonymous door just like a thousand other doors in a thousand other grubby little venues.

To me, the door looked like a luminous portal into a magical world. *She* was behind it.

Before I could reach the door, though, it opened. There she was. Alone. She was walking backwards toward me and calling goodbye to the dim figures in the smoke-filled room beyond.

I stopped. She didn't.

She collided with me just as the door closed behind her and she was turning to walk forward again.

"FUCK! What's your fucking problem?" She howled angrily, but her tone of voice miraculously changed when she looked up and saw who she'd run into.

"HOLY SHIT! It's *YOU!*" She put both of her hands flat on my chest and pushed me hard but playfully as she started talking in the rapid-fire freestyle I would grow to know so well.

"This is like some sort of fucking...I don't know... *FATE!* Or divine intersection! Or some sort of...you know...thing that's like *meant to be* or something! Like every fucking thing in the world is trying to get us together! First I see you, okay? And I look away for a second and I get this thought in my head like, 'WOW! I need to get to know him!' and I look back and *FUCK! You're GONE!* So Big and the guys finish their set and I go backstage cuz I came with Big and I want to tell him that I'm not gonna leave with him cuz I saw this guy who I want to meet and he says, 'What's his name?' and I say, 'I don't know' and he says, 'Well, what's he look like?' and I tell him and while I'm telling him, Barbi—you know Barbi?—she comes in and says, 'Oh, he's looking for you, too!' and I say, 'Did you tell him where I was?' and she's like, 'No, cuz he said the girl he was looking for was *PRETTY,* so I didn't think it could be you!' So I slug her in the gut and I say, 'Well what's his fucking name, bitch?' and she says, 'GUY!' I can't fucking believe it! *GUY!* That's so perfect I could *PUKE!* But she says, 'He said he was gonna go somewhere else, though' and I say, *'FUCK!'* and I go to leave and *BANG!* I slam into you! That is so fucking RAD! Isn't that *TOO FUCKING RAD?"*

I was left momentarily speechless (not that that was unusual for me). I finally regained the power of language after being lost in her eyes for what seemed like an hour but was probably two seconds. For some reason the first words out of my mouth were, "Why is my name perfect?"

"You mean you don't know?" She folded her arms and gave me a skeptical look, head tilted and one lavish eyebrow cocked. "Nobody told you my name. Seriously."

"Seriously."

"It's Girl!" Her arms extended to either side, palms open in a *can you even believe it?!* gesture.

Okay, I admit this is completely idiotic; but with the noise of the band dampened by a cement block wall but still loud, I honestly thought she said "Squirrel." I'd heard *The Ghastly Giggle* and in my mind that would be a perfectly understandable nickname considering the noises she was capable of.

"Okay, Squirrel. So what does that have to do with MY name?"

"KEEEEEEEE-HEE-KEE-GH-HICK-GHEE-HICK-EE-H-H-KEE!!!!"

Somehow it was actually kind of cute now. Maybe because this time it was me that made her do it.

"No, you silly fucking asshole!" she yelled with a huge grin, "G! I! R! L! *GIRL!!* You're GUY and I'm GIRL! We TOTALLY have to go somewhere and get to know each other!"

On the way up the stairs arm in arm with the woman who would completely change my life, I shouted to Todd, "ME FIND GIRL!" just as the band ended a song. For that one moment my voice was the loudest sound in the club and the friends who I had asked about her started a wave of applause that spread through the whole place and followed us as we exited, bowing, to the street.

CHAPTER 3

On the way over to Girl's house for the first time, I had a couple hits of grass to steady my nerves.

Her father answered the door wearing tan slacks and a raspberry polo shirt. "Hi! Come on in! I'm Rudy. You must be Mr. Mann."

Stepping over the threshold, I examined him with weed-vision. Rudy Zamora was a study in averages. Not notably tall or short, thin or fat. Not especially ugly nor particularly good-looking. Hair not freshly-trimmed but not overgrown either. Latin-American but you'd maybe assume Italian if you didn't hear his surname.

"Oh, please. Call me John," I answered, shaking his hand. It was neither too warm nor too cold. *This one's just right* said a little Goldilocks voice in my head.

I wasn't used to commuter dudes like Rudy looking me in the eye and shaking my hand. When Girl and I had met three days prior, my hair had been lime green and laminated into a crown of deadly-looking points. I'd been wearing a spiked and studded leather jacket, red Doc Marten boots with extra thick waffle stomper soles, and tight plaid pants with dangling decorative bondage straps.

People like Rudy had been known to cross the street to avoid interacting with me. If I had walked up to his front door some evening looking like that, I would have been greeted by the neighborhood rent-a-cop with a flashlight shining in my face.

Tonight, though, my yuppie drag was on point: A visit to Goodwill had yielded a light blue dress shirt, a maroon tie in a tasteful floral print (loosened at the neck like I'd just come from a long day at the office), gray pants, and black loafers. My hair was dyed brown, parted in the middle and swept back just covering the tops of my ears.

I was only nineteen years old, but I'd been six feet tall since middle school. I'd been getting into bars without anyone even asking to see my (fake) ID for ages. In my current guise I easily passed for a young suburban dad. I was still worried that something about my appearance wasn't legit, though; Rudy was looking at me funny.

He said, "I feel like we've met before. Were you at the advance screening of that John Candy movie last week?"

I breathed a sigh of relief. I've always had one of those familiar-looking faces. "No, I'm not in the film business," I replied, "I work for...

um…" Shit! I hadn't thought about this part! *wheredoiworkwheredoiworkwheredoiwork…* "The DMV! It's not exciting but the benefits are great," I said, thinking fast, "…though I *am* working on a screenplay!" I had to throw that in. In Los Angeles it's like "aloha."

"Well, good luck with that. Let me know if you'd like me to read it. I'm in budgets and finance over at Orion, but I have friends on the production side of things. Abbey will be right down." He got a crease between his eyebrows as he continued, "I gotta say I was surprised when she told me she was going to babysit. That's…um… uncharacteristic. How did you find her?"

Okay, this part Girl and I had rehearsed: "A classmate of hers watches our little twin girls sometimes but she's overseas in an exchange student program so she gave me your daughter's number."

"I hope she works out for you. She's… She can be a little…let's say… rebellious?" He chuckled nervously and showed me a forced-looking smile, "But then again weren't we all at fifteen?"

Yeah, so it turned out Girl's sixteenth birthday was still months away. I had just about shit myself when she'd told me. The ladies who stamp hands at LoLo aren't exactly what you'd call strict about verifying the ages of the patrons. Hell, *I* was underage, too! Even so, I had figured Girl was at least *screwing*-legal if not *drinking*-legal! By the time the truth came out, though, it was a little late for me to care. For one thing, I was sloppy in love. For another, I'd technically already committed statutory rape three or four times depending on how you count variations.

And then there she was—coming toward me through the hallway from the back of the house. Even with all the time we'd spent together over the weekend, the sight of her still floored me. I had to keep from laughing, though. She was Good Girl head to toe. A new-looking yellow sweatshirt with her school logo topped a pair of indigo Guess jeans with crisp creases. The pink baseball cap covering her punky hair matched the backpack slung over one shoulder.

Looking Girl in the eyes, I addressed Rudy. "My wife and I might be out pretty late. I hope that's not a problem. I know it's a school night."

Meeting my gaze, Girl answered—for him and to him — "It's fine, daddy. I'll just crash on the couch after the kids are in bed if I get sleepy. See you later! Don't wait up!"

"Bye, princess!" He called as we walked out to the driveway where the car I'd borrowed from a roommate was parked. Then he added, in a serious dad-voice, "Be *good!*"

As we drove away I finally relaxed. I couldn't believe it had worked! When Girl first suggested this method of spending time together on weeknights without her father freaking out over our age difference, I didn't understand why we needed such an elaborate scheme. After all, the night we met she had been out all night and had started the evening in the company of a hardcore punk band composed of guys way older than me! According to Girl, though, Rudy had thought she was attending a sleep-over party that night. Plus it was a weekend so no big deal. Weeknights were different, apparently. She had a strict nine p.m. curfew. Also, Rudy expected to drop his little Abbey off at school on his way to work, so spending the entire night together was a no-go. With the babysitter cover story, though, I could drop her home really, really late. I had to hand it to her; she knew how to work people.

I was surprised by how normal Rudy Zamora had looked.

Girl and I'd had long phone calls every night since we'd met. My apartment had a single, pale pink telephone covered with stickers, which was mounted on the kitchen wall. I stretched the extra-long, spiral cord down the hallway and clamped it in the door to my bedroom for hours, causing a major choking hazard for any roommate on their way to the bathroom in the dark.

During these conversations, Girl had given me the impression that her father was some sort of devil. After seeing him for myself, though, I thought he seemed nice enough for an old dude and as we drove away from that first meeting, I told her so.

Big mistake.

Girl slammed both hands flat down on the dashboard and turned in her seat to face me. "Don't you *ever* say anything nice about him again!" she shouted, her voice rising an octave above normal. Then she slumped down in her seat, folded her arms, and looked out her window quietly for several blocks. When she spoke next, her voice was low and quavery. "He's a monster. They should do, like, an After School Special about my perfect fucking daddy. I'll tell you all about him later. We'll see if you still buy his Joe Happy act then."

Around midnight we were leaning over the little perimeter wall of my apartment building roof, watching the comings and goings at the gay and lesbian bar across the street. Bears and butch girls looked remarkably alike from above. We made a game of guessing the genders of the patrons.

"Dudes?" Girl conjectured.

"Nope. Gay dudes don't wear wallet chains that thick. Besides, I know the one on the right." I stood up and waved, calling, "Hi, Becky!"

Becky looked up and smiled.

"Hey! 'Sup, Good Guy?" She blew me a kiss which I returned.

Becky put her hand casually into the back pocket of her date's jeans and the two of them continued into the club. I bent back down, resting my elbows on the wall. It came up to my waist; Girl's chest.

I was necking a forty ounce malt liquor. My cassette player was hanging by its carrying handle from a TV antenna behind me, The Buzzcocks playing from its shitty little speaker. Girl was bopping along to "Ever Fallen In Love," sipping a plastic liter of Boone's Farm Strawberry Hill, a syrupy sparkling pseudo-wine drunk exclusively by underage girls. Her breath smelled like a bubble bath as she reached one arm around my neck and pulled me into a long, tongue-filled kiss.

When we separated, she reached back and pushed "stop" on the mixtape. She put her back to the low wall, set her half-full bottle on top of it, and spun me the origin story of Abigail Zamora.

According to Girl, Rudy got her mother pregnant at fourteen years old. Rudy was a student teacher at the school in Portland where Lily—Girl's mother—was a pupil. He was a junior in college and not yet twenty-one. The school board and Lily's parents all wanted to avoid negative publicity so no criminal charges were filed. Rudy was kicked out of school and blackballed from teaching in the state of Oregon.

Between a young girl's romantic idealism and the religious convictions of her family, it was decided that

Lily would keep the baby. During the pregnancy, Lily's parents tried to keep Rudy away from their daughter, but he started stalking her, lurking outside her home and calling at all hours. They were granted a restraining order.

The night Lily gave birth, a heavy rain was blowing sideways. Portland's streets were slick and sirens howled through the city like wayward coyotes. Wearing scrubs, Rudy walked purposefully through the hospital's chaotic emergency room and took the elevator to the third floor. The elevator doors opened and Rudy followed the arrows labeled *MATERNITY*.

In the midst of the evening's turmoil, nobody questioned the young nurse carrying a newborn through the hospital's exit doors. He opened his umbrella and melted into the rushing darkness.

Rudy fled with his daughter across the border into California. He bounced from town to town, eventually settling in the sun-blistered suburbs of the San Fernando Valley. He found work in and around the movie industry. To his neighbors he was an ordinary single parent. Behind the walls of the one-level Spanish-style bungalow in Glendale they moved into when Girl was seven, though, things were not at all normal. Rudy treated Girl more like a wife than a daughter. She was expected to keep his home clean, do his laundry, and cook his meals. If she got "out of line" or "talked back" she was beaten.

Eventually Rudy started suggesting that there might be other wifely tasks his daughter should perform.

On his little princess' thirteenth birthday, Rudy Zamora took his daughter to the circus. Afterward he took her home. There he took her virginity.

Girl and I were standing toe to toe on the roof. I was looking at her. She was looking through me, her tiny palms warm against my chest. In the glow of the streetlights, tears traced silver snail trails from the corners of her eyes to the point of her chin as she recounted in heart-breaking specificity what her father had done to her; what he had made her do to him.

The pink backpack was on the ground beside our feet. Girl dropped into a squat and unzipped it as she continued her crushing story. "Afterward, he told me how much I looked like my mother. He left me laying there naked on his bed and I heard him rummaging around in the hall closet. Then he came back and handed me this."

She pulled a clear Ziploc sandwich bag from the backpack. Still squatting, she handed it up to me. Inside was a slightly rumpled school portrait photo. It could have been Girl a couple of years earlier but for slight differences; a wider nose, no gap in her teeth. I flipped it over and saw *Lily, 12 yrs.* in a slanting, feminine hand.

"He always got, like, all sentimental about my mother after he fucked me. That's how I ended up learning the whole story. I knew I could ask him anything about her when he was all...like...post-collidal or whatever."

"But... I don't get it—why didn't she ever come looking for you?"

"I guess her parents tried to find me for a while, but they were probably glad to be rid of me. Who wants their little kid to have a little kid?"

She took the photo back and gazed at it, leaning her forearms on the little wall. She stood there for a long time, gazing at the picture in silence. When she finally spoke it was with a quiet wistfulness. It was so unlike her usual high-energy patter that it made the hair stand up on my neck.

"I think about her all the time. That poor little girl who had her baby stolen away. I imagine she still dreams about someday seeing me and holding me and loving me and taking care of me..." Her voice trailed off and she slipped into another quiet reverie, seeing nothing but the photo she cradled between her hands like an injured bird.

When she suddenly turned to me and spoke again, I startled and knocked my beer bottle over the edge of the roof. "But now *you're* here!" The bottle shattered against the sidewalk four stories below, punctuating her proclamation with a cymbal crash.

"It's like a fairy tale where the princess is being held captive by an *evil monster* and her one true love comes riding in on this big white horse and *kills it!*"

She flung her arms around my neck, knocking her own bottle off the edge in the process. The plastic *clunk* when it landed was the perfect cartoon sound effect as I swallowed hard and choked out, "What the fuck are you talking about?"

CHAPTER 4

Okay, so her plan was completely unhinged and I was out of my mind to go along with it. I'd officially been rendered Girl stupid.

"It'll be soooo romantic!" Girl gushed as "Teenage Kicks" by The Undertones played on the turntable across the room. "You'll be my knight in, like, shining armor and you'll crash into the evil lair and slay the beast! Then we'll jump in our carriage and ride off to the castle where the queen will welcome her long lost princess with open arms!"

Girl was higher than a kite on this really great hash that had come up from Tijuana hidden in my roommate's underwear. Naked except for a choker made from a cross-section of fishnet stocking, she was monologuing while jumping up and down on my mattress with her arms over her head. A black candle was on the floor beside the bed. Inky wax pooled into a china saucer, transmorphing Victorian roses into Gothic ones. Golden light shone upward.

In the candle's glow, Girl's flawless olive skin made her look like a Botticelli. Every bit of her was rounded. Her arms, her neck, that little wrinkly part at the back of her knees. Her pubic hair was completely shaved, adding to the impression of a Renaissance painting come gloriously to life. She was perfection.

I gazed worshipfully up at her. I was laying on my back, hands interlaced beneath my head. My hard-on was so full it hurt even though we'd already had sex. How could I argue with her? Even about something as insane as metaphorical beast-slaying? I had to at least play along. I wanted her to be that happy forever.

"So let me get this straight," I interrupted with a smile, "Dragons and castles aside; here in the twentieth century, you're proposing that I break into your house and *kill* your father. Then we steal his car and drive to Oregon where we attempt to *somehow* find your mother based on a photograph of her when she was twelve. At which point...what? We'll all live happily ever after?"

Girl dropped to her knees straddling my legs and enclosed my boner in both of her little fists.

"That's why I'm so crazy about you, Guy! You understand me!"

There was no way on Earth I was actually going

to commit murder, but I figured I could at least help Girl find her mom. Maybe we could just sort of...*borrow* Rudy's car and go on a road trip without him having to know about it.

If we *were* going to turn Girl's dream of reuniting with her long-lost mother into reality, though, the first thing we had to do was find Lily's current whereabouts.

In Girl's view of the world, we could just drive around Portland and we'd somehow be mystically guided to the woman. Her belief went something like this: It was evil forces which were keeping her and her mother apart. Therefore, if the two of them were simply brought within a reasonable distance of each other they would be drawn together by their mutual love.

I reminded her that we didn't even know if Lily was still *in* Portland and managed to convince her that having a starting zip code for our quest wouldn't be cheating the fates. We agreed to search Girl and Rudy's house for evidence of where Lily might be living now.

I met Girl in front of the high school on a Tuesday afternoon as classes were letting out for the day. She sat on the front steps smoking a clove cigarette as the other kids filed out around her, shooting her dirty looks. We walked three blocks and took a bus the rest of the way. When we arrived at her house, she let us in with a key that she wore around her neck on a wide shoelace with Care Bears printed on it.

Rudy wasn't due home anytime soon so I took my time looking around. I hadn't been beyond the entryway before. Stepping past a couple of closed doors, I saw a kitchen to my right. Turning to the left I saw a central hallway leading to bedrooms and bathrooms. Down two pointless little steps was a living room with a picture window view of the street.

A monolithic oak entertainment console dominated one wall of the living room. Girl stepped up to it and rotated a gold-tone knob with a resonant *click* and the FM tuner came to life. Spinning another dial, she tuned to KROQ. A song by The Teardrop Explodes filled the house, the singer wailing about how the object of his affection made him go bop bop babba dabba whoa.

I knew how he felt.

We started our exploration in the kitchen. Girl shuffled through untidy stacks of papers in a cluttered telephone nook. I examined a junk drawer full of matchbooks and business cards, looking for hand-written addresses and phone numbers. I didn't find anything useful. Two more drawers full of maps and back issues of *Variety* were equally fruitless.

In Rudy's bedroom the closet, dresser, and nightstand yielded nothing worthwhile.

"Does your dad have a place he keeps, like, photo albums and shit?" I asked.

"For sure! There's a box of old snapshots and stuff

on the shelf in the front closet!" she announced, skipping back down the hall to the home's foyer. She opened one of the two closed doors I had seen when I entered.

Leaning into the spacious coatroom I looked up and saw a shelf crowded with boxes on which were written things like *winter hats/scarfs* and *xmas lights.*

The shelf was well within my reach. I could have retrieved any box Girl wanted. Instead, she put her back against me, raised her arms above her head, and said, "Pick me up."

Obediently, I bent down and wrapped my arms around her hips. I then stood straight, lifting her to shelf level.

I thought Girl would bring down containers for us to go through. Instead, she started taking lids off of shoe boxes and rummaging through their contents while I held her aloft.

My face was pressed into the small of her back and I could smell her skin through the thin fabric of her T-shirt—a libido-goosing mix of clove and soap and teen girl sweat. You could have bottled that fragrance and sold it for five hundred dollars an ounce. I closed my eyes and nuzzled into Girl's warmth. One perfectly rounded buttock engulfed each of my collarbones as I hugged her pelvis.

In the living room Brian Ferry was singing about being a slave to love. I swear, radio DJs always managed to play music that exactly described my life at that moment. Love had me enslaved, alright.

Girl was belting along with the chorus when she broke off and yelled, "Holy shit! Holy shit! Let me down!" She started kicking her legs and trying to turn around at the same time.

I loosened my grip and Girl slid down the front of my body, twisting so that we were face to face. Her little gumdrop breasts pressed against my stomach as she shoved a red greeting card envelope up into my face. It was too close to read. I took it from her and held it at a comfortable distance. The empty envelope was addressed to "Rudy + Abigail Zamora" in bubbly, feminine cursive. Girl was repeatedly poking a stiff index finger at the return address:

Lillian La Fleur

Liberty Rose Hotel

608 SE Tacoma St

Portland, OR 97202

"La Fleur?" I said, "So you're what? Half French?"

"I don't know—I guess so. Who cares? I found her! I really *found her!*" Girl pressed the envelope to her face and inhaled deeply through her nose, trying to catch some lingering aroma of the mother she'd never met.

"But Girl, look. The address is a hotel. She was probably just staying there for a day or two."

She slapped me playfully on the chest and laughed,

"Why would anybody stay for a day or two at a hotel in the same city where they already live, you big stoop? She probably, like, rents the penthouse or something. I bet she's a fashion designer or a singer! Anyway, that doesn't matter! We found her! That means we can do it *today!!*"

She turned away from me and opened the door to the right of the closet.

"Let's get ready for daddy!" she sang in an unnerving schoolyard nya-nya tune as she disappeared through the doorway.

We hadn't actually discussed *when* we'd carry out Girl's demented plan. I was still trying to figure out how to talk her out of it. I certainly wasn't prepared to just kind of *do it* at the drop of a hat. Apparently, though, Girl very much was. She'd been paddling around in Loco Lake for a long time. I'd only recently been pushed in. And I didn't even know how to swim.

I told myself that we would teach Rudy a lesson. We would hurt him (not kill him—certainly never that). I was working on the side of justice. I tried to feel like the hero Girl wanted me to be. I *was* the Good Guy here, after all. And Rudy was very definitely a bad guy.

I took a deep breath and followed Girl through the door into madness.

I found myself in an attached two-car garage. To my right was a wide aluminum garage door. Attached to the top of this was a track that ran along the center of the ceiling to an electric motor. Across the empty space, a series of workbenches lined the far wall. Woodworking tools occupied the pegboard above, each with its own painted outline.

"The garage is pretty soundproof so you can use like power saws and stuff without annoying neighbors or whatever. When I'm totally stressed out with life I come in here and scream as loud as I can. Nobody can hear a thing. It's perfect."

Perfect for what, exactly? I thought.

A wooden straight-backed chair with worn and peeling white paint covering about half of its surface was upturned on the workbench amid a clutter of spent sandpaper, rags, and solvent jars. Girl lifted the chair, turned it right-way up and set it down in the center of the garage floor. She stepped back and looked at the chair, then approached it again and turned it slightly. Stepping back again, she nodded, apparently pleased with its positioning.

"There's some rope and duct tape in that cupboard, I think," she told me, pointing to a row of cabinets high along the garage's rear wall.

Standing on a plastic milk crate that was lying on its side full of old record albums, I opened the cupboard and found the items. When I turned around, Girl was looking at the chair and pointing her finger at the spot above it where the person's head would be if someone were sitting there.

She was frowning and baring her teeth and her lips moved soundlessly as she delivered a silent tongue-lashing to an invisible audience. Suddenly, she lurched forward and spat in the phantom's face. The glob of saliva sailed through empty space and landed with a quiet *splip* on the cement floor.

She blinked a couple of times and shook her head like she was coming back to reality, then bounced back into the house, calling, "Leave those things on the chair and come with me. You can help me make Daddy's last meal!"

CHAPTER 5

"This is really good, Abbey. Nice and spicy the way I like it."

It was a typically warm Southern California night and the kitchen window was open, allowing me to hear every word from my hiding place in the bushes outside.

An untrimmed holly plant grew along two sides of the property, hiding me from the street and the house next door. I stood in the shadows of the shrubbery with the hood of my black sweatshirt up and my hands in its pockets. White lace curtains covered the window on the inside. Girl had assured me that Rudy wouldn't be able to see me looking in at this time of evening with the kitchen lights on.

Girl and her father were perched on wooden bar stools eating dinner facing each other on opposite sides of an island countertop. I watched Rudy's face as he ate. I watched the back of Girl's head. Framed in the twilit gloom of the muggy Glendale evening, the brightly-lit scene was like a view into another world. A movie within a movie within the unreality which my life had become since I met Girl.

I'd started thinking of my life in terms of B.G.—my life *Before Girl*, and A.G.—my life *After Girl*.

My life B.G.: Carefree punk kid working slacker hours at convenience stores and movie theaters so I could afford a cheap apartment and spend my free time riding skateboards and going to clubs at night.

My life A.G.: Lurking in bushes spying on the man I was supposed to be helping murder.

Even though I knew in my heart that I was *not* going to murder Rudy, I had to let Girl think that I was. When she was happy I was king of the world and no drug-induced high I'd ever felt could compare with the feeling of being around her. When she was sad my life had no purpose except to make her happy again so I could get my fix.

From the other room I could hear the radio. Robert Palmer smugly reminded me that I might as well face the fact that I was addicted to love.

Seriously, DJ? I thought, *You really have to fuckin' rub it in?*

"I'm glad you like it, Daddy. Here, have some more." Girl spatula'd another helping of beef enchiladas from the baking dish and slid it onto her father's plate.

"You sure you don't want to try some, Princess? It's delicious."

"I told you, Daddy. I'm not eating meat anymore."

This had taken Rudy only slightly by surprise. He'd been living with a teenage girl long enough that abrupt diet and lifestyle changes barely phased him. Girl's sudden vegetarianism provided the perfect excuse to prepare a separate entree for herself.

Rudy cut a big piece with the edge of his fork and shoveled it into his mouth. He had no idea that the tangy sauce *just the way he liked it* was masking another, less pleasant, flavor.

While Rudy was at work Girl and I had taken three packages of over-the-counter sleep aids and popped all of the little gelatin capsules from their plastic bubble cards onto a plate. Seventy-two pills.

Girl opened a large can of enchilada sauce and dumped its contents into a pot. This she placed over a low flame on the stove and stirred in some Tapatio and a liberal amount of cayenne pepper.

On Girl's instruction, I busied myself with sliding apart the halves of the sleeping pills and pouring their white powder into a cereal bowl. While she was distracted with her sauce preparation, though, I pocketed every third pill. I was determined to undermine the fatality of her plans every chance I got.

"Okay, Guy—add the secret ingredient!" Girl

instructed with an evil grin.

I poured the little pile of white powder into the saucepot. I put my hand in the pocket of my jeans and fingered the couple dozen pills there. I would flush them the next time I was in the bathroom alone.

I was still trying to put together the pieces of Girl's plan. I asked why we needed the soundproof garage. "Aren't the pills going to kill your father?"

She told me that a friend of hers had tried to commit suicide a year earlier by downing a whole package of this same brand. This friend woke up in an emergency room with a raging headache and her throat raw from the stomach pump tube. Rudy was bigger and the pills would be dissolved in a whole pan of enchiladas, she explained. He'd only actually end up consuming maybe a third of a package. She just wanted him out of commission long enough to move him to the garage, where we could dispatch him at our leisure with no resistance.

Maybe I had held back enough capsules that Rudy wouldn't even lose consciousness. I crossed my fingers and paced nervously outside the window as he consumed bite after bite, washing down each mouthful with Mexican beer, while I looked for signs of the drug's effect.

Rudy Zamora's daughter had been "babysitting" for "Mr. Mann" a few times a week for nearly a month and I'd been observing him carefully. I could *not* picture him raping his daughter. Nothing I saw tonight made me feel any different. Making smalltalk over dinner, the look in his eyes wasn't that of an obsessive child molester; it was the look of a loving father.

Then all at once it was the look of a loving father in extreme pain. His eyes closed tight as he grabbed his guts with both hands, digging them into his midsection like he wanted to claw himself open. When he spoke, his voice was a barking whisper.

"Abbey! Call 9-1-1! I think I'm having a heart attaaaaaggg..." His eyes rolled backward into his head and his face rolled forward into his enchiladas.

I stopped pacing. I could hear my heart beating. Nothing moved.

Girl's back was still toward me. She pushed against the counter with one hand and slowly swiveled the seat of her stool until we were face to face. In her eyes I saw the same hungry gleam as the night she watched the preppy beat-down in the basement of the Lola Lounge. The sound coming out of her mouth was the same as well:

"KEE-H-KEE-GH-HEE-HEE-H-H-GHEE-EE!!"

CHAPTER 6

When Girl looked through the window at me and I heard The Ghastly Giggle, I could feel my scrotum instinctively contract with the primordial urgency of fight or flight. My monkey brain chose flight, stumbling me backwards out of the bush into the dark yard. I couldn't breathe. I didn't know if I was pirouetting in circles or if the world was spinning around me.

I was overwhelmed by the feeling that I had crossed a line. Not just a moral line in the sand but a border between dimensions. I didn't recognize this universe. My vision was tunneling, an inky blackness closing in on me.

Then suddenly the darkness was banished and Girl was there, framed in the light of the open door. She grabbed the waistband of my pants and pulled me into her fluorescent-lit world. She was kissing me and fumbling with my clothing and I was doing the same to her. She leaned against me, steering me with her mouth against mine until my back was pressing against Rudy's, smashing his face further into his food and knocking his Corona over to puddle around his plate. Girl and I slid down the back of his stool and ended up in a writhing knot of arms and legs and asses and clothing, tumbling from one side of the kitchen to the other.

I hated to admit it to myself, but the sex Girl and I had on that kitchen floor with her unconscious father blowing bubbles in his enchilada sauce above us was the best sex I'd ever had.

Eventually, panting and laughing, we collapsed onto our backs on the hard linoleum. After a few minutes of quiet afterglow, I crawled to my jeans and pulled a joint out of the pocket. Leaning naked against the wall, I lit up. "Now what?" I croaked, holding the smoke in.

She took the joint and sucked hard and long. "Now we finish him," she croaked back and started laughing. "We totally sound like a couple of gangster frogs!" she coughed out, cartoon speech balloons of smoke framing every word.

We killed the rest of the joint while amusing each other by puffing out our lower lips and making *ribbit* noises.

Eventually I stood up, unsteady from the buzz, and started to put my jeans back on. Girl stopped me with a hand on my back.

"No. No clothes. That way, if we get blood on us we can just shower it off." Inside my skull the cannabis-coated walls echoed back *ifwegetbloodonus... ifwegetbloodonus... ifwegetbloodonus...*

She was standing now and wearing rubber gloves. Just rubber gloves.

"Where did..." I murmured.

Handing me a pair of my own, she said, "Here. Fingerprints. Let's get him in the garage."

My hands slid into powdered latex. It smelled like condoms.

I opened my mouth to ask *why* we might get blood on us, but just then Girl shouted, "Trust fall!" and grabbed a fistful of Rudy's hair, yanking him backward. His arms pitched limply out to his sides as he spilled off the bar stool into my arms, spattering enchilada sauce into my open mouth.

"Gross!" I spat, "Warn a brother!"

Laughing, Girl bent down and lifted Rudy's ankles. We hobbled and baby-stepped his dead weight into the garage. We tumbled him into the chair and Girl started tying his ankles to its legs with pieces of clothesline.

"Get his hands," she directed, nodding at the roll of duct tape which sat on the floor beside her.

"I don't get it," I said, binding Rudy's wrists with tape to the wooden arms of the chair. "Why tie him up and all this shit? Why don't we just leave him and get out of here?"

"Because my perfect daddy has a big-ass gambling problem. He's in debt up to his eyeballs to some really gnarly dudes. I caught him talking on the phone about it one night when he thought I was asleep. We're gonna make it look like some gangster shit happened here. If it's brutal to the max, there's no reason for the police to suspect me. They might even think I was kidnapped or something!"

She's so cute when she's vicious, I thought. *Her nose gets all wrinkled up and her lip does that Elvis thing and...* Woah. I was really high. I got a big wave of paranoia.

"But what about all the sleeping pills in his system?" I asked, close to panic.

Girl stopped working on her knots.

"Oh, shit!" She said, putting one hand to her forehead and cracking up into a fit of laughter, "KHEE-HICK-HEE!! I didn't think about that!"

For some reason that got me laughing again, too, until both of were us lying naked on the cold cement floor rendered helpless by a case of pot-induced giggles until Rudy the buzzkiller decided to wake up.

"Whaaa...oooh..." He started making little moaning noises as his eyelids flickered, showing nothing but whites.

"Quick!" Girl yelped, "Tape his mouth in case he

starts screaming or something!"

Wondering why I was bothering if the garage was so very soundproof, I stripped a piece of duct tape from the roll and pressed it against Rudy Zamora's mouth. Almost instantly he started shaking and bucking. Half-digested enchilada mixed with beer sprayed out of his nose all over my naked groin.

"Shit! He's puking!" I yelled and yanked the duct tape off of his mouth.

Two things happened when I did this, neither of which I had anticipated: First, the tender skin of Rudy's lips came away with the duct tape, peeled off as cleanly as a Band-Aid. Second, the well of vomit which the tape had dammed came rushing out through the bloody hole of his mouth.

Even though I'd already been showered with stomach contents once, I didn't think to step aside before I ripped away the gag. This time I got a full bath, chunks of beef and bile splashing off my bare chest and dripping down the front of my arms and legs.

"God *damn* it!" I yelled, reflexively swinging a backhanded fist. The glove ripped where my knuckles connected with Rudy Zamora's right cheekbone, knocking his head to the left and splashing blood and barf onto Girl's face. She didn't even seem to notice. She just hopped up and down on tippy-toes, her hands making little patty-cakes in front of her neck, the *Ghastly*

Giggle in full force. She was *loving* this!

Rudy, meanwhile, was out again, his brief attack of consciousness having passed. He slouched forward as much as his bound hands allowed, his head hanging down so that his chin touched the collar of his blue-striped dress shirt. Stringy strands of blood hung from his ruined lips as if a spider had spun crimson webs connecting mouth to groin.

"Oh, man..." I began shakily, "I'm not liking this, Girl. This isn't fun. Let's wrap it up and get out of here. What do we do next?"

Girl swiped a hand down her face and absentmindedly wiped it clean on her bare belly, leaving a red palm print. Turning away from me, she went over to her father's workbench and squatted down on her heels in front of a large lower cabinet. She opened the cupboard and pulled something out.

She stood up and turned around. She was holding a mysterious shape covered with an old workshop towel. She took a step toward me, executed a very pretty curtsy, and with great flair pulled away the cloth like a naked, bloodied magician's assistant presenting a brightly-colored prop. I half expected doves to fly out of the gaudy object.

"What the fuck is *that* thing?" I asked.

"This, my dear, is the murder weapon!"

She placed into my hands a bright orange power tool

as big as a large man's work boot but about ten times heavier. I turned it over in my hands and read the label on its side: *Chekhov Cordless Nailer w/ propane propellant system.*

She'd handed me a goddamn nail gun!

Sliding behind me, Girl pressed her bloody torso against my bare back and reached around under my arms to press a switch on the side of the apparatus I was holding awkwardly in front of me. It shuddered slightly then was still.

"There's a safety by the trigger," she purred, standing on tip-toe to reach my ear, "Flip it off and give him one right between the eyes."

After a few moments of fumbling with the heavy nail gun, I found the proper way to hold it and disengaged the safety catch. Gripping tightly with both hands, I hooked the front under Rudy's brow and used it to lift his head so that he was facing me. A sliver of white showed between his eyelids and a bruise was starting to form on his right cheek where I'd hit him. I pushed the business end of the nail gun hard against his skull. I took a deep breath and held it.

My finger was on the trigger. If I pulled it, there would be no going back. I would be a killer. A murderer. An executioner.

My hands started trembling, rattling the tip of the tool against Rudy's brow ridge. His head bounced limply.

"I can't do it," I said quietly, my voice shaking.

Girl was still pressed up against me, her arms encircling my ribs. I could feel the warmth of her lower belly against my buttocks. Her breath was hot on my shoulderblade. I felt Girl's hands slither down my slime-coated torso until they found my own tool. Slippery from the fluids on my stomach, her hands slid up and down the shaft, waking it up.

I closed my eyes. "Stop," I gasped, "You're gonna make me—"

There was a sudden *SSSSS-PWAP!* and Rudy's skull snapped back then rebounded forward, knocking the heavy device from my unsteady hands to clatter against the cement floor. Rudy's head fell forward to rest on his chest once more, a new bloody thread dangling from the fresh wound in his forehead.

I took a staggering step backward, my legs tangling with Girl's and almost bringing us both down.

"Oh shit oh shit oh shit oh shit fuck *fuck FUCK!!*" I was half crying and half laughing as I groped for Girl, hugging her tightly. She hugged me back.

I stared at Rudy's unmoving body.

Still embracing, Girl and I stumbled clumsily to the door that connected the garage with the house. Bursting through, we slammed the door behind us and stood with our backs against it in the darkened vestibule, staring at each other.

The only light came from the kitchen behind Girl. In the darkness of the evening its golden glow back-lit her spiky blonde hair like a halo. Her big dark eyes shone in the gloom like an exotic animal glimpsed in passing by the side of a country road at night. In spite of everything, she was the most beautiful sight I'd ever seen.

After a moment of silent eye contact, she spoke.

"You... are so totally... my *HERO!*" She threw her arms around my neck and kissed me long and hard. The sweet taste of her pink tongue and soft, full lips mingled with the sour tang of her father's blood and vomit. I didn't care. When I was kissing Girl, there was nobody in the world but us.

I drank deeply the heat of her breath as she spoke against my mouth, "Come on! Let's get cleaned up!"

Taking my hand, Girl pulled me down the hallway to the bathroom. We peeled off our rubber gloves and I flushed them away down the toilet. Girl turned on the shower and stepped in. I joined her and we spent a long time washing the evidence of our misdeeds from each others' bodies and hair.

Toweling off, I walked nude to the kitchen where my clothes still lay crumpled on the floor. Girl went to her bedroom to put on a fresh outfit. When I was dressed, I picked up her clothes and took them to her room.

I stopped in the doorway. She didn't see me watching her. She was doing a little dance to some music in her head while she pulled a pair of black jeans up over the soft, round magnificence of her ass. She turned to pull a shirt from a drawer and saw me.

"Hey! Tie me!" she said.

She held a white T-shirt that had been cut apart until it was just a shirt front with two strips of cloth at the neck and two more at the bottom. The two at the top were already tied together forming a loop which she slipped over her head. She presented her bare back to me and held the bottom ties out so that I could take them and join them in a bow behind her back just below her ribs. She stepped back, turned around to face me, and posed with one arm above her head and the other held out to her side. The front of the shirt had a black and white photo of a handgun with the words "Penis Envy" above it in mismatched ransom note letters. The bottom was cut into a ragged fringe, exposing her gibbous, cafè latte belly.

"How do I look? Good enough for a road trip?"

"You're the hottest thing I've ever seen," I told her truthfully.

She put her hands behind her back and dug her toe in the ground like a shy little girl, looking at me from under long eyelashes. "I bet you say that to all the girls right after you snuff their parents."

Girl turned and dropped down on all fours, reaching under her bed. She pulled out a vintage child-sized suitcase. The hard sides were orange and pink plaid and covered with band stickers.

Bouncing back up to her feet she exclaimed, "I'm all packed, Jack! Let's hit the tarmac!"

I realized that despite all the talk about pulling off this insane caper, I hadn't taken it seriously enough to pack a bag and I told her so.

I grabbed a handful of underwear and socks from Rudy's room along with a couple pairs of jeans and a stack of T-shirts. I shoved them into a gym bag we found on the floor of his closet.

Walking out the front door, we tried very hard not to look like two people fleeing the scene of a crime.

Rudy's car was perfect for our purposes. Like its owner, the car was so unremarkable that it was practically invisible; medium-sized, medium blue, European-made but not at all sporty. I got in behind the wheel and Girl slid into the passenger seat. I held out my hand to her. "Give me the keys."

She looked at me. Her eyes started to fill with tears. Her lower lip trembled.

"What? What's wrong?"

"Promise you won't get mad." Like I could get mad at that face.

"You're scaring me, Girl. What is it?"

"I forgot to get the keys."

"So what? Tell me where they are. I'll go get them."

"They're in Daddy's pants pocket."

CHAPTER 7

When I was a little kid, I remember my mother's brother told a joke to a bunch of other grown-up relatives. It was a silly, stupid story about a guy who buys a dolphin at a pet store. It's some kind of magical dolphin, though, and it will live forever as long as you feed it a special diet of myna birds (I told you it was a dumb story). The guy figures this won't be a problem, since he has a tree in his backyard where a flock of myna birds gathers every morning. Each day the guy walks to the tree and grabs a bird to take to the dolphin. One day, as he's going to the tree, there's this lion lying across the path sleeping. The lion's wearing a Penn State sweatshirt. The guy steps over the lion, grabs a bird, and goes back to the house—but as soon as he steps back over the lion again, a policeman appears and arrests him. When asked what the charge is the cop says, "Transporting a myna across state lions for immortal porpoises."

I didn't get it.

I thought about that joke often over the next few years. The adults in the room had laughed. Some moaned, saying things like "Christ! What a terrible pun!" But I didn't *get* it! It was a meaningless string of random words that was somehow supposed to be funny. I felt left out, but I was too embarrassed to ask anyone to explain the joke to me.

Because I had laughed, too.

I pretended to get the joke so my parents and aunts and cool older cousins would think I was sophisticated and mature. But now I lived under a curse, doomed to *never* get the joke. For a few years I lived in fear that someone would confront me with it: So just *why* do you think that joke's funny, Guy?

I wished. I prayed. I begged the universe to reveal the key to me. Then, one day... It happened!

I was watching an old black and white episode of "Perry Mason" after school. I was thirteen and I thought Mason was wicked the way he'd get up in front of the judge and jury and persuade them that justice should be done. I could never be that slick.

I was half listening to the show while I sprawled on the couch and leafed through the new issue of *Dynamite* magazine. As I finished reading an article and turned the page, I looked up at the television. The charges against this week's defendant were being read to the court.

The man before the judge was accused of... Wait for it... *Transporting a minor across state lines for immoral purposes!* I finally got the stupid lion/myna/porpoise pun! As the episode progressed, it even explained—in euphemistic terms palatable to a 1960s TV audience—what the phrase meant. I felt like a load had been lifted off my shoulders!

As I climbed the front steps of the Zamora porch on my way to play pocket pool with a dead guy, I thought about that joke and the TV show and I realized that I was about to transport a minor across state lines. And if fleeing the scene after executing that minor's father with a nail gun wasn't an immoral purpose, I didn't know what was. I pictured Girl as a big myna bird and started laughing (Okay, so maybe I'd had a little more grass while I was getting dressed in the kitchen).

I laughed as I entered the house. Still laughing I threw open the door to the garage. With feigned confidence I strode through the door. I held my chin high and threw back my shoulders, making myself big. Pumping myself up.

I got this. Show no weakness. Just reach in and grab the keys and run the fuck out of there.

I stopped.

Rudy was gone.

The chair we'd left him bound to was also gone. All that remained was the nail gun, a roll of duct tape and a surprisingly small smear of blood on the floor.

I freaked all the way out. My shoulders hunched forward as I folded in on myself, paralyzed. I was already on edge because of what we'd done and feeling paranoid from the weed. I ran over to where I'd last seen Rudy. Silly as it sounds, I actually waved one shaking hand through the air where the chair and its occupant used to be, as if perhaps the body had only become invisible. I was totally losing it.

Suddenly, bright light and loud rumbling! I snapped to attention. Turning toward the direction of the noise, I saw Rudy. He was still alive. He was also still lashed hand and foot to the chair, but somehow he'd managed to hop over to the wall-mounted button which opened the garage door. He was standing on his tip-toes, stretching up as far as he could from his semi-seated position and pressing the button with his tongue, his mangled lips leaving a big, red kiss mark around the switch.

Adrenaline transformed my fear into anger. I reached him in two long strides. I slapped one palm against the button, stopping the door at half-mast. With my other hand, I pushed Rudy's face away from the wall.

He slammed back down to a sitting position, but the momentum kept him going, tipping him backward onto the two rear legs of the chair. He balanced like that for a comically long time, bobbing his head like a chicken in an attempt to right himself. I reached out to steady him, but he flinched back from my hand and overbalanced. He crashed backward, his head hitting the concrete with a sound like a head hitting concrete.

I pushed the switch on the wall again and the door rumbled closed. I hoped nobody in the house across the street had seen their neighbor lying in his garage with a nail sticking out of his head and bloody clown makeup rimming his mouth.

Rudy's eyes were closed again and I didn't see any sign of life. Kneeling beside the fallen pedophile, I leaned slowly toward his face to listen for breathing. When we were almost nose-to-nose, his eyes opened wide and he shouted, *"BLUH!"*

I tumbled backward onto my ass and scrambled frantically, crab-walking in reverse toward the nail gun, which lay on the floor a couple of yards behind me. When I reached it, I grabbed the unwieldy apparatus and swung it around to aim at Rudy with both hands.

As much as I wanted to, I couldn't just walk away. A few minutes ago I had believed myself to be guilty of homicide. Now I knew that I wasn't but I couldn't enjoy the reprieve. Rudy might not be dead—yet—but he had looked right at me. I had to finish the job I had started.

I raised up onto my knees, then stood and walked over to his head. He was on his back, strapped to the chair like an astronaut preparing to blast into orbit. I stood so that his skull was between my feet. He faced me upside-down with eyes that kept glazing over and rolling up behind their lids then snapping back to focus on me again. The silvery head of the nail sparkling in a bruised circle on his forehead gave Rudy the look of an Indian mystic.

I let the weight of the nail gun hang from the limp ropes of my arms. I bent at the waist until its muzzle touched a spot midway between Rudy's hairline and the first nail. I took a deep breath and held it. I closed my eyes tight and pulled the trigger.

Nothing.

I opened my eyes and stood up straight again, looking for the switch that Girl had pressed before. It must have flipped to the *off* position when the nail gun dropped to the floor earlier.

"She's not really your babysitter, is she?"

DAMN IT! He got me again! I spasmed, losing my grip on the weighty power tool, dropping it onto the face between my feet. There was a gristly crunch as Rudy's nose broke, blood splashing out from one nostril in a fan pattern. The nail gun spun away across the floor.

"God damn it! Stop that!" I shouted as I descended to hands and knees and scrambled after the weapon.

I got it and turned back toward Rudy. He looked like shit but he was still alive and still awake. He looked right at me. His eyes were full of tears. I didn't know whether they were caused by grief over his imminent death or the blow to his nose or something entirely else. As I turned my attention back to the nail gun, determined to get it functional and finish the job, he spoke again.

"You don't look like a killer. How did she talk you into it?" For a man facing his mortality, Rudy's eyes held a baffling mix of resignation and sympathy.

"*SHUT UP! SHUT UP! SHUT UP!*" I tried to disregard the pitiable figure in front of me and concentrate on everything Girl had told me about her father—the kidnapping, the abuse.

I got the gun's power on and safety off and pulled the trigger. Nothing happened.

It dawned on me that there was an additional safeguard at the end of the barrel and I used the first two fingers of my left hand to engage it. I pulled the trigger again and this time a nail shot out between my fingers.

Yes!

I started firing wildly at Rudy's face from about three feet away, sitting on the floor with my legs out in front of me, screaming the whole time, "*How do you like that, motherfucker?!? Huh? Huh, big man? That'll teach you to rape my girlfriend, you sick asshole!!*"

A few nails lodged in his shoulder and face, but most tumbled wide, clinking away on the cement floor. I got my legs under me and knee-walked toward Rudy until the front of the gun was only an inch or so from his face. He clenched his eyes shut and turned away from me as I kept shouting abuse and squeezing the trigger again and again, leaving a neat line of finishing nails across his temple and around the side of his head, one of them pinning his ear tight against the skull.

Eventually I stopped. Rudy didn't move. I reached down to feel his neck for a pulse. I wasn't entirely sure where I was supposed to put my fingers, but I didn't feel anything and he looked pretty damn dead. I threw the nail gun away from me and ran out of the garage, crossed the foyer and exited the front door.

Girl was still sitting in the car where I'd left her. The car! The keys! Shit! I retraced my steps and patted down Rudy's hips, feeling for the keys. There they were, in his right front pocket. I reached in and grabbed them. One last look at the body to make sure it was still inanimate and out the door I went again.

When I got into the car and started the engine, Girl turned to me with a smile and said, "That was quick!"

CHAPTER 8

As we drove north out of Glendale, the scene of the crime in our rearview, adrenaline was still surging through my body. My limbs tingled and my mouth was dry. I gave Girl an abbreviated version of what had happened when I went back into the garage and found Rudy still alive. I told her about how I had kept shooting nails into him until he stopped moving.

She listened wide-eyed while twisted sideways in her seat, holding my bicep in her small hands. "You're so brave!" she gushed.

"I guess..." I said. "I don't really want to talk about it anymore for a while if that's okay..." My hands were still shaking.

I turned on the radio and twisted the knob to the bottom of the dial to KXLU, the Loyola Marymount University college station. I turned the volume up loud and let myself wallow in the gloomy echoes of Bauhaus singing about Bela Lugosi being dead.

As the song hit its nine-minute mark, Girl joked that the DJ must've had to take a shit. That made me laugh and I started to feel like everything would eventually be okay.

I decided to concentrate on the road trip ahead with denial-charged focus. With the vague nature of Girl's plans, one thing we were missing was money. We had maybe forty-five dollars and change between us. This wouldn't get us to Oregon's southern border, much less all the way to Portland at the far northern edge of the state. Gas alone would cost more than that plus we'd need to eat eventually.

It was around eight o'clock in the evening when we left Los Angeles County driving north on the I-5. We figured we'd get as far as we could on the half-full tank in Rudy's car and after that we'd make shit up as we went along.

Around midnight our fuel was running low. I took the next exit. A sign on the off-ramp promised, *GAS FOOD LODGING CAMPING NEXT RIGHT*. We rolled into a service station which sat on a lonely strip at the crossroads between the freeway and a dusty country lane.

I pulled the Volvo alongside one of a half-dozen self-serve pumps. When I opened the fuel hatch, I saw the words "DIESEL ONLY" encircling the perimeter of the gas cap. I got back behind the wheel and moved to the next filling station and lifted a diesel nozzle.

While I filled the tank, Girl walked over to chat with the pimply-faced local who was minding the till to see if she could figure out where we were and come up with some sort of plan to make some money.

As I was screwing the gas cap into place, she walked back to me swinging her hips more than usual and looking coyly over her shoulder at the attendant behind his little bullet-proof window.

"What was that all about?" I asked her.

"Well, little ugly dick and I had a very interesting conversation," she said, leaning against the car and waving with her fingertips toward the guy. He waved back. "So this is the gas. The food and lodging are in a town called Los Banos about eight miles that way," she pointed to the east, "and the camping is at something called 'Turtle Terrace RV Resort' which is two miles the other way." She pointed in the opposite direction.

"Doesn't 'Los Baños' mean 'The Bathrooms'?" I asked.

"I don't know and I don't care. The important thing right now is that mister smelly balls said he'd give me twenty dollars plus the tank of gas for a blowjob and I said okay."

I started to protest, but she stopped me with a hand on my crotch, the gesture hidden from the cashier's leering gaze by the side of the car. She started rubbing me through my jeans.

"He's watching," she continued, "Act chilly. I'm not really gonna do it. Anyway, I told him you were my brother and wouldn't care. I told him you were super tired from driving and wanted to take a nap in the car anyway. Pull around behind his little building where traffic can't see you. There's a door back there where he'll let me in. Give me a few minutes, then sneak in and bash him over the head with something. We'll take the money out of the cash register and make our getaway."

She was grinning ear to ear, high on the excitement of pulling off an actual robbery. I could feel *The Ghastly Giggle* bubbling just below the surface. I'd swear that Girl's mood swings could make the air pressure around her change. Sometimes I felt like my ears would pop just from being around her.

"I can't hit an innocent kid over the head!" I objected.

"Okay, how about if you saw him touching my tits and stuff? Could you hit him then?"

I didn't even have to think about that. "Let's do this," I said and slid behind the wheel. I figured I could wrestle with questions of moral ambiguity later. I rolled to the back of the building, the tires crunching on oily gravel. As I rounded the corner I looked over to see Girl skipping to the window.

Behind the gas station I swung the car around in a K turn and backed into the shadow of a large propane tank in the corner of the lot. Facing the back of the building,

I slouched down and watched from the darkness. There was a closed door on the rear wall.

After a minute Girl came around the side of the small structure. The kid opened the door but straddled the threshold, blocking enough of the opening that Girl would have to squeeze by him. She made a show of it, turning around and sloooowly sliding her ass across the front of his jeans as she passed. The kid followed her in, pulling the door closed behind him.

I slipped out of the car as quietly as I could. There was an empty coffee can on the ground, half-full of cigarette butts. I turned it over and stood on it with the ball of one foot, raised up on tippy-toe so that I could look through a small window set high in the wall beside the door.

I was looking down into a meager workspace. There was a counter with a cash register and a rack of maps, in front of which sat a thread-bare desk chair. On one wall was an old set of kitchen cabinets with no doors. Its grimy shelves held an assortment of spark plugs, motor oil and windshield wiper blades. A portable television stood atop a waist-high refrigerator in one corner. In another corner, a stack of pornographic magazines all but hid a shit-colored microwave oven.

From my elevated vantage point I could see that the kid was now sitting. I watched as Girl bent slightly, took hold of the arms of his chair, and swiveled it so that it faced away from the door. She straightened and began doing a strip tease for the zit-faced little hick. She was still wearing the *Penis Envy* T-shirt she'd cut into a halter top. With one hand she lifted the back of the neck loop up and over her head. She opened her fingers and let the strap drop, the fabric of the shirt only held in place over her breasts by her other hand starfished against her sternum. She flung her free hand in the air and let that arm flop across the top of her head while she closed her eyes and swayed her hips slowly back and forth.

I don't know about the pump jockey, but *I* was turned on as hell.

I stepped down from the can and started looking around for a rock or some other heavy object I could use as a weapon. Nothing. The lot around the little shed was surprisingly well maintained. I couldn't find anything heavier than an old basketball shoe. This was on the ground near the restroom doors which filled one side of the building.

I stepped into the men's room and looked in there. Nothing. I started to walk out again, but stopped when I saw movement out of the corner of my eye. I turned toward the motion, fists raised.

I was facing what remained of a mirror. It was missing part of its glass and my reflection only filled half of the frame. The top of my head had been deleted in a diagonal line, one blue eye staring back at me accusingly.

As I turned my head one way and then the other, my looking-glass twin smirked and sneered as he deformed across the remaining facets.

I pulled the largest, pointiest piece from the metal frame, fashioning a handle by wrapping paper towels around the wide end of the triangular shard.

Back at the entrance to the office, I turned the knob as quietly as I could and eased the door open. Sliding my head through the crack, I could see our friend the pump jockey with his back to me. He had one hand on each of Girl's tits and was squeezing them like he was trying to decide if they were ripe enough to purchase. Girl could see me over his head. She rolled her eyes and looked bored.

I felt a wave of jealousy when I saw Girl being groped, but not a big enough wave to stab the poor kid. Instead, I silently moved behind him and pulled his head back with one hand on his shiny, pimple-encrusted forehead. With the other hand I pressed the edge of my makeshift blade against his neck.

"Tell the lady how to open the cash drawer," I snarled into his ear, "or I'll slit you wide open."

The kid became literally paralyzed with fear. His whole body went rigid, a breast still held tight in each hand. Girl pulled free and stepped aside to tug the front of her shirt back up, but the boy's arms remained stretched out in front of him, his fingers like a hawk's talons grabbing for a fish. Girl turned and gestured toward the register.

"Well?" she snapped her fingers twice in front of the kid's bulging eyes.

His arms didn't move, but his mouth started working, "Umma umma umma you um you push the um gray the um big gray button um twice."

She did and the cash drawer slid open with a cheerful *cha-ching!*

In the corner that I hadn't been able to see from the window sat a rusty wire-mesh waste basket. From this, Girl dug out a McDonald's bag, its bottom translucent with fry oil, which she filled with money from the till. There were several twenties and a handful of smaller bills and change in the black plastic insert that divided the drawer into sections. Lifting the insert, she uncovered two hundred-dollar bills and a fifty as well as two paper-clipped bundles of five twenties each.

"Is there any more money in here?" I demanded, bearing down harder with the broken piece of mirror.

The kid's claw-like hands started trembling and he shook his head in tiny little twitches so as not to risk cutting his throat. "NuuhhNO! Just my wallet. You can take my wallet if you want it! Just don't kill me! PleeHEEeeease..." He started crying then, his words breaking up into hitching sobs and sniffles.

Girl got on her knees in front of the terrified townie

and reached around his body to fish the wallet from his back pocket. Inside were three sweaty singles, a condom so old it was crispy, and a school photo of a rather tragically cross-eyed teenage girl.

Girl looked at the back of the photo, then held it up for me to see. Written there was: *Corey— I'll never forget this summer. Luv always, Megan.*

Girl replaced the contents of the wallet and shoved it down the front of the kid's pants. She leaned in close to his ear.

"Okay, Corey," she half-whispered, "If you ever want to see Megan again, you'll do exactly what we say. Now, Corey, when your boss and the police ask who robbed you, how will you describe us?"

His voice was as quiet and breathy as Girl's, but much shakier: "Uuuuhhhuh…really um pretty and um sexy?"

Girl looked at me. "Kill him."

I cut Corey's skin just a bit with the edge of the glass. He went into instant freak-out mode. His arms were waving and his head was twitching around. He acted like somebody had given him an enema with battery acid.

"NO!! NO!! DON'T KILL ME! PLEASE! I'LL SAY WHATEVER YOU WANT! Just pleeheeeese don…duhon't huh huh huh…" He was back to sobbing.

Girl stroked his hair to calm him and spoke gently into his ear again, "Let me ask you the question once more, Corey. When your boss and the police ask who robbed you, how will you describe the *three Black men* who did it?"

Corey stopped trembling. He sat up straighter, looked Girl in the eye, and smiled. "Oh! Oh, okay! I get it! Yeah! It was three big Black guys! One of them put a knife to my throat and another one got the money..."

"Very good, Corey," Girl said, putting one hand on each of the kid's cheeks and giving him a little kiss on the mouth. "But you're forgetting one thing."

"What's that?" He looked worried again.

Girl stood and took a step over to the cabinet. She grasped a steel oil can by its flexible spout. "One of them hit you," she said, swinging the thick metal base around in a fast two-handed arc to connect with Corey's right temple, knocking him unconscious.

CHAPTER 9

I'm not a violent person. I've never been in a fight that amounted to more than a couple of drunk dudes shoving each other around because one of them got a little too rowdy in the slam pit or put the moves on the other one's girl. I had committed more violent acts in the last eight hours than in the previous nineteen years combined.

As I lay in the dark listening to Girl snoring quietly beside me, I pondered my motives. What was it about Girl that made me forget about things like ethics and conscience and the law?

A couple of hours ago as we drove away from the gas station, leaving the acne-faced attendant unconscious and drooling in his sad little box, we had *laughed!* We'd just committed our second felony that evening and we could Not. Stop. Laughing.

Girl had been in the passenger seat, her bare feet against the glove compartment. The grease-stained

McDonald's bag was in her lap. She was counting bills as she pulled them out, the stack in her other fist growing, "...five ninety-five, six hundred, six oh one, two, three, four— Holy shit! There's six hundred and nine dollars here!" She rummaged in the bottom of the bag, "And eighty-seven cents!"

"*Rad!*" I shouted, beep beep beeping the horn, high on the thrill of the moment. "Let's go get a room for the night and rest up!"

We were at the intersection just beyond the gas station. We could go one of three ways: forward to continue north on the freeway, right toward Bathroomville, or left away from town. I turned on my right-turn signal.

"Not that way," Girl said, putting a hand on my arm. "Too visible. I think we should lay low tonight. Let's check out that Turtle place."

I shrugged, indifferent. I turned left.

The sparse brush on either side of the road thickened to pine forest as we climbed slightly in elevation. After a couple of miles, the way forked. In front of us were dashes painted on pavement—yellow and white lines disappearing into the inky night like my memories of a normal life. To the right, a roughly tent-shaped metal sign with a reflective arrow painted on its surface directed us down a narrow drive of packed dirt which carved a serpentine path through the woods.

Turning the steering wheel to the right, my headlights illuminated a larger sign arching overhead with the words *TURTLE TERRACE* crafted from scrap iron. At the apex of the arch was a misshapen creature composed of discarded machine parts. I think it was supposed to be a turtle with wheels, but it looked more like a lizard being run over by a lawn mower. Below all of this, a smaller metal sign had *RV Resort + Campground* welded into its surface. The words *and nature park* had been added as an afterthought in white paint.

We drove under the watchful gaze of the turtle's gear-shaped eyes with their wing-nut lashes and came to a dark office that appeared closed for the night. I killed the headlights and rolled quietly past a small cluster of prefabricated buildings. A full moon illuminated the "resort". A dozen or so sizable motor homes were scattered here and there around the perimeter of a large clearing, parked within lines marked with white spray paint on the dirt. Each space had poles and pipes coming out of the ground with electric and water hook-ups. The huge vehicles were tethered to these like moored pleasure boats surrounding a cove.

A grassy park filled the interior of the circle. To one side was a handful of picnic tables and barbecue grills, some under simple wooden shelters. Across the clearing from these, a rust-pocked set of playground equipment emerged from encroaching ivy, bent fingers of broken monkey bars reaching toward the moonlight. A roundabout which must have once hosted squealing children pushing each other in dizzy circles was angled into the dirt like a crashed UFO.

The centerpiece of the clearing was a round, rock-walled fire pit about twenty feet across. This was surrounded by a mis-matched collection of camp chairs and patio furniture. Within the circle, smoking embers sent occasional fountains of sparks cracking into the air, evidence of a gathering recently dispersed. I parked Rudy's car in a space hidden from the office by an expensive-looking land yacht with a large bumper sticker on the back that said *RV There Yet?*

We'd catch a couple of hours sleep in the car and try to slip out before the manager caught us. If we were discovered, we could always pay for our use of the site at that time. Girl and I reclined the front seats and told each other goodnight. She was asleep almost instantly, apparently untroubled by the appalling acts she'd committed that evening. Considering all that had happened in the last few hours, the innocent smile on her face as she slept gave me an uneasy sense of discomfort.

I closed my own eyes, trying not to think about what would happen if the police figured out that we were the ones who nail-gunned Rudy. Girl seemed to have planned everything pretty well; maybe there was a chance we could get away without being caught. Even if the authorities never caught up to us, though, the judge and jury inside my head were determined to mete out justice in the form of torturous nightmares.

I awakened from a dream in which Girl had me tied to the table saw in her father's garage. She was cutting slices from my head, tossing them into a frying pan where they sizzled and popped. They smelled like bacon. Every slice that hit the pan was accompanied by chirpy, tinny, arcade music. When I squinted and blinked my way to consciousness, the sun was shining in my eyes through the windshield. I still smelled bacon. I also still heard that video game noise—like a robot bird greeting the morning somewhere in the distance.

tweedleedleedleedle...

As the fog of sleep dissipated I became aware of my surroundings. I was still in the reclined driver's seat of the car we'd stolen from Rudy Zamora. I looked over at the passenger seat. Girl was gone.

tweedleedleedleedle...

Where the hell was that sound coming from? I pulled the lever, returning my seat to an upright position, and reached for the window crank. I rolled the window down a few inches.

tweedleedleedleedle...

The sound didn't get any louder. The bacon smell

got stronger, though. That, I could tell, was coming from the open door on the side of the luxury motor home we'd parked beside.

tweedleedleedleedle...

But what was making that goddamn noise? It must be something inside the car. I sat up and cocked my head to the side, trying to pinpoint the direction the sound was coming from.

tweedleedleedleedle...

There. Under the seat. I reached between my feet and felt a handle. Grabbing it, I pulled out a rectangular black case the size and weight of a lunch box with a brick in it. A coiled phone-cord-looking cable was sticking out of one corner, the other end connected to the car's cigarette lighter outlet. *Motorola* was embossed into the case's faux leather top flap, which fastened with a plastic clasp.

TWEEDLEELEEDLEEDLE...

It was a car phone! I'd seen them in TV shows, but I'd never actually used one. I opened the lid and located the handset. It was a long, black, futuristic-looking paddle with an intimidating array of flat buttons with cryptic markings covering one surface, along with a little rectangular display like the face of a digital watch. As I tried to puzzle out which of the cluster of symbols you pushed to answer a call, the twittering stopped. In the vacuum of the sudden silence, I heard Girl's voice from beyond the camper door. It was too muffled to make out more than an occasional word amid the machine gun patter of her animated monologue, but I was pretty sure I heard the word "eloping."

CHAPTER 10

I placed the phone's receiver back into its recessed compartment and clipped the lid shut. As I returned the case to its spot under the seat, my head was full of questions: Who was trying to call Rudy on his fancy Hollywood car phone? What would happen when they couldn't reach him? How long until somebody went looking for him at his house? What really nagged at me, though, was the question of whether to tell Girl about the telephone; and more to the point, why was I seriously considering *not* telling her?

Before I had time to fully ponder these questions, Girl appeared in the doorway and hipetty-hopped down the RV's aluminum steps, a glass of orange juice in her hand. She let out a joyful little whoop when she saw that I was awake. Turning her head, she called over her shoulder, "Dale! Tony! He's up!"

A woman answered from the camper, "Well it's about time that fiancé of yours joined the livin'!"

I looked beyond Girl toward the source of the voice. From the silver-rimmed orifice of the doorway emerged an orbicular middle-aged lady in aquamarine spandex leggings and a lemon-colored tube top. To say this woman was egg-shaped would be selling her short; she was *eggs*-shaped. It was as if a child, while coloring Easter eggs one Spring morning, decided to assemble a whimsical egg person. A turquoise belly egg sat below two enormous, orange, spray-tanned egg tits sitting pointy side down in their yellow basket. The left one was decorated with a rose. Atop these sat the woman's amazing egg head, crowned by a teased and laminated hair egg the color of pumpkin guts. On the front of her head egg, a warmly smiling face had been painted in lipstick and eye shadow.

This spectacular creature took the four low steps like a force of nature, plump egg arms swinging and egg fists clenched. When she reached ground level, I realized that without the towering shock of hair, she was even shorter than Girl's modest height. On squat eggy legs she stomped the four strides to where I waited, amazed, in the car. She grabbed the outside handle and yanked the door wide. Standing her full height she was looking me in the eye while I sat in the low driver's seat.

"Good mornin', sleepyhead!" She reached out and took my upper arm in both her hands and pulled me forcefully from the car. "Come on inside 'n' let's get some food in that belly!" She patted me on the stomach. As the little woman turned back toward the camper, she said to Girl, "After the menfolk are done with breakfast, I'll show y'all where yer wedding's gonna be!"

Girl winked at me behind the woman's back as Dale stamped up the steps ahead of us. From this angle I could see that the egg lady's mischievous sculptor had scrambled the eggs which filled the back of her stretch pants.

I mouthed, *"WEDDING?!"* Girl responded by breathing on her nails and polishing them on an imaginary lapel as she took me by the hand and led the way into the enormous vehicle.

Inside Dale and Tony's spacious mobile retirement nest, the smell was heavenly. Bacon and coffee and a hint of incense. A breakfast buffet that would have fed a modest crew of lumberjacks filled a sturdy rolling island. Beside this, a removable-looking table on a single metal pole was surrounded by a crescent of lavishly comfortable sofa-style seating. Rustic woven blankets and crocheted throws covered the leather upholstery. A picture window behind the sitting area looked out on a corrugated metal building which formed an L shape with the office. A stenciled sign on its wooden door read *PLAYROOM.*

We were standing between the table and a full-sized kitchen. The entire space was larger than I expected based on the outside of the vehicle. On closer examination, I realized that one whole section of the camper slid outward while parked, expanding the interior.

"Tony's takin' a shower. He's lookin' forward to meetin' you, though, after what-all your gal was tellin' us!" Dale had already set a plate for me. She was loading it with French toast, bacon, crispy patties of pan-fried corned beef hash, scrambled eggs, and a wedge of cantaloupe. My portion barely made a dent in the smorgasbord.

"Think you made enough?" I joked with a grin.

"Well not with you two surprise guests, but Tony'll just have to make do," Dale replied. She showed zero signs of being ironic.

Girl was still holding my hand. I could feel her vibrating with gleeful anticipation. She knew something I didn't.

I heard the shower stop. After a few moments, a door opened somewhere and the bus-sized vehicle tipped to one side beneath my feet. The wheeled cart full of food rolled several inches to starboard before the floor tipped the opposite way, sending the cart gliding gently back to its original position as the RV over-corrected then returned to level.

At the end of the corridor was a bedroom illuminated by another large window. As I watched, the light was blocked by a hulking backlit figure whose shoulders barely cleared the walls on either side. As he stepped out of the shadowy hallway and into the sunny common area, there was one thing I knew for certain about Tony: He was uncircumcised.

I was so surprised at the huge man's nudity that I fixated on his dick for an awkwardly long time. A neatly trimmed pompom of white pubic hair topped the impressive girth of Tony's shaft, which tapered to a point where the smallish head was draped in foreskin. Framed on either side by Tony's clean-shaven scrotum, it looked like a cone of vanilla ice cream being held in a child's fist.

"Eyes are up here, brother!" Tony boomed jovially. He pointed to his grinning face with his left hand as he thrust his right toward me to shake. I offered my own hand which vanished into a fleshy cocoon of fingers. My gaze moved up, taking in an expansive, ivory-furred chest bracketed by tanned and tattooed biceps whose size rivaled the cantaloupes on the breakfast tray. A thick pedestal of a neck supported Tony's bald, bearded head.

Looking at the man's smooth cranium and luxurious silver whiskers, I felt like a kid reading *Highlights* magazine with its trick drawings of faces which, when turned upside-down, miraculously became entirely different faces. Knitted brows turned into double chins. Beards became bouffants. I resisted the urge to invert my own head to get a better look at Tony's clean-shaven proxy. If I had, I'm sure his bushy eyebrows would have made a spectacular mustache.

I thought that the big, naked man would return aft and put on some clothes after introducing himself but instead he strode past me and heel-kicked a lever that unlocked the plush driver's seat from its forward-facing position, rotating it to face the dining area. While Dale picked up a big, oval platter and began constructing an epic tower of food for her man, Tony dropped heavily into his chair, genitalia proudly presented between wide-spread tattooed thighs.

"Don't just stand there gawpin', son. Eat up!" Tony had a voice that sounded like it came from low in his chest, filtered on the way to his mouth through small, sharp rocks. "I know I'm pretty, but I ain't sweet as Dale's cookin'!"

"You're full o' shit but I love ya." Dale kissed him on the cheek and pulled a folding metal TV tray from somewhere. Balancing Tony's breakfast in one hand, she whipped the tray open with the other, set it between Tony's knees, and thunked down the heavy platter of food.

I was so distracted by the surprise exhibition of beefcake that I'd forgotten all about my own heaping breakfast. I sunk into the seat in front of my plate and dug in. I hadn't eaten anything since before we'd dispatched Rudy in his garage the previous evening and my stomach gurgled gratefully as I chewed a mouth full of French toast. It was light, fluffy, and full of cinnamon. Delicious!

Girl nestled in beside me. Dale sat across from us. Nobody spoke for several minutes as Tony and I dug enthusiastically into our meals. Girl and Dale, who had apparently already eaten their fill, sipped orange juice and coffee respectively. With Tony's junk shielded from view by his breakfast tray, the scene took on a comforting, domestic feel.

Girl broke the silence. "So. Tony. Nice cock."

I nearly gagged on my corned beef hash, but Dale and Tony just smiled at each other and raised their eyebrows.

"Thanks, little lady!" Tony beamed. Addressing me, he added, "I understand this is y'all's first time in a clothing-optional resort." I turned and looked at Girl. It was clear from the way she was grinning at me that she had been waiting to see my reaction when I found out what sort of place we'd stumbled into.

Through the window behind Girl's head, movement caught my eye. Looking over her shoulder, I saw the door to the campground rec room open and a pair of senior citizens emerge. Between them, they were wearing two pairs of flip-flops, a daisy-print terrycloth hair wrap, and a wristwatch. I'd never seen naked people of such advanced years before. "Wow," I said, "Gravity's a bitch."

The ladies and I were misted with juice as Tony exploded into deep, contagious laughter which infected each member of our little group until we all had tears running down our cheeks.

CHAPTER 11

The food was delicious. Listening to the women's conversation while I ate, I learned that Dale had spotted us parked in the neighboring camping space when she woke to make an early-morning supply run into town in their "get-about"—a little yellow AMC Gremlin which got towed behind the camper when they were on the road. Upon returning from the grocery store, Dale had found Girl sitting on the stones of the firepit and invited her inside. There, Girl explained our situation.

According to the story she told the couple, we were running away to get married against the wishes of our families who forbade our love because of a blood feud which stretched back generations and involved a patent dispute from the turn of the century. It seems we were convinced that if we eloped and then revealed our union, both sides would come together and end the silly quarreling once and for all.

And we were getting hitched today. Here. At this

nudist camp. *My life A.G.*

Dale made it clear that she was *very* excited and would be planning everything (along with her inner circle of naked ladies). Apparently it had been a few years since they'd had a wedding at Turtle Terrace. The owner of the camp was an old friend and a certified justice of the peace registered in neighboring Los Banos. And, according to Tony, "All the gals here get mucho worked up for weddings and baby births."

I finished my last bite of eggs and leaned back in the overstuffed seat, full and happy and looking forward to whatever came next. Dale stood and started clearing plates and cutlery. Girl joined in with the cleanup. Pushing aside his TV tray, Tony stood and stretched. I examined the corner where the wall met the ceiling, not positive I could resist staring at the eye-level penis in front of me if I relaxed my gaze.

"Fantastic food as always, baby!" Tony patted Dale on the fanny, then turned to me. "Join me outside for a smoke, bud!" Tony grabbed the small towel he'd been sitting on and draped it around his neck. Slipping his feet into a pair of flip-flops, he opened a drawer to one side of the sink and pulled out two gigantic cigars the color of dark chocolate. Without looking to see if I was following, the big man disappeared through the door.

I caught up with Tony outside on the far side of the camper. He was seated on his towel on one of a quartet of low-backed chairs crudely chainsawed out of girthy logs surrounding a bulbous terracotta Mexican wood stove with a top-hat chimney. As I sat down on the chair beside his, Tony produced a wooden match from somewhere (seriously—where was he hiding that?). Holding the match tightly in his right fist, he popped the head into flame with the thumbnail of that same hand. He performed an elaborate lighting ritual that involved sucking and puffing and rolling the end of the cigar in the flame. Tony's head and shoulders quickly vanished behind a haze of bluish-white smoke. The smell was like leather oil and raked leaves. When the cloud disbursed, he was holding the lit cigar out to me and saying, "Here ya go."

I took the cigar. I thought the end would be wet from Tony's mouth, but it was perfectly dry. As Tony repeated the process on his own smoke, I took a tentative pull on mine. This was my first experience with what was obviously a very expensive cigar. My tongue went numb as I held the smoke in my mouth with minimal inhalation. After a moment of savoring the flavor I let the smoke pour out my nose.

As the haze between us dissipated, Tony whistled, wide-eyed. "Not a single freakin' cough! Real good!"

It surprised me how much this man's manly and man-to-man compliment moved me. I didn't feel like not coughing made me masculine. I was just such a pothead that my throat was immune to smoke. Still—his simple praise was more effort than my own father ever made at male bonding.

"Heh. Thanks," I chuckled, "I don't know shit about cigars, but this is nice!"

"Then that's all you *need* ta know, brother!" Tony nodded with a mock-serious scowl.

I took a longer draw this time and blew a couple of smoke rings. Blowing smoke rings is one of those skills that's supposed to pass from father to son. Or maybe it's taught by an older brother sneaking butts behind the garage. I learned from a book.

In sixth grade I went through an amateur magician phase, schooling myself on all aspects of prestidigitation. Most of this priceless and arcane knowledge came from the library or from slim, cheaply printed pamphlets procured through order forms snipped out of comic books.

One of these booklets had a whole section on the art of cigarette manipulation (This was the 1970s and a cigarette was as logical as a coin or a watch if you were going to do slight of hand tricks with a prop provided by your audience). The slim volume was published in England and the chapter in question was titled *Fancy Fag Flourishes!* Besides teaching how to vanish and reappear "fags" in various and whimsical ways (Up your nose and out your mouth! From behind a child's ear!) and how to throw a cigarette with pinpoint accuracy (Into milady's cleavage! Into a child's ear!) there were "flourishes" which were done while actually *smoking* the cigarette. The forbidden nature of these techniques made them irresistible to eleven-year-old Guy.

Walking to school one day, I stopped at the bodega where I always bought comics and bubble gum cards. I put an Archie Double Digest and a pack of Marlboros beside the cash register and said, "They're for my grandma. She's stuck in bed. She had hemorrhoid surgery."

The middle-aged man behind the counter wrinkled his nose in distaste as he rang up the items and muttered, "Eighty-five cents." I counted out change. He put my purchase in a paper sack. I took it and left. Not once did he bother to question my story or even really look at me.

I went through that pack of Marlboros over the next month, practicing tricks with both lit and unlit fags. It was during this time that I got really good at smoke rings (To this day I can also grip the filter end of a half-smoked cigarette with my tongue, open my mouth, and gently reverse the whole thing behind my teeth so that the lit end is now pointing toward my throat. In this position I can close my lips and blow smoke out my nose, pretend to drink, and generally chill out as long as I want before flipping it back out still lit).

Tony took an almighty pull on his cigar. With a face

like a howling wolf, he blew a big smoke ring which hung in the air heavier and longer than a cigarette's would. My mouth already full of fragrant fumes, I pursed my lips in a tight little o against my teeth. With upward jerks of my lower jaw I sent a sequence of tiny smoke rings parading through Tony's larger one. Tony beamed a fatherly grin in my direction and slapped me on the back. *That* made me cough.

We finished our cigars, smoking and chatting comfortably. The time flew by and I didn't once think about Rudy's corpse.

I heard the door open on the opposite side of the RV, then feminine voices and laughter getting louder as Dale and Girl came our way. Perched on our logs, Tony and I turned to look in the direction of the sound just as the pair came into view. Between them they were wearing a shoulder-length bridal veil held in place with a jeweled tiara, pink Converse All-Stars, and a pair of yellow suede Birkenstocks.

To boner or not to boner? That was the question. Looking at Girl I could feel my crotch tightening. The fact that she wasn't *completely* naked was crazy sexy! Shoes usually come off *before* you shed your other clothes, you know? Wearing *only* shoes says, "I'm going to walk around in the nude. Outside. For everybody to see. Deal with it." *Yowza*. Now I was fully turgid.

Thankfully I was still clothed. When, inevitably, I was encouraged to strip off like everybody else, would my stiffy be seen as a naturist faux pas? I needed to take arms against my hard-on and by opposing end it. My attention had been exclusively on Girl since the women had rounded the end of the camper; in an attempt to cool my visible arousal, I decided to concentrate on Dale's naked form. I dragged my gaze away from Girl and turned it toward the peeled egg lady.

Uh-oh.

The sight of Dale striding toward me cunt-first made me grow even more firm. The woman was every aboriginal fertility totem; every Freudian breastfeeding hangup. She wore her self-assured sexuality like a Kevlar vest. Proud. Unbreakable.

Dale's breasts were magnificent. Surprisingly for her age and their size, her ghostly areolas—only slightly pinker than the surrounding skin and the size of tea saucers—were directed straight at me. They looked like they'd follow you around like Mona Lisa's eyes. An inscrutable belly button smiled tight-lipped beneath. The rose which I had seen peeking above the rim of Dale's tube top was the northern terminus of a tattooed bouquet which cascaded down her softly rolling rib cage to the voluptuous hillock of her left hip. Following it down, my eyes were drawn to the inviting tuft of her bush, trimmed to a tidy triangle and dyed the same orange as her hair!

The two ladies stopped in front of us. Dale stood fists on hips, elbows and knees akimbo, pelvis thrust forward. On my low wooden seat I was eye-level with her very pretty pudendum. At this rate I was *never* going to lose my erection.

As it turned out, I didn't need to worry. I was invited to go inside and disrobe in private to whatever level made me comfortable. Dale and Tony reassured me that there was never any pressure. Their whole deal, I was informed, centered around freedom and comfort and being part *of* nature instead of apart *from* nature and all sorts of other hippy shit that actually sounded really nice. By the time I was on my own inside the trailer, my penis was flaccid and I was eager to see what all the fuss was about.

Wearing white tube socks with a navy and orange stripe around the top, Israeli military surplus combat boots, and a pair of black Ray-Ban knock-offs, I palmed open the aluminum door and stepped out into the sunshine. I was alone on that side of the RV. A light breeze tickled the hairs on my scrotum. The heat of the day lovingly cupped my butt cheeks.

I raised my hands high above my head and slowly

spun once around, luxuriating in the sun's kiss on brand new parts of me. Armpits. Legpits. All my pits. *Mmmmmm...* I could get used to this.

CHAPTER 12

T he wedding was pretty ridiculous. It was also kind of beautiful.

At one point somebody had placed a top hat on my head so now I was wearing that and my boots, standing in front of thirty naked people seated on towel-covered folding camp chairs. It was shocking how quickly I had lost my self-consciousness. Between the chilled out attitude of the RV Park's residents and Tony's helpful advice ("Hard-ons happen, brother."), I found myself settling easily into the lifestyle. It was just so... *comfortable!*

News of the wedding had spread quickly through the tight-knit community. Girl and I were instructed to relax and take it easy while preparations were made. As Dale and two other sturdily-built ladies had begun collecting chairs from the campers and arranging them in rows with an aisle in-between, Tony stomped into the woods with a fireman's ax over his shoulder. After a while, he had emerged with a bundle of long, thin saplings under one burly arm and begun fashioning them into a leafy archway at the front of the assembly of chairs.

Now here I was, standing naked under the arch and waiting for Girl to walk down the aisle in front of me. Over my right shoulder stood Hank, owner of Turtle Terrace and local justice of the peace. He was a leathery little Latino in his mid-sixties. He sported a tiny gray mustache which he clearly straight-razored to a pencil line daily. He had a full head of hair styled into a glossy salt-and-pepper pompadour with a matching thatch poking out around the spiral notebook which he held in both hands at crotch level. On his chest, a constellation of tight white ringlets against walnut skin framed a pair of blue-rimmed reading glasses hanging on a braided gold chain.

Looking around the congregation, I recognized several people who had introduced themselves and congratulated us as we lounged beside the fire ring earlier on a pair of oversized Adirondack chairs, their vertical slats painted the colors of the rainbow in spectrum order. On the flat surfaces above our heads, glittering gold crowns were rendered in metallic paint and glass gems.

As we'd held court side by side on these splendid thrones, Girl and I had been presented with refreshments including bottles of beer, a whole kielbasa, a big bowl of mixed fruit and a fat joint that we passed back and forth, getting delightfully baked while the California sun warmed our bare bodies.

At one point a skinny little dude with black-dyed Elvis hair—sideburns and all—sauntered bow-legged up to us, his long, narrow pecker swinging like a pendulum, and introduced himself as "Chuck! Your wedding photographer!" He had a Polaroid camera hanging from a strap around his neck. He opened the hinged top, held it to his eye, and instructed us to "Strike a pose!"

I reflexively crossed my legs, hiding my genitals from the gaze of the lens, and gave Chuck a toothy smile with double finger guns. The shutter clicked and the undeveloped picture whizzed out of the slot in the camera's front. Chuck said "Nice!", handed me the print, and walked away.

Girl leaned over the arm of her chair in my direction and I inclined toward her, holding the snapshot between us so we could both watch it develop. The greenish-gray square gradually resolved into an image of the two of us on our rainbow seats of honor. There I was, grinning crazily and pointing my fingers at the viewer while beside me, Girl had one hand behind her head, elbow out to the side, with her other palm against the inside of one of her wide-spread thighs. Her eyes were half-closed and her lips were puckered into a kiss.

Standing under the arch later, I saw Chuck take his place in the front row of chairs, camera in hand to record the ceremony for posterity.

Just then, a door opened across the clearing on the side of a gleaming silver Airstream the size of a B-52 bomber. An ancient Creole woman named Lady K who had given us a tarot reading earlier in the day ("Before you...the six of cups. You'll be reuniting with an absent loved one soon," she had intoned. Girl squeezed my arm and whispered, "Mommy!") leaned out and waved in my direction. Beside me, Hank said, "Go time!" and waggled his notebook at a pale, red-bearded gentleman in a plaid flat cap who stood and began playing the Wedding March on bagpipes. He paced in a circle as he played, his freckled todger bobbing in time.

I hadn't seen Girl since a giggling gaggle of aunties had spirited her away around three-thirty. It was quarter after five as I stood waiting for her to appear.

And then there she was.

All day, Girl had been wearing a flimsy party-store veil meant for bridal showers and her pink Chuck Taylor sneakers. As she exited the Airstream to the other-worldly droning of the pipes and slow-stepped toward me flanked by her entourage of middle-aged bridesmaids, I saw that her wedding attire had been upgraded. Now she had on a pair of knee-high white patent-leather go-go boots with four-inch heels, white lace gloves and a diaphanous veil which draped from a crown of white silk roses all the way down to her ribcage, where delicately crocheted lace defined its bottom edge.

Even though I was quickly getting used to this whole naturist gimmick, I couldn't help chubbing up a little as Girl approached me, a white bouquet clutched between veiled bosom and exposed loins. A happy murmur of appreciation spread through the crowd at my visible show of affection.

Girl handed her bouquet to Dale, who sat down in the front row with the other members of the bridal party. As I took Girl's hands in mine and looked into her eyes, Flat-Cap stopped playing and sat back down, his pipes wheezing out an anticlimactic *honk* as leftover air escaped his bag.

Up close, I could appreciate the magnitude of my bride's makeover. The *walkin'* boots weren't the entirety of the Nancy Sinatra theme; a blonde ponytail fall had been clipped into Girl's platinum pixie. I could see frosted pink lips and blue eyeshadow through the filmy fabric of the veil. My semi went from six-thirty to eight o'clock. "Aaaaaawwww..." the congregation sighed in chorus. To my left I heard the *click—whiz* of Chuck's Polaroid.

Hank put on his reading glasses and opened the notebook to a page marked with a sticky note. "Friends and lovers both old and new, we are gathered here today to celebrate a promise of love. An oath of commitment. A declaration of cooperation and trust..."

Trust.

"Do you trust me?" Girl had asked as we sat watching preparations being made for the wedding and the party to follow. In the firepit, five naked men were stacking wood into an intricate tower for a bonfire later. Without their clothes, I found myself guessing what these dudes did in the outside world based on hairstyles and tattoos. Footwear was no help since flip-flops and leather hippy sandals were nearly ubiquitous (except for the fellow in the ostrich skin cowboy boots; there's always one rebel).

"Trust you how?" I asked.

"To keep us safe. To stop us getting arrested."

She went on to say that she'd been thinking about our situation. Technically, we weren't on the run since nobody was chasing us. We didn't need to use fake names or lay low. In fact, she explained, this wedding was the perfect high-profile alibi in case we *were* considered suspects in Rudy's death. One could argue that the only crime we were guilty of was underage love. We simply borrowed her dad's car to run away and get married and Rudy was still alive when we did so.

Girl and I both had IDs with our real names and fictional birth dates. Mine was made by a friend with access to a color Xerox machine and a laminator. Girl told me she had bought hers from a senior at school.

They were good enough for indifferent doormen in dimly lit dive bars. Turns out they were also convincing enough for an off-duty naked court officer squinting and muttering his way through the details of a marriage license on a small, red, portable typewriter balanced on his bare knees while he was perched on the edge of a canvas director's chair with "STARLET" in sequins across the back.

"Do you, Guy Montague Larsen, take Abigail Maria Zamora to be your lawfully wedded wife, for richer and poorer, in sickness and in health, through the good times and the bad, forsaking all others today and forever?"

Did I?

As we had lounged about, eating and drinking and smoking while the camp bustled around us, Girl had talked me through *her* thinking, wedding-wise.

"When I made up that whole story to Tony and Dale about our families and eloping and shit, I didn't think they'd throw us a wedding *today*, but then I figured— what the fuck. I love you."

Matter-of-fact. Not even looking at me. Passing me the joint. It was the first time either of us had said those words.

As I was taking a hit, attempting to mentally recover from the unexpected L-bomb, she had leaned over the wooden arms of our chairs and grinned at me, her voice lowered. "Besides, we are going to be *showered* with cash wedding presents! These people are all estranged from disapproving families and they're...whattaya call it...living vicariously or whatever. Their *own* kids would never even *attend* a nudist wedding, much less have one *themselves!*" She leaned over farther, plucked the joint from between my lips and kissed me on the mouth. Settling back into her own throne she had exclaimed, "We're the most exciting thing that's happened here in a long time!"

"I... I Do."

Why did I hesitate? This was all play-acting, right? The marriage would never hold up in court... *Right?*

I still hadn't told Girl that I loved her, too. She hadn't said it to me with any expectation of reciprocation. I wasn't sure she even really realized that she'd said it. Right after that, the bridal brigade had shown up to take her away for her bachelorette party-slash-beauty appointment.

Now she was in front of me and the sight of her took away any misgivings I might have been harboring. *"I love you,"* I mouthed as Hank turned his head to the right and addressed her.

"Do you, Abigail Maria Zamora, take Guy Montague Larsen to be your lawfully wedded husband, for richer and for poorer, in sickness and in health, through the good times and the bad, for today and all of your tomorrows?"

"YOU BET I DO!" Girl shouted into my grinning face.

"Well then," said Hank, taking off his reading glasses and lowering his notebook, "By the power vested in me by the great state of California, it brings me immense joy to pronounce you husband and wife. Please let us all share in your first kiss as a married couple."

So we did.

The reception was every bit as lucrative as Girl had predicted.

Two of the picnic tables had been pushed end-to-end into a single long buffet. A three-tiered white cake sat in the middle of this bounty, somehow baked from scratch inside one of the whale-like buses whose amber-eyed windows glowed along our lamp-lit party's quickly glooming edges.

A third picnic table had been positioned perpendicular to—and slightly apart from—the food table. Along its front edge hung a hand-markered paper banner: *GIFTS*.

As the bonfire licked the stars and naked bodies danced in and out of its glow, spurred on by chaotic bongos and banjo, frantic flute and mandolin, a pile of envelopes grew on the gifts table. Every time I looked, more greeting cards thick with cash had been added to the stack. This tribe who was feting us only numbered ten or twelve couples and a few singletons, but I could swear at least two dozen wedding presents waited to be opened.

We partied late into the night before retiring to the "bridal suite" prepared for us in one of the cluster of buildings around the office. Behind the *PLAYROOM* trailer which housed bumper pool and foosball along with a TV and a modest bar, there was a corrugated metal shed labeled *LIBRARY*.

Inside was an eclectic collection of books displayed on stainless steel industrial shelving. Between the bookcases a queen-sized air mattress had been inflated, filling nearly the entirety of the bare plywood floor. A heavy comforter in a cheetah print and shiny, gold satin sheets made up the bedding. A gauzy red scarf had been draped over a battery-powered lantern on a shelf, the resulting blush transforming the little storage unit into our own rose-tinted love nest. Already naked, Girl and I kicked off our shoes, slid inside the slippery bedding and consummated our union as the raucous music of the reception's ongoing after-party echoed through the trees outside.

CHAPTER 13

We woke to a communal breakfast already in full swing. The tables had been left in place from the night before but now the leftover cake was joined by a huge, Sterno-warmed tray of scrambled eggs. This was flanked by platters of bacon and sausage, stacks of waffles and a deep cookpot of maple syrup-laced oatmeal. The smell was sublime.

Everywhere I looked there were naked asses on towels. Happy greetings were tossed our way as Girl and I walked among the breakfasting naturists, a few of whom had never called an end to the previous night's celebration. The fire was still being stoked. One old hippy with a battered acoustic guitar noodled pretty melodies into the morning air.

Bellying up to the mouthwatering spread, I dispensed coffee from a tall chrome cylinder into two Styrofoam cups and handed one to Girl. We each filled a paper plate. Dale and Tony were on a couple of the log chairs beside their motorhome, drinking from matching mugs with embossed Harley Davidson logos. Towels had been placed on the two empty seats. Taking that as an invitation, we strolled over and joined them, setting our plates on our bare thighs and our coffee cups on the ground beside us.

After some polite small-talk about how well we slept and how hung-over everyone was, Tony set his mug on the ground and leaned forward, forearms on knees.

"Dale and I been talkin' and we think you shouldn't go right back to your families. That's just gonna be a metric shit-ton of drama that you don't need to rush into. You got a nice chunk o' change there," the big man jerked his head toward the *GIFTS* table, still laden with envelopes (though the size of the pile looked more realistic in the sober light of day). "Take yourselves a honeymoon. Go someplace fun. Have an adventure you'll never forget. Give everybody back home time to worry a little. Miss y'all a little. All the bullshit'll still be there in a week."

It felt awful lying to these sweet, generous people. I wanted to unburden my troubled conscience. I wanted to scream, *There is no family! There is no feud! We're criminals! We're killers! We've scammed all of you!*

But I didn't do that. These folks were happy. Girl and I had brought joy into this little circle of covered wagons in the woods. My selfish desire for honesty would only tarnish that bliss.

It felt strange standing there fully dressed, hugging all of our new naked friends good-bye. With the exception of a few full-time RV-ers (including, it turned out, Dale and Tony), most of these people had real lives and stationary houses elsewhere. Pieces of paper were pressed into our hands with phone numbers and addresses in the Midwest, Utah, Rhode Island. These were accompanied by sincere invitations to visit if we were ever in the area.

We waved our arms good-bye out the open windows of the car. A group of people followed, waving back, as we turned onto the rough road out of camp. My rearview mirror was full of dicks and tits being sprayed with dust kicked up from our tires. Ahead through the windshield I saw the back of the wheeled tortoise atop the arching sign at the camp's entrance. From this angle he had a welded set of cock and balls. Below him was painted: *NOW LEAVING TURTLE TERRACE — PUT YOUR DAMN CLOTHES ON!*

We reached the end of the private drive and turned right onto an artery road that fed into Interstate 5, heading north toward Portland. Girl snapped the radio on and picked up the top envelope from the stack on her lap. As Depeche Mode wondered aloud what makes a man hate another man, Girl opened the envelope. Inside were two fifty-dollar bills and a tarot card; the six of cups. Written on the card's back was, "May the Goddess smile on your journey! —Lady K".

As we made our way northward, Girl continued to open envelopes. The gifts inside were mostly money along with a few checks made out to "cash" and one two-hundred-dollar savings bond with a picture of FDR on it. Most of these were enclosed in blank greeting cards with heartfelt messages penned inside and holiday-neutral images on the front. There were a pair of cardinals on a budding branch, a country meadow with a fawn looking at a butterfly, an old-timey woodcut of a European village.

It's a universal truth that old people always keep a box of blank greeting cards around—even old nomadic nudists.

The amounts of the gifts ranged from twenty dollars up to Dale and Tony's card (a watercolor of an orange and red tree frog), which contained seven crisp hundred-dollar bills!

Green signs over the freeway displayed the distance in miles to each of the cities to our north. I did some mental arithmetic. "If we drive straight through to Portland, we'll get there just after dark."

Girl put her bare feet up on the dashboard and leaned back into her seat with one hand behind her head.

With the other hand, she spread out a stack of bills and fanned herself with them. "Ooooorrr..." she dragged the word out into a melodramatic siren song that started high then dropped down an octave before flipping up at the end, "...We can take Tony's advice and make a honeymoon out of it. We got a couple thousand bucks in cash and San Francisco's only a hundred miles away. I've never been, have you?"

I had not. That settled it. We turned west.

As we were leaving the site of *The Gas Station Heist,* as Girl called that chapter of our *Grand Adventure* (also Girl's terminology), I had grabbed a map of the western United States. The front of the folded map featured an illustration of a friendly, uniformed pump jockey smiling and waving beside his friendly pet tiger. Above them was the Exxon logo and below, the words *MAKE EVERY MILE COUNT.* With the map spread across Girl's lap, she called out turns. We made our way into and through Oakland and across San Francisco Bay.

I lived in Los Angeles, the second largest US city in both area and population, but driving the interminable span of the Bay Bridge with its spires and tunnel and towers, anticipation building until I finally got my first glimpse of the City by the Bay across the water, its hillside neighborhoods packed as tightly as bookshelves on the left, a miscellany of skyscrapers to my right (most squared, one pointy), I knew I was entering a *proper* city!

LA had tall buildings, sure. One time I hiked up into the hills with some buddies of mine, jumped a fence, and climbed some rickety scaffolding behind the second letter of the Hollywood sign. Sitting there in the hole of the O, I could see the Capital Records building below me like a stack of chips gambling on the public's taste for boob jobs and big teeth. Beyond Hollywood, I could make out Century City's glass towers blued by smog and distance, a cerulean cathedral to commercialism. But mostly I saw spread-out neighborhoods full of wide boulevards and suburban lawns. Los Angeles' glittering sprawl extended to the horizon in every direction.

San Francisco was different. San Francisco had edges. Located on a peninsula seven miles across, developers had long ago run out of anywhere to build but up.

As we exited the far side of the bridge, we were engulfed by San Francisco. Beneath the low, gray ceiling of the sky and walled in by shoulder-to-shoulder buildings, it was like driving inside. I wove between neighborhoods, through hallways of filigreed row houses, into bustling shopping streets with increasingly Chinese signage, up hills and down; taking random turns. Girl was playing tourist, hanging out the passenger side and "Wow!"ing.

As we passed a big, brick Catholic church, Girl pulled her head in the window and pointed. "Pull over here!" I swung into an empty spot along the curb. There, next to a cross-topped signboard announcing times for confessionals and High Mass, was an otherwise normal four-sided glass phone booth with an ornate red and gold two-tiered Chinese pagoda roof. Because San Francisco.

"Yellow pages! Let's find a swanky hotel!" Girl exclaimed, bouncing in her seat and thrusting two index fingers toward the payphone, "Let's get the, like, honeymoon suite and live like a couple of...you know...*hotel-living people!* Like my *MOTHER!*" Wait for it... Here it comes...

"KEE-HEE-GHEE-EE-HICK-HE-KEE-GH-HEE-H-KEEHEE!!"

There it was. God, I loved that stupid sound.

CHAPTER 14

Eight hundred sixty-four dollars bought us the "Romantic Escape" package at a stately old hotel with a uniformed doorman and a restaurant off of the lobby. For about a third of our bankroll, we got five nights all-inclusive with meals (excluding cocktails), a menu of available activities (in-room couple's massages, guided tours, tickets to drag shows...), a daily bottle of chilled champagne, and general toadying from the attentive staff. Girl and I checked in with our shitty luggage, giggling and tipping like rock stars.

Our deluxe room featured a little Victorian ironwork balcony accessed by ducking through a gate-hinged window and stepping over the sill. We sat on the balcony's cold, slatted floor, passing our first day's bottle of bubbly back and forth and watching the nightlife below us on Market Street. A somber mood had settled over us as the excitement of the wedding and the naked partying and the road had given way to the reality of our actions. All the adrenaline had left the building. I could feel Rudy's ghost lurking over my shoulder. I tried to distract myself with romantic smalltalk; "You looked very pretty at the wedding, Mrs. Larsen."

"Everybody could see that you thought so, Mr. Larsen."

We were flirting out of habit, but our hearts weren't in it. We barely made eye contact. We sunk back into silence, passing the bottle, lost in our own thoughts. The champagne only deepened our funk.

At around four-thirty in the morning, we left the empty bottle on the balcony, crawled over the sill, pulled the black-out curtains shut, shed our clothes, and slithered between cool, skin-smooth sheets from opposite sides of the immense bed. We didn't touch. I occupied my discreet expanse of luxuriant cotton; Girl had her own patch over there somewhere.

We slept.

Bright light assaulted my face, waking me instantly and searing the inside of my skull like a branding iron. I raised a hand to shade my eyes from the blinding sunshine and saw Girl silhouetted, topless, her fists still gripping the heavy drapes she had just thrown open. The back of her panties had a picture of Eeyore's ass with his nailed-on tail.

From somewhere in the room, Robert Smith was singing about jumping someone else's train. Girl spun toward me dancing to the music. The front of her underwear had Eeyore's sad-sack face with the words, *MONDAY AGAIN* in arching letters above his head. As The Cure's locomotive guitars faded into the drum and harmonica intro of New Order's "Love Vigilantes," the DJ layered in a field recording of a group of girls shouting over club noise: *"DON'T TOUCH THAT DIAL! IT'S GOT CUM ON IT!"*

Girl bopped over to a TV/radio combo that filled the top of a long, low dresser against the wall that faced the foot of the bed. "I found the good radio station! K-O-M-E! Like CUM! KHEE-GHE-HE-HICKUP!" She turned the volume dial and the music got louder.

My pulse was pounding in my temples completely out of time with the music. I swung my feet over the edge of the bed and used both hands against the mattress to hoist my upper body vertical. I moved too fast; when my brain caught up, it slammed into place with a meaty jolt.

"I'm never drinking champagne again," I grumbled. My tongue had grown large and sticky. "I think I'm allergic."

With monumental effort, I hauled myself upright(ish) and got my legs under me (more or less). I began the ordeal of sliding my feet one at a time toward the far distant bathroom. When I finally arrived, I pissed for a hundred years then retraced my steps, ready to fall back into bed.

As I shuffled my way past the hallway door, I heard two quick raps—very discreet. I opened the door a crack, making the *Do Not Disturb* gimmick swing beneath the outside knob. I saw a hotel employee retreating toward the elevators. I looked down. On a tray outside the door, a fresh bottle of champagne nested in an ice-filled silver bucket. A white cloth napkin was tied artfully around the neck, securing a long-stemmed red rose to the side of the bottle.

I bent down and grabbed the edge of the bucket, leaving the tray behind, and straightened back up. I hipped the door closed and made my way wordlessly to the big window. Without stopping, I dropped the bucket next to the TV with an icy rattle and handed Girl the rose. I stepped naked onto the balcony, twisting the little wire cage off of the bottle as I went. I popped the cork, sending it sailing in an arc across the street. It landed on the roof of a stopped city bus. I held the bottle aloft in a morning toast to the commuters looking up at me, put the neck to my lips, and tipped its base toward the sky.

There was a half-smoked Djarum propped on the edge of a brown glass ashtray at my feet next to a mostly-depleted matchbook. I lowered to a squat then dropped backward onto my bare ass, my legs flopping out in front of me. I picked up the clove cigarette, lit it, and took a deep drag. I sat there on the balcony, the latticework floor waffling my buttocks, and let the sunshine, nicotine, loud music and fizzy hair-of-the-dog sweep the cobwebs from my frontal lobes.

Half a bottle later, I stepped inside feeling like a new man. Girl was dancing back and forth between her little suitcase, open on the bed, and one of the big room's two closets. She was hanging up everything she had brought with her. Every item of clothing got its own fancy hotel hanger, including a white belt studded with silver crucifixes and a pair of knee-high argyle socks.

The gloomy mood of the night before had evaporated. Girl had driven it away with loud music, determined cheerfulness and naked titties. We decided to enjoy the day and take advantage of our all-inclusive package. I called down to the front desk and booked a bicycle rickshaw tour of historic San Francisco landmarks.

I opened the gym bag I had filled with clothes from Rudy's room when we bugged out. I pulled on a pair of jeans. The waist was fine, but Rudy's legs were longer than mine, so I folded up the bottoms into big, oversized cuffs.

While I was packing, I had found an entire drawer in Rudy's dresser full of neatly-folded promotional T-shirts for Orion Pictures movies and had grabbed a handful at random. I pulled a gray shirt from the bag. It featured the logo for *Beat Street*—yellow, orange and pink tenement buildings that formed the title were surrounded by little break dancers.

I found a sewing kit in the closet Girl *wasn't* currently filling with underpants on wooden hangers. I used the kit's scissors to cut the sleeves off of the shirt and pulled it on.

The bathroom counter held an extensive selection of toiletries including styling mousse and hairspray. I chose instead a thick, creamy hand lotion. I squeezed a generous amount into one palm, rubbed my hands together, and applied it to my hair—fisting and twisting and pulling it into a messy mane.

Girl slid into view in the big, wall-to-wall mirror. She gently nudged me aside so that she could access the sink. Her hair had grown out some since we met, so now it was spiky white with ebony roots, like animal fur. She still had a long, hot-pink front piece that hung down to the tip of her nose. She ran some water on her hands and wet the magenta forelock. She parted it in the middle and manipulated the two halves into an open heart shape, each side curving up and away from the center parting and meeting again at a point in the middle of her forehead. She flattened the heart with her palms, then picked up a can of hairspray from the beauty bar and, shielding her eyes with her free hand, sealed everything in place.

She was wearing a black half-slip with *MOTOR CITY BABY* in big, bubbly glitter letters on the front over silver spandex capris. She had a white cat collar around her neck with a little bell on it. Her eyelids were a smoky charcoal and her plump lips a shiny, iridescent oil slick color. On her feet were her usual pink Converse high-tops. She was stunning.

Our bicycle rickshaw driver was standing in the lobby when we stepped out of the elevator. He was long and lean, with Aztec features and elaborately highlighted hair that tumbled in bouncy waves on the top of his head over brunette short back and sides. He was wearing high-waisted dark chocolate zoot suit slacks and a matching vest unbuttoned over a white wifebeater. His shoes were shiny, two-tone tan on mahogany wingtips. He was holding a sign that said "Maria & Monty Larsen".

During the road trip from Turtle Terrace to San Francisco, we'd been struck with the revelation that our middle names both started with the same letter. These had become our pet names for each other and it was those names we had used to check into the hotel.

In a lilting Mexican accent, the driver introduced himself as Guillermo. I shook his hand and said, "Monty. This is Maria."

Girl held out her hand. Guillermo sandwiched it

between his palms and gleefully exclaimed, "Ay! That is my drag name! Maria Tortilleria! Now I *know* we will have fun together!"

The rickshaw "bicycle" parked at the curb was actually a tricycle, with a wooden two-person passenger seat bolted between the rear wheels. Girl and I pressed together on the hard, narrow bench under a ribbed canopy of lavendar nylon which featured the hotel's name in tatty gold embroidery on each side.

Our seat was down low and the driver's saddle was positioned quite high to accommodate Guillermo's long, Rockettes-worthy gams. As he swung gracefully up onto his perch, his shapely bottom right in front of our faces, Girl commented that he must be a vision in stockings. Guillermo exclaimed, "Por supuesto, Mami!" while effortlessly extending his right leg fully vertical. The loose, pleated trouser leg dropped to his knee, revealing a hairless, tightly-muscled calf.

Lowering his foot once more, Guillermo pedaled us into traffic. As we made our way along Market Street and turned onto Castro, Guillermo began rattling off facts with sincere enthusiasm.

"Across the intersection over there is Twin Peaks Tavern, the oldest gay bar in the whole country! It has been there since the thirties. Can you imagine the *courage* needed to run a gay bar in the nineteen-thirties? And right there on the corner! Then around thirteen, fourteen years ago they open those big windows! Windows! In a gay bar! Pride, *amigos*. That is what The Castro is all about!"

He wheeled us down a few more blocks, past boutique shops and an ornate old movie theater. There was very little car traffic. This was a walking neighborhood. Pairs of men strolled hand in hand knowing—*knowing*—that they were safe from harassment! Even in liberal LA, there still weren't many parts of the city where a same-sex couple could be that self-assured.

As Guillermo's musical voice narrated everything we were seeing, we moved away from The Castro and cruised along Haight Street and through Golden Gate Park and past the "Painted Ladies" houses before skirting the edges of Chinatown and finally stopping at a burger place called Zim's around noon.

Guillermo turned around in his seat and said, "I know all of your meals at the hotel are paid for, *amigos*, but this is the very best American food I have had. Would it be okay with you if we stop for lunch here?"

We agreed and extricated ourselves from the rickshaw seat with a helping hand from Guillermo. As we approached the restaurant, a pair of uniformed policemen were just exiting. The younger of the two— a handsome Filipino with an athlete's body and floppy boy-band hair parted in the middle—stopped and held the door open for us. Guillermo entered first. Crossing the threshold, he looked openly at the cop's tight pants then slid his eyes upward, taking time to appreciate the utility belt, the badge, the radio mouthpiece clipped to his left epaulet, the wispy mustache. Finally, he looked the blushing rookie in the eyes and purred, "Thank you, officer."

The other policeman was a caucasian fifty-something veteran with an iron-gray flattop who stood to one side, smiling and shaking his head, arms folded across his barrel-shaped torso. Guillermo turned to him and said, "Hi, Jordan. Tell Rachel thanks for that recipe. He absolutely loved it."

"Will do, Maria." the older cop replied.

Guillermo wasn't wrong; the food at Zim's was as good as American diner food gets! We had big, juicy burgers on amazing buns with flavorful fixin's that dripped down our chins while we talked and laughed and Girl asked probing questions like, "Do you wear a fake pussy when you perform?" and Guillermo delighted in providing candid answers. (For the record: He owned three very convincing mirkins and an undergarment which gave him realistic cameltoe in tight pants.)

All of the employees knew Guillermo, but it was clear that everyone in the neighborhood called him

Maria. Over slices of apple pie with cheddar cheese melted on top (crazy delicious), he told us he was one of the stars of the pre-screening drag shows at the Castro Theater—the big, fancy movie house we had pedaled past that morning. It was Friday and he was performing that night. Our honeymoon package at the hotel included two tickets, so we made plans to attend.

Our bellies full, Girl and I were dropped back at the hotel. I approached the doorman, a Black dude with a military bearing who had introduced himself earlier as Daryl. His close-cropped hair was gray at the temples as well as in a patch the size and shape of a credit card over his left eye. He could have been forty-five or a well-preserved seventy.

"Hey Daryl, any idea where I could get my hands on some..." I looked both ways and stage whispered, "...marijuana?"

He spoke in a scratchy smoker's voice in the back of his throat, like Kermit the Frog being strangled. "I'll send the boy up," he rasped. "C.O.D." he added, holding up a cautionary hand as I pulled a wad of money out of my pocket. I pressed a five dollar bill into the palm for his trouble and thanked him.

Back in our room, girl stripped off her road-stale clothes, dropping them in her wake as she walked to the bathroom and half-closed the door. I heard the shower start.

I sat on the bed and pulled out the gym bag to pick out fresh clothes to wear to the show that night. Among the movie tees was a white ringer with baby blue neck and cuffs promoting the remake of *Breathless* from a few years earlier with a photo of Richard Gere looking seductively into the camera. I thought it would be a hit with the Castro crowd and laid it out to change into after I cleaned up. I took my shirt off and placed it in the clear plastic bag provided by the hotel for laundry. I was wondering if I had time to join Girl in the shower before the doorman's "boy" arrived, when I was startled by a series of five sharp raps on the entry door. It sounded like the knocker had used something hard, like a big ring or maybe a billy club. I walked over and cautiously opened the door. The boy walked briskly into the room, stopping with a snappy hundred eighty degree turn to face me. I closed the door and turned to look at our friendly neighborhood drug dealer.

He *was* a boy! I made him to be seventeen years old —eighteen tops. "Lance." He introduced himself, offering a hand to shake. I took it. I was holding a delicate cluster of fingers inside of a soft kid-leather glove in dove gray. It matched his spats.

Lance was a rather camp white boy with a prominent chin and a toothy smile, dressed in the finery of a Victorian dandy. A colorful jacket and equally gaudy vest that somehow managed to both clash and complement each other framed a shiny silk cravat in a bold paisley knotted around a high, detachable collar. His trousers were the color of merlot with a wide gold satin stripe down each outseam. His left hand rested on the head of a walking stick. The top of the stick was a sphere of pink marble. I assumed that this was the door knocker. A yellow suede messenger bag sat on his right hip, its strap hanging across his narrow torso like a pageant sash. I liked him immediately.

"So! So, so, so, so..." Lance leaned his staff against a wall, opened his bag and busied himself at the end of the bed with his back to me. After only a few moments of this, the boy turned around and stepped to one side, wafting a graceful hand out to present his wares. Across the foot of the bed was an array of illicit drugs in a variety of bags, bottles, and boxes.

"Take your pick, good sir!" Lance proclaimed, "I have grass, coke, H, acid, shrooms, whippets, poppers, bennies, barbies, and blues.

Girl came out of the bathroom as the dealer was listing his wares. She had let the water run her eye makeup into black Alice Cooper tears. She had a white hotel towel around her hips and another draped around her neck, the two ends hanging in front of her chest. "Oooooo..." she cooed, "I love a smorgasbord!"

I selected a Ziploc containing ten expertly-rolled joints and a small mustard-colored cardboard carton with the brand name "Vaporole" on it. This box contained a dozen little mesh-covered ampules of amyl nitrate. When the glass tube inside one of these "poppers" was broken, the cloth was saturated with the drug and the fumes inhaled. Intended to treat certain heart maladies, poppers were all the rage in the gay community for their euphoric effects and their ability to enhance erotic pleasure. I'd enjoyed them the one time I tried them while dancing at a club, but I'd never had sex on them. I intended to remedy that.

Girl picked up a baggie containing some wrinkly, gray-brown chunks of dried plant matter. She pinched it by a corner, pinky extended, and waved it in front of my face like a hypnotist's pocketwatch. "You ever done shrooms?" she asked.

"No, but I've always wanted to! I've just been…I don't know…a little intimidated, maybe?"

"Well, then! I know what *we're* doing tomorrow!" She sang, spinning excitedly in place. The centrifugal force of her rotation made the ends of her neck towel fly out sideways, exposing her breasts. Lance raised his eyebrows in mock scandalization and performed the most flamboyant sign of the cross I'd ever seen, snapping his fingers with a little head toss at each of the four points. We all laughed, Lance quoted a price, and I handed him a fistful of wrinkly bills from the pocket of my jeans. He smoothed the banknotes out as he counted them before sliding them into a wallet he kept in an inside jacket pocket. He shook my hand again, blew a kiss to Girl, and left.

Once we were alone, I stepped out of my jeans (Or were they *Rudy's* jeans? I needed to get myself some clothes that didn't remind me that I was a murderer!), laid them beside the *Breathless* shirt on the bed, and showered. When I exited the bathroom naked, toweling my hair, Girl was also naked. She was draped seductively across an antique-looking chaise longue. She had a lit joint in one hand and was sucking on a clove cigarette held in her other, providing an acceptable cover smell for the pot odor. I walked to the window and opened it, dissipating some of the smoke.

Girl handed me the joint and waggled her eyebrows up and down. "Break out those poppers, Monty! I wanna see what all the fuss is about."

We had hours before the show started that evening and we filled a few of them with blissed-out, drug-fueled lovemaking.

As sunset was reddening the sky, I called down to the desk and ordered supper, along with today's newspapers. Seeing those cops at Zim's had gotten me thinking about our misdeeds of a few days ago. I wanted to see if there was any mention of the gas station robbery or Rudy's death in the papers. I was confident that we had avoided leaving any evidence linking us to either crime, but then again you never know. Corey the gas monkey might have ratted us out. A neighbor of Rudy's might have seen something and spoken up. I also wasn't wearing gloves when I returned to the garage for the keys, so now my fingerprints were all over the nail gun. I'd never been arrested, though, so there was nothing in the system to compare them to.

I heard the room service cart and opened the door for the bellboy—actually a chubby Chinese girl in a too-tight red uniform jacket. She rolled the food in, I tipped her, and she left. We had ordered one of each item from the appetizers section of the menu. As we enjoyed deep-fried things and stuff on sticks we paged through the Examiner, Chronicle, and Daily Post, reading every headline. Not surprisingly, there was nothing about either of our crimes. After all, they didn't happen in San Francisco. I made a mental note to pick up a Los Angeles paper when I got a chance. I had noticed a comprehensive-looking newsstand down the block from the movie theater on Castro Street. I figured I'd pick up the Sunday LA Times day after tomorrow and have another look then.

The Castro Theater drag show was an absolute revelation! I had seen a few campy lip-sync performances at open mic nights and there was an LA punk-funk fusion band called The Urethra Franklin Blues Explosion made up of cross-dressing bodybuilders, but Guillermo/Maria and the rest of the Castro troupe took drag to another level!

The double feature of movies that night was *Funny Face* and *Funny Girl,* and the highlight of the live show was a duet between Maria Tortilleria as Audrey Hepburn and a drag queen who went by the convoluted name of Barb Bitch-You-It whose Streisand was extraordinarily convincing. They did all of their own singing—with live piano accompaniment! Girl and I watched from the third row as they performed a hilariously vitriolic rendition of "Anything You Can Do (I Can Do Better)" which escalated in intensity with every verse until ultimately devolving into a professional wrestling styled fight complete with stripe-shirted referee. The climax was a run-in by a drag *king* dressed as Hulk Hogan who threw them both off the stage, then ripped "his" yellow shirt down the middle, exposing full breasts with black electrical tape Xs over the nipples and a patch of glued-on chest hair. The crowd went nuts!

Girl and I stood, cheering and whistling and stomping along with the rest of the packed house as the performers took curtain call after curtain call. It was one of the most entertaining pieces of live theatre I'd ever seen.

There was a brief intermission before the film

portion of the evening's entertainment started while the brightly-painted stage setting was cleared from in front of the movie screen. As Girl and I were sharing a clove cigarette in the lobby, trying to decide if we really wanted to stick around for the rest of the show, Maria came through a door off to one side of the popcorn counter and spotted us. She waved and headed in our direction. She worked her way through the appreciative throng like the diva she was, acknowledging the applause and compliments that rippled outward from her in waves.

She was still made up like Audrey Hepburn, a tight brunette chignon showing off her long neck, but the strapless red ballgown and diamond necklace she wore onstage had been replaced by a navy and white striped boatneck top with half-length sleeves and a pair of white capris that were tight enough to show off her ersatz lady bits. Navy deck shoes with embroidered gold anchors completed the yachting ensemble.

She gave Girl and me each a hug and exclaimed in a breathy falsetto, "I'm so very glad you both came! Have you ever seen *Funny Face*?"

I had fond memories of watching it along with *Breakfast at Tiffany's* on TV one afternoon in fifth grade when I was home sick from school and I told her so. Girl confessed to being completely unfamiliar with the film. Maria invited us to sit with her and her fellow performers up in the balcony. She implied that it was *the* place to be for the show.

I said, "You two go ahead. I'll catch up. I'm going to move the car while I'm thinking about it."

For a large and crowded metropolis, San Francisco had a surprising amount of free parking available as long as you obeyed a few rules; a car could be left at the curb for anywhere from twenty-four to forty-eight hours, depending on the neighborhood, as long as it was moved in time for the street sweeping trucks to roll through as scheduled. Like many businesses in the city, our hotel didn't have a dedicated parking lot so we'd left Rudy's car on a side avenue a couple of blocks away, halfway between the hotel and Castro Street. I had checked the posted ordinance as Girl and I were walking to the theater and seen that the car needed to be moved before the following morning.

It was starting to look like we'd be partying with the drag queens late into the night and I didn't want to have to search for a fresh parking place in whatever state I might find myself later so I figured I'd dash over and move it before the evening's gaiety recommenced.

As I strolled along Castro, this time without a female companion, I received a *lot* of attention.

"Hey, Richard Gere! I got a gerbil for you!" called a mustachioed gentleman, grabbing his leather-clad crotch.

"Mmmmm… Slow down and let me look at that ass!" moaned a shirtless, hirsute, pot-bellied fellow wearing a sailor hat and cut-offs so short that the pockets hung below their frayed denim edge.

I decided at that moment that every sexist asshole who cat-called women on the street should be made to walk through The Castro on a Friday night.

I reached the car and read the details on the nearest parking sign. If I simply moved to the other side of the street I'd be good for another two days. There were a number of open spots available so I pulled out, executed a U-turn, and slid into place along the opposite curb.

As I glanced down to turn off the ignition I spotted the curly charging cable hanging down from the lighter socket and disappearing under the seat. I'd been thinking about Rudy's car phone ever since Turtle Terrace. I still hadn't informed Girl of its existence.

Since I had a few minutes alone to scrutinize the device now, I lifted it from its hiding place, set it on the passenger seat, and opened the case. I picked up the handset and examined the face of it. Below a grid of number keys was a bunch of square buttons with confusing abbreviations like *FCN* and *RCL* on their surfaces. One was labeled *PWR*. Guessing that this was short for "POWER," I pressed it. The little screen at the top of the receiver lit up with two rows of symbols rendered in squared-off clusters of red dashes like the score on a pinball machine. These flashed a couple of times, showing their default "8" patterns, then resolved into "MSGS: 3."

Somebody had been calling Rudy's fancy Motorola and leaving him messages. Were they looking for him? Had he been reported missing? Had the body been found? I started getting that white tunnel vision rapid-breathing sensation that had overtaken me outside of the kitchen window when I'd seen Girl's father flop face-first into his enchiladas the night I had... *dispatched* him.

I closed my eyes and leaned back against the headrest, trying to slow my breathing. I gave myself a silent pep talk: *"You got this. Nobody knows you ever even met Rudy. He never heard your real name..."*

I opened my eyes and tried to figure out how to listen to the messages. After some experimentation and lucky guesses, the writing on the display changed to "CALL MSGS." A green button in the lower right corner was now illuminated. The text on the button read *SND*. I pushed it and held the phone to my ear. There was the sound of ringing, a loud *BEEP*, then a robotic female voice stuttered through static, "Fir... —essage".

A few seconds of silence followed, then another beep and the mechanical lady was back: "—ext mess..."

Then I heard a voice I thought I'd never hear again. It sounded far away, nearly drowned out by crackling and hissing. Only some words were intelligible, but it was unmistakably Rudy!

"John, I ho..." *CRACKLE HISS* "...what Abbey tol..." *HISS POP* "—all me back..." *CRACKLE* "—xplain every..." *HISS*

Then there was another beep, the female voice said, "Nex..." followed by more static and then the line went dead.

What the actual fuck? Had I just heard a message from beyond the grave? And why was it so garbled? Was I doing something wrong? I thought these portable phones were supposed to...you know... *WORK!* Didn't rich people rely on these things for business?

I looked in the case and saw a slim instruction booklet tucked in beside the recess where the receiver fit. I pulled it out and looked at the cover. Against a field of pastel pink horizontal stripes was a line drawing of the handset floating in the foreground, tethered to a rendering of the case hovering in mid-air at an oblique angle. Also pictured was a stubby antenna with a fat round base.

The antenna! Of course! I had seen cars with little aerials magnetted to their roofs all around Hollywood in recent years, but Rudy's car didn't sport one of these. Could that be why the call quality was so shitty? I looked again at the case and saw that a second cable, this one straight, extended from its bottom edge and back to the floor.

I got out of the car and kneeled down to look beneath the driver's seat. The wire continued back toward the rear of the car, hidden beneath the floor mats, to where it went out of sight under one corner of the back seat. I pulled the key from the ignition, walked around and opened the trunk. There, nested in a coil of cabling, was an antenna identical to the one on the cover of the user manual.

I looked at my wristwatch, a Swatch knockoff I had purchased the day before from a skinhead selling cassette tapes and trinkets laid out on the Haight Street sidewalk. It had a black and white checkerboard band with the 2 Tone Records dancing ska dude mascot on the face. The movie was scheduled to start fifteen minutes ago. I had to decide whether to spend more time putting the antenna on the roof and trying to listen to Rudy's message again, hoping for a clearer signal this time, or head back to the theater.

If Rudy really *had* survived the nail gun attack, what did that mean for our plans? Should I tell Girl about the phone? Should I tell her about the message? I needed time to sort things out.

On the one hand, if Rudy was still alive that meant that I wasn't a murderer. I felt a surge of relief about that. On the other hand, that also meant that Rudy had certainly talked to the police by now. They were probably looking for Girl and me.

I closed the trunk and started walking. I'd sleep on it, come back to the car later, and listen to the whole message if I could. Maybe I was reading the situation all wrong. I was ninety percent sure that was Rudy's voice I had heard, but I didn't know *when* the message had been left. It could have been weeks old for all I knew.

Then again—why would he call his own phone? He had clearly said "John", which was the name he knew me by, but maybe he shared the phone with somebody else named John…? I was grasping at straws.

As I retraced my route along Castro Street to the movie house, ignoring the shouted propositions and whistles aimed my way, I felt unmoored from reality. Was I going to prison? Would I ever again see my eccentric, ever-revolving cast of roommates and lay on my unframed mattress while I fell asleep to the pumping house music from the gay bar outside my window? For the first time in days, I truly felt like a fugitive from the law.

Back at the theater, before I could present my ticket stub, the doorperson—a dead ringer for Diana Ross who stood at least six foot eight with heels and hair— recognized me and waved me in, pointing to a set of stairs through a doorway on the other side of the lobby.

I ignored the "Balcony Closed" sign and climbed. The skunky smell of marijuana smoke grew stronger with every step.

As I emerged into the balcony, Audrey Hepburn was twirling about in a dark bookstore far below me, wearing a giant yellow hat. Girl was above me in the top row of seats wearing an auburn beehive wig and magenta-sequined opera gloves, lounging across the laps of three drag queens and smoking a joint held in a long mother-of-pearl cigarette holder.

When she saw me, she whooped, "GUUUUUYYYY!!" and bounded from her human couch. She skipped down the risers, jumped into a full-body hug—wrapping her arms around my neck and her legs around my waist—and planted a smoky wet kiss on my mouth.

In the second-to-last row of seats, a stocky man dressed like a lumberjack turned to Maria, who was sitting beside him with one hand casually resting on his knee, and said, "How come you never greet *me* like that?" The other members of the balcony crew chuckled affectionately.

Girl removed her wig and pushed it down onto my head, stuck the joint holder into my mouth, grabbed my hand, and led me to the uppermost tier. I settled into an empty seat and Girl sat next to me sideways with her legs draped across the armrest between us, her feet on my thighs. I found myself at one end of a row of off-duty performers, some of whom were still in full drag (I later learned that there was to be another live performance during the interim between films) while others sported various stages of post-performance casual wear. The Hulk Hogan impersonator from earlier was beside me, the remnants of her torn T-shirt still displaying her tape-pastied tits. Her yellow handlebar mustache remained glued in place, but she no longer wore a blonde wig on either her head or her chest. Her own hair was an ashy mullet—short and spiky on top and hanging below her collar in the back. She handed me a half-full fifth of Jack Daniels. I traded her for the joint, holding up the whiskey bottle in a toasting gesture before taking a long pull.

"Cheers, mate" she said in an Australian accent. She took a toke and passed the dutchie on her left-hand side.

I snugged down into the worn red velvet as a theaterful of strangers below me sang along with song after song like a church congregation belting familiar hymns.

For the next several hours I decided to forget about Rudy's voice crackling cryptically through the ether. As the evening wore on I drank, smoked, snorted, and swallowed whatever I was handed as I deliberately nose-dived into *The Fog of Partying.*

The night soon fractured into a series of soft-focus montage vignettes: Making out with Girl. A dressing room full of half-naked bodies. Making out with Diana Ross. Looking out at rows of laughing faces, my outspread arms across two sets of broad shoulders holding me up as I Rockette-kick in heels across a stage, boa feathers clinging to my sticky lips. A smoke-filled lobby with a noisy mob of theatergoers flowing around me to the street. A popcorn fight in that same lobby, disco music blasting from a boombox on a glass counter. A projection booth crowded with esoteric machinery and film posters full of French words. Looking up from the floor of the dressing room at Girl's grinning, lightbulb-framed reflection, *The Ghastly Giggle* echoing off the walls. Hugging Daryl the Doorman during a crimson sunrise, whispering "Sailors take warning" into his ear. The fresh linen smell of a hotel pillow.

Noonday painted the room in a golden glow.

I looked at myself in the bathroom mirror, my palms against the edge of the sink, elbows locked to support the leaden weight of my head and upper torso. Orange and turquoise eyeshadow filled the space between my lids and the high, surprised-looking eyebrows drawn an inch above my own. My cheekbones were defined by brick-red swaths of blush. My lips had clearly been lined and filled at some point, judging from the dark smear running from my mouth to my right ear. I was shirtless. My nipples had been rouged to twice their natural size.

Girl came into the room and handed me a clear plastic tumbler of champagne. "Those queens know how to party," she said in an uncharacteristically deadpan voice.

"I'll drink to that," I replied, draining my cup.

We made eye contact with each others' reflections. She was wearing as much makeup as I was, but her motif was glitter. Silver glitter eyeshadow. Red glitter lips. Gold glitter sparkling in platinum hair.

I turned to face her. She had on a white camisole with nothing on the bottom. I pulled it up and off, then tugged down the tighty-whities I was wearing and kicked them away. Taking Girl by the hand, I stepped over the edge into the tub. She followed and pulled the curtain closed as I turned the shower on hot.

Glitter and greasepaint swirled down the drain while we spent the next half hour washing off the previous night, taking more time than strictly necessary on perfectly clean body parts. Her little hands made me big and my big hands made her gasp. Afterward, we dried each other with the fluffy hotel towels.

Despite the previous night's cathartic bacchanal, the shower's afternoon delights had left my head shockingly clear. Almost too clear; *thinking about Rudy again* clear. I longed for further escape even as I told myself that I needed to figure shit out and soon.

Girl provided the perfect solution. "You still up for

taking these today?" she chirped, holding up the baggie of shrooms.

CHAPTER 15

When I was working at the Pussycat adult cinema on Santa Monica Boulevard in West Hollywood, there was a grizzled old dude named Edwin who ran the projection booth. One day he showed me the set-up inside his dimly-lit garret. Each feature-length porno arrived at the theater on several ten-minute reels of thirty-five millimeter film. These were spliced together into a continuous strip which was pulled through the projector from one big horizontal roll with no human oversight necessary.

Because of this arrangement, Edwin had nothing to do except kill time while he waited for a movie to end. After the final money shot he would turn off the machine and raise the house lights, causing the patrons to scatter like startled roaches, their faces averted from each other. Another group of masturbation hobbyists would shuffle in, avoiding eye contact, Edwin would thread the film back through the projector, start the movie playing again, and have another hour and a half of leisure.

During these idle times in his (inexplicably unionized) job, Edwin would emerge from his citadel and descend a narrow flight of stairs to hang out outside my ticket window. We had long, largely one-sided conversations as he soliloquized through the little round hole in the glass in front of my face.

These chats often took on a surreal, mountaintop guru quality when Edwin was tripping on mushrooms at work—which he did quite often. I learned early on that if I had a life challenge I was struggling with I could ask Edwin's advice while he was shrooming and he would provide a completely unique perspective which I would never have thought of on my own.

Now, sitting on a cross-town bus with Girl while we waited for the psilocybin psychedelics to kick in, I was hoping for some Edwin-level insight into The Rudy Situation.

We had ordered two chocolate malt milkshakes from room service and dumped half of the dried-out mushrooms into each. We stirred them up and choked them down while preparing for our Saturday afternoon psychotropic walkabout. As we got dressed I expressed my paranoia about attracting attention from authority figures with our obviously drug-addled behavior, so Girl suggested that we forego our usual punk-rock accouterments and aim for a combination of comfortable and inconspicuous. Each of us put on jeans with one of Rudy's movie shirts (*Lone Wolf McQuade* for me and *Desperately Seeking Susan* for Girl). It was drizzling outside, so I added a black zip-up hoodie over my shirt, while girl wore a denim jacket over hers, first removing the oversized *FUCK REAGAN* button and the dozen safety pins which radiated out around it like sun rays.

We had discussed our options and decided to pick a destination, make our way there by public transportation while the drug took effect, then enjoy the trip (literal and metaphorical) during a long, leisurely walk back to our homebase.

In the lobby, we looked through a rack of tourist brochures in search of destinations within reasonable distance from the hotel and chose Coit Tower, a 200-foot cylindrical spire on Telegraph Hill north of Chinatown just over three miles away. Doorman Daryl pointed out where to catch a bus which went directly there in just about the amount of time it should take for the shrooms to do their thing.

Girl was in a wild, hyperactive mood as we boarded the bus. While I leaned back in a sideways-facing seat, anxious and apprehensive about the sensations which would soon be overtaking me, she couldn't sit still. She bounced around in the aisle, perching briefly on my lap or in the seat across from me then jumping back up, swinging from the handrails and talking a mile a minute.

"You're gonna have SOOOOO much fun!! I can't *believe* you've never done shrooms before! It's like escaping from your own body and your own mind and like experiencing, like, all your senses through different lenses! Colors make sounds and noises smell funny and when you touch something you can like taste the textures and shit! KEEE-HEE-GHEE-EE-H-KEE-HEEEE!!!"

On and on she rambled, block after block, as riders entered and exited around her. Our fellow passengers were mostly older Chinese women with wheeled shopping baskets and aggressively blank expressions who refused to even acknowledge Girl's forceful presence.

At the rear of the bus, three Black youths wearing Adidas track suits and thick gold chains were clearly relishing Girl's antics as they slouched across the back bench, eyeing her from under the brims of their Kangols, smiling and pointing and commenting into each others' ears. A boombox at their feet was loudly playing "It's Tricky" by Run-D.M.C.

The Asian aunties swayed in unison as the bus tilted and rocked along the roller coaster San Francisco roadways. I became convinced that they were all deliberately moving in time with the music.

The shrooms were kicking in.

I closed my eyes for what felt like five seconds and

vividly re-lived the moment when a bruised and bloodied Rudy looked tearfully up at me and said, *"You don't look like a killer. How did she talk you into it?"*

I flung open my eyes. The bus ladies were now wearing blue uniforms, moving cans down a conveyor belt. I blinked and looked around. By some mushroomy mix of autopilot and time dilation, I had exited the bus and I was now standing in the lobby of Coit Tower, facing a series of murals depicting 1930s industrial workers.

I spun in a circle and realized that Girl and I were in line for the elevator to the top, surrounded by a throng of gabbling tourists sporting gaudy vacation wear. These sightseers blended with the life-sized painted people on every surface of the curved walls to create a claustrophobic crush of humanity that extended to infinity in every direction.

I was hemmed in on all sides—arms and legs and torsos and faces wherever I looked. Voices filled the cavernous space like water, gurgling and burbling in languages I couldn't understand. I had to get out of there! Fast!

I located girl's face amidst the morass of real and illustrated humanity and shouted into it, "I CAN'T BE HERE!"

I moved away from her as her voice cut through the maelstrom behind me, "But, Guy! We already paid!"

"You go up! I need outside!" I wondered if she could

even hear me over the flood of voices. I couldn't even be certain that I was speaking English.

I looked around wildly, searching desperately for the word *EXIT*, but the murals were full of writing: newspaper headlines, picket placards, factory signs. I spotted an open door with grass visible beyond and heaved myself through it.

Emerging into cool fresh air, I dropped gratefully down onto hands and knees in an open patch of unoccupied green lawn. I rolled onto my back and closed my eyes again.

Rudy's sad, bloody mouth was inches from my eyes, moaning, *"She's not really your babysitter, is she?"* Rudy's face then seamlessly morphed into that of Gas Station Corey, blubbering, *"Duh-don't kill me!"* as Girl's voice echoed from far, far away: "guuuuyyy...loooook at meeeee..."

I opened my eyes and was paralyzed by a wave of panic! I was high in the air, falling down the side of a cliff toward a storm-tossed sea! I was going to die!

I flailed my arms and legs and felt solid ground beneath my back. My perspective flipped vertiginously and I realized I was looking *up*, not down. The cliff face was the concrete expanse of Coit Tower looming over me. What I had taken for waves beating against a rocky shoreline far below were rainclouds against a slate blue sky. Girl was in a window high above, leaning over a railing and waving her arms above her head, calling down to me, "hiiiiii, guuuuuuuyyyy... kee-heee-hick-kee-gheeee..."

I poured myself up to a standing position. Bracketing my mouth between my hands, I shouted, "Please come down! I'm kinda freaking out!"

I spotted a bench nearby, teleported over to it and sat down. Girl was somehow already sitting there beside me and she put a hand on my cheek, pulling my head gently onto her shoulder, whispering, "Sssshhhhh... It's okay. I'm here, Monty." Madonna looked up at me from the front of Girl's shirt, a cigarette smoldering in one gloved hand. "I'm here, too," she said.

Eventually the panic and time-jumps ebbed and I started to enjoy my trip. The intermittent sprinkling rain felt cold and refreshing on my skin and the sun winking in and out between clouds kept popping up surprise rainbows that sounded like violins.

We floated down the staircases of Telegraph Hill and into the bustling, colorful streets of Chinatown, where we pointed and grinned at the crispy ducks hanging absurdly in windows with their horseshoe necks and inverted heads. We stood in aromatic doorways of open storefronts covered in writing we couldn't read, smelling smells we'd never smelled. We turned down random alleys, using distant skyscrapers as landmarks to continue moving vaguely south-southwest, arm in arm, rambling and laughing and stumbling down hills.

We pitched to a clumsy stop at the bottom of one steep street, where we found ourselves beneath a big, elaborate gateway with three huge, green-tiled Chinese pagoda roofs that arched overhead topped with sculpted dragons.

As we stood getting our bearings, we were suddenly swarmed by a multitude of developmentally challenged kids being guided by a pair of women, one at the front of the throng and one at the back. The children all had big, innocent smiles on their faces. Everyone, including each of the adults, was wearing a bright yellow T-shirt featuring a grinning cartoon face and the words, "UP-SIDE DOWNS."

The kids were all shorter than me but a similar height to Girl. As the mob flowed around us she was subsumed into their mass and I lost sight of her. The crowd stopped with me in their center. Looking out across the tops of their heads, I felt like an oversized messiah. I spread my arms out, my hands hovering above them in hallucinogenic blessing.

One of the ladies—who seemed not to notice me in their midst—pointed upwards and spoke loudly and slowly to the assembly: "This is the Dragon Gate. It was a gift from the country of China."

The faces surrounding me all looked up. I looked up, too. I found myself spellbound by the gate's rococo beauty. I stood gazing upon its florid wonders for what might have been a minute or an hour.

When I looked back down, the kids were gone and Girl with them! I looked in every direction, but I couldn't spot them anywhere! I felt myself starting to panic!

I ran to the next corner and looked both ways at the intersection. Then I repeated the process in the opposite direction. There, way off in the distance, I saw the congregation of little yellow bodies with their bobbing heads just curving out of view far down at the end of the next block. I ran toward them but by the time I reached the crossroads they were gone again. I sat down heavily on a bus stop bench to collect my thoughts.

A tiny old white lady who looked like she was wearing every piece of clothing she'd ever owned walked up and stopped directly in front of me. She thrust a slightly bent cigarette upright in my direction, pinching the stained filter end between her grimy thumb and forefinger.

"I got a menthol!" she shouted, drops of spittle showering my face, "I hate menthol! Trade me for one that's not!"

I rummaged in the pocket of my hoodie, feeling around keys and the amyl nitrate poppers box. I found a crumpled pack of Djarum Blacks with a few left. I pulled out the black and red box and offered it to her saying, "I have cloves?"

She screamed, "FUCK YOU!" and stomped off down the sidewalk.

A bus appeared in front of me and started expelling its cargo of middle-aged Chinese ladies with their ubiquitous shopping trollies. I stood and looked around the front of the bus to the readout above the windshield. It was the same route number we had taken earlier!

I waited for the disembarking passengers to clear the entrance and I mounted the steps. I asked the driver if she was going toward Market and Castro and she gave a vertical jerk of her head and a vaguely affirmative grunt. I dug out the necessary change, dropped it in the receptacle, and took a seat near the front where I'd be able to see when it was time for me to get out.

Girl had said earlier that if we got separated we should find our way back to the hotel individually. We had divided our money, which up to that point I had been carrying, each of us stuffing a fat roll of bills in the pocket of our jeans. At the time, I had questioned why we even needed such a contingency plan, since *obviously* we wouldn't let each other out of our sights!

She had chuckled, shook her head, put a hand on my shoulder, and said, "Virgin."

Now I sat, riding alone, looking out the bus windows, keeping an eye out for Girl or the Up-Side

Downs crew. It was starting to get dark and the city was lighting up, streamers and tendrils drifting along behind the illuminated logos and letters as they glided past my pharmaceutically-enhanced eyes.

Soon I began to recognize familiar buildings. I saw the neon "Zim's" sign with it's over-sized Z trail past. A few blocks later, there was the hotel, its flood-lit awning simply displaying the street number. I got momentarily lost in thinking about how classy it was to name a business after its address and by the time I pulled the cord to signal that I wanted to get off the bus we had overshot my destination by three blocks.

The bus stopped. I got off. I started walking back toward the hotel and realized that I was passing where I'd left the car. This was the perfect opportunity to figure out what Rudy had been trying to say to me on his car phone's messaging system while Girl was—safely, I hoped —off somewhere on her own adventure.

I walked down the side street where I was parked. As I approached the car, the yellow sodium street light overhead came on with a low buzzing sound, throwing Rudy's normally blue Volvo into sharp-shadowed monochrome like something from a film noir detective movie. I looked at my hands in the creepy light and saw that I, too, had been leached of color.

The psilocybin in my system overlaid film grain speckles over my vision. I pulled the keys from the pocket of my gray jeans with my gray hand and opened the gray trunk. The antenna lay in a nest of coiled cable, its round, magnetic base like a cobra's hood. I pulled the sleeping snake from its basket and stuck it to the roof of the car with a flat *donk*.

I opened the driver's side door and slid behind the wheel. The interior of the car was briefly rendered in technicolor as the dome light came on, then plunged back into black and white when the door shut.

I started the engine to maximize battery power, reached down between my legs, and birthed the heavy case up onto my lap, the twisted black umbilicus wrapping around my ankle. I extracted the receiver, pressed the *PWR* button and watched the garish light show as the phone woke up.

Once again it took some trial and error before I was able to access the voicemail system, but soon I had the cold plastic brick pressed to my ear, listening with singular, drug-sharpened focus to the electronic drama; now clear and static-free:

"First message"

(Breathing, then a heavy sigh)

CLICK

BEEP

"Next message"

(Another big sigh) "John, I hope you get this. I don't know what Abbey told you to make you do what you did, but... I *Do. Not. Blame. You.* Please, *please* call me back. John... Don't... Don't believe her stories. She's not well. I'll explain everything. Just... Just be careful. Please. I don't want anybody else to get hurt."

CLICK

BEEP

"Next message"

"Hey, Rudy buddy! It's Chris. What's goin' on, man? I been tryin' your house and I just got your machine for like two days. Everybody here's worried about you. Well, except Barf Breath. He's just pissed that the quarterly forecasts weren't ready for his presentation and he's getting shit from upstairs. But whatever. I hope you're okay. Call me."

CLICK

BEEP

"End of messages"

I sat there staring out through the windshield with the leatherette bulk of the battery-laden case squeezed between my stomach and the steering wheel, the now silent face of the phone paddle still pressed uselessly against the side of my head, trying to process what I had just heard: Rudy was alive. Rudy had not called the police on me. Rudy was concerned for *my* safety.

She's not well.

Be careful.

Rudy's words echoed through the shadowy grotto

inside my skull as my feet carried me autonomously toward the hotel. I touched my thigh and felt the shape of Rudy's key ring in my pocket, so I must have turned off the ignition. I must have returned the phone to its cradle. I must have opened the car and gotten out. Daryl was holding the door and saying "Evening, Mr. Larsen" so I must have.

I don't want anybody else to get hurt.

My room number was in front of my face, so I must have pushed the button. Stepped onto the elevator. I must have pressed "3" and stepped out again when the doors opened. I must have.

Don't believe her stories.

I must have pulled out my room key and opened the door, because there was Girl face down on a massage table in the middle of the room with a towel draped across her torso, her bare legs being rubbed by a thick-waisted older woman in pink nurse scrubs. Room service trays full of food were on every surface. The radio was turned up loud. From its speakers, Lene Lovich was lamenting her way through "What Will I Do Without You."

When she spotted me standing stupified in the doorway, Girl jumped off the table completely naked, the towel flying off, and shouted, "GUUUYYY!!" She jumped onto me like a monkey, arms and legs encircling me, and planted a long, wet kiss on my mouth. I put my hands on her waist and pulled her off of me, standing her onto her feet.

She grabbed a fistful of french fries and shoved them into her mouth, talking and chewing, "You look terrible! Heidi!" She turned toward the masseuse, "This is my husband! Monty! Doesn't he look like he needs some Muskelerweichung?" Girl took my hand and led me toward the massage table. "Heidi taught me that word! It means 'muscle softening'! HEE-GHEEE-EE-HICK-HEE!"

Heidi patted the table and said, "Up you go now! Let us get you fixed up."

I had to admit a massage sounded great after what I'd been through. I could think about Rudy later. I didn't know how to feel about what he had said on the phone anyway. Who was telling the truth here? Who should I believe—my wife or her molester?

As I stripped off my *Lone Wolf McQuade* T-shirt in a daze and prepared to get some *Muskelerweichung* from Heidi, Girl pulled a shirt on. It wasn't *Desperately Seeking Susan*, though. The shirt she was wearing now was yellow and read, "UP-SIDE DOWNS."

CHAPTER 16

As Heidi softened my muscles, Girl fed me cocktail shrimps and french fries and champagne from a straw up through the face hole in the massage table while she told me about her journey from the Dragon Gate back to the hotel.

When the kids had overtaken us beneath the gate, Girl had found herself eye-to-eye with a girl named Molly on one side and a boy named Brian on the other, who tapped her on her shoulders and introduced themselves. As soon as everybody had finished looking up at the elaborate structure, Molly and Brian had taken Girl by the hands and led her away with the rest of the group, asking questions and telling her about themselves as they walked hand-in-hand along the street.

They explained that they were on a special Saturday field trip organized by an activity club for young people with Down syndrome, which they were all members of. They were just finishing up a walking tour of "interesting things to see in our city" when they encountered us. The Dragon Gate was the final stop on their itinerary and they were now on their way to the "Big Banana," the organization's second-hand school bus, which was parked a few blocks away waiting to take them all back to the community center from whence they had begun their day.

Girl boarded the bus along with the group, shroom-happy and content to go with the flow. One of the adult supervisors, Judy, entered first and moved to the back of the bus, but it was the other grown-up, Lenore, who spotted Girl in the rear-view mirror as she was sliding in behind the steering wheel. She jumped from her seat and spun around, confronting Girl and asking who the hell she was and what she was doing there.

Girl answered truthfully that she had been in the middle of a very pleasant hallucinogenic drug trip when she was adopted by Molly and Brian. She asked politely if they could please drop her off at her hotel if it wasn't too far out of their way, because she was still very high and didn't know if she could find it on her own. Lenore —a hippy chick in her forties and Molly's mom—agreed, started the bus, and turned onto Market Street.

At some point along the way, Brian said to Girl, "I like your shirt. I think Madonna is sexy!"

Girl answered, "I like your shirt, too!" And so they traded.

Girl kept talking and Heidi kept rubbing and I fell into a deep, dreamless sleep there on the massage table.

When I next opened my eyes, it was the middle of the night. I was still looking through the padded opening where my face rested. I could hear rain tinging on the metal balcony and pattering against the windowpanes. In the glow from the streetlamps through the window, a glistening string of drool shined like a silver thread connecting my lower lip to a dark spot on the carpet.

I got my hands under my chest and pushed myself upright, snapping the saliva strand with a wet *click*. I staggered to the bathroom, emptied my bladder, and stumbled to the bed where I immediately passed back out for the rest of the night.

Sunday morning came and we rose bright and early. I was remarkably clearheaded. I had that "go with the flow" attitude I had witnessed so many times in Edwin the shroom-loving projectionist. So what if Rudy was alive? That was simply a fact. It meant that the police were not looking for me. So what if I had tried to murder a man? That, too, was simply a fact. I couldn't, after all, change the past, so why dwell on it? More to the point, I had failed. I was not *actually* a cold-blooded murderer! So many sources of anxiety had evaporated with a simple voicemail message.

It was a nice, sunny day in San Francisco. I opened the window. The city smelled clean; purified from the overnight rain. I felt like being outside.

"Let's go for a walk," I suggested.

Girl was sitting up in bed and stretching her arms over her head. "Okay," she yawned, "We can go down to that newsstand and see if they have the Sunday paper from back home. I wanna look again to see if we made the news."

I knew that there wouldn't be anything in the paper about us (unless Gas Station Corey hadn't stuck to the agreed-upon story). No harm in going along with the pretense.

"Sounds great," I agreed.

We each had a morning pee and threw on yesterday's jeans and T-shirts. I tucked the ends of Rudy's over-long pant legs into my combat boots. From the closet I unhooked one of Girl's necklaces from its wooden hanger and clasped it around my neck. It was a thick steel chain with a plastic Saint Patrick's Day shamrock charm hanging from it.

In the bathroom, I spritzed some hairspray on my hair and spiked it up while Girl wiped her finger on a tube of black lipstick and smudged both eyelids liberally then applied matte red from another tube onto her lips, blotting them on a square of toilet paper. Using a plastic comb, she teased the longer pink section of her hair until it was frizzy then pulled, twisted, and sprayed it until it was sticking straight out from her forehead like a unicorn horn.

We nodded in the mirror at how totally bitchin' we looked and headed out.

We said good morning to Daryl as we exited the hotel hand in hand and strolled down Market Street toward Castro, a proverbial spring in our step.

I honestly felt like a million bucks. The last week's events seemed long ago and far away, magically swept away by the mushrooms. My brain felt as freshly cleansed as the wet city streets.

The sun was shining warmly upon us and we kept making each other squeal by bumping the little ornamental trees which lined the sidewalks, causing them to shower us with fat water drops trapped in their leaves from last night's rain.

When we arrived at the newsstand, a truck was just delivering bundles of the absurdly fat Sunday LA Times. We purchased one and lugged it back to the room. Once there, we ordered coffee and breakfast from room service and spent the morning in domestic bliss with music playing and the paper's many sections spread across the floor and bed.

On the radio, KOME was playing Dramarama and Girl was singing along about giving her lover diamonds, pills, and hundred dollar bills.

She was lying on her stomach on the floor, the color comics pages open in front of her face. She rolled over onto her back and picked up a dry piece of French toast from a plate beside her. She took a bite and exclaimed while chewing, "I want *all* our Sundays to be like this from now on! Like a regular married couple reading the paper and shit!"

As I sat back in a chair with my feet up on the bed, leafing through the *City* section with its local Los Angeles headlines, pretending to look for news of our transgressions, Girl moved on from the funnies to the slick Sunday color supplement with its human interest stories and celebrity gossip.

I was just about to say something like, "Well, there's still nothing about your father," when Girl erupted to her feet, the glossy magazine gripped between clenched fists.

"HOLY SHIT!" she screamed, "NO! NO! NO! FUCKING *NO!*"

She flipped the pages over so that what she had seen was facing me and rammed it toward my face.

There, under a banner reading NEWS OF THE WEIRD, was a headline that said, *"Miracle Man Survives Nail Gun Mishap"* along with a black and white reproduction of an X-ray showing a human skull pincushioned by nails which glowed bright white against the gray tones of flesh and bone.

I lowered my feet from the bed and stood to face her.

I took the paper from Girl's hands and read the story:

"Don't drink and drive nails! That was the lesson learned by Rudy Zamora, 37, of Glendale, when he stumbled and lost control of a cordless nail gun he was using to assemble a bookcase in his garage workshop last Tuesday after consuming a six-pack of beer. A triage nurse at Glendale Adventist Hospital emergency room, where Zamora was treated following the accident, told News of the Weird, 'He's lucky to be alive! If the nails were bigger, some of these wounds could have been fatal!' The nurse, who declined to be named for this article, said that she used a pair of pliers borrowed from a hospital maintenance worker to pull one nail from Zamora's forehead and another nine from the side of his skull, as well as one from his cheekbone, two from his jaw, and two more from his collarbone—fifteen in total. Mr. Zamora, an associate producer at Orion Pictures, also sustained a broken nose when the bookcase he was building fell onto his face."

I lowered the paper. Girl was looking at me with an expression I'd never seen on her face before. Her normally twinkling dark brown eyes were wide and black, her smokey eye makeup adding to the ferocity of her Medusa stare. Her lush eyebrows, usually arched and expressive, now formed a straight line against the top of her eyes, nearly touching in the middle. Her full, red lips were drawn into narrow lines, her jaw thrust forward exposing her lower teeth. The corners of her mouth were pulled down and out, her chin trembling.

"You... told me... you finished him *off!*" she seethed with rage.

"I-I-I thought..." I stammered, "He *looked* dead! He wasn't moving! Or, like, breathing or... I felt for a pulse and...whatever..." I trailed off.

Girl had stopped listening. She had opened her suitcase onto the bed and was yanking her clothes violently off of their hangers and throwing them into it, forming a pile that soon buried the little traveling bag.

As she flung clothing, she berated me. "Well don't just stand there, you idiot! We have to get out of here! Pack your shit!"

Girl had never spoken to me like that. Seeing her like this after listening to Rudy's messages I feared that after all of the time we had spent together I was finally witnessing her true self.

I was stunned. Frozen in place. I found myself getting lost in the lyrics of the Orchestral Maneuvers in the Dark song which was pouring forth from the radio, perfectly articulating my feelings of disillusionment and disappointment—both in Girl and in myself for falling for her tricks and twists of mind.

Out of the corner of her eye, she saw me standing immobile and spun to face me. She reached a hand out to the bedside table and grabbed a nearly-full bottle of champagne by the neck.

Lifting the bottle over her head, she heaved it straight at my face. White foam spiraled through the air as the bottle spun wildly in my direction. I bent sideways at the waist to avoid being hit and the bottle smashed into the television, lodging mouth-first into the hole it made in the glass screen.

As champagne poured into the guts of the combination TV and radio, there was a loud electric *POP!* and the music died. The singer stopped crooning about how hard it was to believe he had been so in love.

Now the only sound was Girl's angry breathing as she glared at me with clenched teeth, her fists white-knuckled balls at her sides.

I made myself move. I threw on my hoodie and stuffed the plastic laundry bag containing my previously-worn clothing into Rudy's gym bag and picked it up by the handles.

By this time, Girl had crammed as much of her travel wardrobe into her suitcase as she could and forced it shut, securing the clasps while corners of shirts and toes of stockings and other bits of clothing still stuck out around the edges.

She grabbed my wrist, growled, "Come on already!" and dragged me toward the door. She released me, opened the door so hard that it slammed against the wall, and started stomping down the hall. I pulled the door closed behind me and followed, catching up to her as she was pushing the elevator call button over and over in a machine gun staccato.

The doors opened. Girl got on and I followed. She began mashing the "Lobby" button, giving it at least a dozen stabs in the time it took the door to close. During our brief ride to the ground floor, she paced back and forth within the small space like a caged cat.

When we reached the lobby, she straightened her back and walked toward the exit with her head held high, looking straight ahead. Her crucifix-studded white leather belt was caught in the suitcase's seam and trailed behind her, the skull-shaped buckle bouncing along the carpeted floor.

I followed in her wake. As Daryl opened the door with a deferential "Mrs. Larsen, Mr. Larsen," Girl strode across the threshold without acknowledging him then took off down the sidewalk at a sprint.

I ran after her. As I caught up, I panted, "Where are we going? *Why* are we going?" I grabbed her arm, halting her forward momentum and spinning her to face me. "Think for a minute, Girl! Your dad told the doctors at the hospital that he did all that shit to himself! It's not like the cops are looking for *us!* Nobody even knows that we're in San Francisco! Calm the fuck down!"

"Calm down? CALM DOWN??" Girl dropped her suitcase and started gesticulating wildly while pacing back and forth, ranting at top volume, "Maybe he didn't talk to the police, but I totally guarantee you that my father has *somebody* looking for me! He's got eyes *everywhere!* We can't drive the car anymore. We gotta find a bus station."

She looked around wild-eyed and took off again at a run, stopping at a payphone at the next street corner. I picked up her suitcase and walked down the block toward her. When I reached her, she had lifted the phonebook, which was hanging below the telephone by a chain, and was now cradling it in one hand while madly flipping through it with the other, turning pages so hard they were ripping.

She found what she was looking for; a full-page ad featuring a simplified map of the city showing where bus tickets could be purchased and the location of the Greyhound terminal. Across the top of the page was a running dog next to the Yellow Pages walking fingers logo and the words, *The World is at Your Fingertips!* Girl tore the page out, grabbed her bag from my hand and raced down the street once more. As I jogged beside her, she started explaining her plans.

"First we drive to the bus station. Then we park

the car someplace crowded and swap the license plate with another car. That'll slow down the maggots that're looking for us while we take a bus north to Portland." We had reached the street where the car was parked and we turned onto it, still running. "Once we're there, we can—"

Girl stopped. She dropped her suitcase once more. We were standing behind Rudy's car. The antenna was still magnetted to the roof.

Girl got very quiet. She extended her arm and pointed at the antenna with one shaky finger. She started breathing heavy, like she was going to hyperventilate. She spoke as she panted, each word exploding out on an exhale and followed by another intake of breath.

"WHAT... THE... FUCK... IS... THAT... FUCKING... THING... DOING... THERE?"

I started stammering as I fumbled the car key from my pocket and tried to insert it into the trunk lock with trembling hands.

"I-I-I meant to tell you about that. I... um... kind of found your dad's car phone..."

I had the trunk open and I dropped the gym bag inside beside the jack and tire changing kit. I reached up and tugged the magnet from the roof and started wrapping the cord around the stubby aerial, still stumbling over my words and avoiding Girl's angry gaze.

"He... he called it and left a message..."

Out of the corner of my eye, I saw a blur of

movement as Girl reached into the trunk and picked up the tire iron. I turned toward her just as she swung the solid wrench end against my temple with a banshee scream.

A flash of red filled my field of vision followed by inky black.

CHAPTER 17

A confusion of voices invaded the darkness in which I was floating.

"...a nice, peaceful neighborhood! We don't need any pimps and whores and junkies making trouble!"

"Yes, ma'am. Of course, ma'am. Thank you for being a good neighbor."

"Hey! I know this guy!"

I opened my eyes to see a fuzzy, policeman-shaped blob. I blinked rapidly a few times and the blurry image came slowly into focus.

I recognized the cop as the young rookie Guillermo had flirted with in the doorway of Zim's during our bicycle rickshaw adventure. He was kneeling beside me with one hand on the Volvo's rear bumper. I was on my back in the street behind the car.

I pushed up onto my elbows and pain exploded in my head. White sparks made lazy circles around the edges of my vision. The officer placed one hand gently on my chest and said, soothingly, "Take it easy, now. It looks like you have a pretty serious head injury…"

His words faded into a distant echo as blackness bled into everything and the world spun me back down to unconsciousness.

I don't know how long I was out for. When I opened my eyes next, I could still hear a woman's voice going on about how her street wasn't a place where lowlifes and drug pushers were welcome. Something soft was beneath the back of my skull now, cushioning it from the hard ground.

I let my head loll to one side and saw the older policeman I had met the other day—Jordan, I remembered, so I couldn't be *that* badly concussed—walking a gray-haired Black woman in a bathrobe and slippers up the steps of her house with an arm across her shoulders. I heard him say, "Thank you again, Mrs. Shingle. We'll take it from here," as she disappeared behind her front door.

Officer Jordan finished tucking Mrs. Shingle away and walked over to his partner and me. I managed to sit up with no fireworks this time and the world stayed in place. I wrapped my arms around my raised knees. I looked back behind me and saw that my head had been resting on a rolled-up nylon jacket with SFPD insignia on the sleeves. One patch was stained with blood. I felt my temple. My hand came away red and sticky.

"Sorry about your jacket." I said to the younger cop.

His partner joined us, dropped to one knee, and replied for him.

"Don't worry about that. I remember you. You're Maria's friend." He gestured back over his shoulder with a thumb. "The lady called in a complaint. Said she heard screaming. Said she looked out her window and saw a young woman attacking—her words—her pimp. Then she said the girl smashed up the car and stormed off."

I realized for the first time that I was sitting amongst pieces of broken taillight and pebbles of safety glass. With the help of the two nice policemen, I got unsteadily to my feet and inspected the damage. Girl had apparently taken the tire iron to the side windows, the lights, the wing mirrors, and—most distressingly— the car phone. Its leatherette case was on the sidewalk, no longer rectangular. The receiver had been pulled out by the roots, the frayed ends of the cable sticking out of the mangled case. The handset itself was splintered into slivers of black plastic and green circuitboard.

I felt my pockets. I still had my half of the cash in one front jeans pocket and a baggie of joints in the other. My hoodie yielded clove cigarettes, poppers, and sunglasses in one pocket and the stack of Polaroids taken by Chuck during our wedding at Turtle Terrace in the other.

"Looking for these?" The younger officer held up Rudy's key ring. "We found them in a bush across the street where the old lady said your woman threw them."

I took the keys and pocketed them. "Thanks," I said.

Officer Jordan put a hand on my shoulder. "How are you feeling, young man?" He pointed toward the sky and said, "Follow my finger."

Concussion was not well-understood in those days. I spent one high school semester as the team mascot during football games. Dressed in a plush bee costume (we were the Fairview Yellowjackets), I got to hang out with cute cheerleaders, wiggling my stinger at the crowd and miming fisticuffs with opponents' mascots. From my position on the sidelines, I saw first-hand how head injuries were treated. A player would be carried limply from the field after "having his bell rung" and as soon as he was able to stand upright, the coach would yell in his face to "Man up!" or "Walk it off!" and back into the game he would trot.

The gray-haired cop swung his index finger back and forth while I tracked it with my eyes. I didn't get dizzy or puke or anything. That was apparently sufficient evidence that I'd be just fine. Walk it off.

"Let's get you cleaned up. Our shift is about over anyway." He turned to address his partner. "Tan, you run the cruiser back to the station. I'll take..." He looked at me and raised his eyebrows.

"Guy" I filled in.

"I'll take Guy to my place." He flashed a fatherly

smile. "Rachel loves a stray."

Officer Tan gave a little two-fingered salute and said, "Whatever you say, boss." He shook my hand, gave me a tight-lipped little nod, and moved off toward their police car parked down the block.

Rudy's car ran fine, though it was pretty chilly without glass in the side windows. The burly middle-aged cop, whose name turned out to be Jordan Jones, was at least concerned enough about my condition to recognize that I probably shouldn't get behind the wheel quite yet. I handed him the keys and rode in the passenger seat while he drove.

"Thank you for this," I said, leaning back against the headrest and closing my eyes. The cool breeze felt wonderful on my throbbing skull. "I don't quite get why you're going above and beyond for me, but thanks."

Officer Jones was quiet for a few minutes. My eyes still closed, I felt him place a fatherly hand on my wrist.

"My wife and I had a son," he explained. "He was about your age when we lost him. Beirut."

We sat in silence for the rest of the short drive. When the car stopped, I opened my eyes. We were parked at the curb in front of a mauve Edwardian-era building across from a city park.

We entered the Jones apartment. It was a cozy

second-story walk-up with its own street entrance. In the flat's living room, rose-patterned vintage barkcloth drapes framed a big bay window with a view across the park to a church with a fancy domed belltower. On a round table stood a framed photo of a sober young man in dress blues and a white service cap. A second, triangular, frame held a folded american flag.

Officer Jones' wife, Rachel, was a ruddy-faced, grandmotherly woman with heavily-freckled arms. She took one look at my bleeding head and bustled me into the bathroom, sat me on the terry cloth toilet lid cover, and cleaned my wound with the skill and efficiency of a nurse.

It turned out she was a retired veterinary technician. She told me this as she wiped and dabbed and patched me up, reassuring me soothingly that everything would be alright and generally mothering me while never once asking probing questions.

Rachel finished and left me alone in the bathroom to change and freshen up. I looked in the mirror. I was still wearing the *Lone Wolf McQuade* T-shirt, which was now filthy and blood-spattered. My left eye was surrounded by dark bruising which extended to the hairline. A series of three little butterfly bandage strips ran along the cheekbone on that side, closing the wound which had been the source of all the blood. I gingerly touched the area and involuntarily sucked air through clenched teeth.

The bones around my eye felt fractured.

I met my reflection's gaze. The white of my injured eye was bright red around the blue iris. I looked frightful. The maimed eye was also very light sensitive, causing me to squint and tear up from the light over the mirror. My hoodie was on the floor beside me. I reached into the pocket and pulled out my cheap imitation Ray-Bans and put them on.

I peeled off my shirt and washed my armpits and chest in the sink. I held my head under the faucet and ran my hands through my hair. I had brought the gym bag full of clothes in from the car. Digging through the bag, I found one last clean movie shirt and pulled it over my head.

I faced the mirror again, the shades making the light easier to bear and concealing my injuries. On my chest, *The Terminator* glared back at me with a matching look; sunglasses and spiky brown hair.

I removed my pants and cleaned my lower half, then put on fresh underwear and socks. I still had one unworn pair of black jeans which I had lifted from Rudy's room and I put them on, once again tucking the overly-long pant legs into my army boots, and shoved my dirty clothes into the bag. I tied the sleeves of the hoodie around my waist and opened the bathroom door.

Walking out into the hallway, I followed voices and found Jordan and Rachel in the kitchen, sitting at a round wooden breakfast table beside a window, drinking coffee from orange mugs and gabbing affectionately. The coffee smelled great. There was a third mug on the table and without my having to ask, Rachel reached over to the mustard-yellow Mr. Coffee machine on the counter beside her, lifted the glass carafe from the warming pad, and poured me a cup.

I was still standing in the doorway. Officer Jones pulled an empty chair out from its spot under the table and said, "Come on in. Have a seat."

I put the bag down beside the door and walked into the cheerful, homey kitchen. I sat. In the middle of the table were a sugar bowl and creamer that matched the mugs. Rachel slid them closer to me. I shook my head, muttered, "Thanks," and picked up my coffee, sipping it black. It was hot and rich and felt wonderful on my parched throat.

"Thank you both for everything," I said, letting the mug warm my palms, "It was really nice of you to help me out. If I can maybe use your phone, I'll make a couple calls and get out of your hair. I don't want to be any more trouble."

Rachel and Jordan looked at each other and then at me. He spoke. "Are you ready to tell us what happened back there?"

I thought for a minute. How many of the actual details should I volunteer? I was sitting in the home of a cop and I'd committed some pretty heinous acts in the last week—at least a couple of them blatantly criminal.

"My girlfriend and I are on our way to Portland. We were staying in a hotel for a couple of days." I began. I worried that describing Girl as my wife might prompt more questions. Best to keep things simple. "We had a fight. She's really mad at her father and she found out that I'd been in contact with him. She got...well, pretty upset." I touched my temple.

"Is she okay out there on her own?" Rachel asked, "Do you know where she might have gone?"

"I'm fairly sure she was planning to take a bus the rest of the way to Portland," I replied. "I might be able to catch up with her along the way if I can find out the bus schedules or whatever..." I trailed off.

I really didn't have a great idea how to proceed. I'd been thinking it over and I'd decided to try to get Rudy on the phone and see if he had any suggestions. He had seemed pretty eager to talk to me. It had been clear from Rudy's message that somehow he wasn't holding a grudge. I had tried to kill him yet still he was concerned with my safety.

I got the impression that he was also concerned with Girl's well-being. *She's not well*, he had said of Girl. Not *she's evil* or *she needs to be stopped*. He had sounded concerned, not angry. This was a man who loved his troubled daughter.

I loved her, too. In spite of what she had done to my face; in spite of the things she had said. My heart ached at the idea that Girl was out there someplace by herself without me to protect her. She was angry. She was hurt. She thought that I had betrayed her. That broke my heart. I had to find her and tell her how much I adored her. I wanted to hold her and rock her and protect her from the big, bad world.

Officer Jones spoke up, snapping me out of my musings. "That car isn't going anywhere in that condition. I certainly can't let you drive it without taillights; you at least need to get *those* fixed. I got a car guy. He mostly works on lowriders—big American cars and shit—but he's patched up my VW Bug a couple times. Let me give him a call and see what he says. It won't be free, though." He raised one eyebrow and gave me an appraising look. "You got any money?"

"Yeah, I can pay him. Thanks, Officer Jones."

"Jordan," He said with a smile.

Jordan's car guy turned out to be an automobile enthusiast and sometime police informant named Hector. I gathered he had a somewhat complicated relationship with local law enforcement. I drove Rudy's battered Volvo to Hector's place following the written directions I was given.

From what Jordan had told me about Hector's desire to assist the police in keeping hard drugs off of "his streets" and the fact that he made a living dropping hydraulics and nitro systems into '57 Chevys for San Francisco's underground street racers, I had pictured a back-alley chop shop. Instead, I was surprised to find that Rollerz, as Hector's place was called, was a legitimate mechanic business between a gas station on one side and a Jack in the Box fast food restaurant on the other, located on Geary—a bright, busy, six-lane boulevard in the Richmond District.

The front of the building featured the garage name rendered in beautiful chrome-styled graffiti lettering above a spray-painted mural of a tricked-out hotrod surrounded by scantily-clad barrio girls. I pulled into the large front parking area next to a lime green Impala which had a naked woman embracing a leopard airbrushed on the expansive hood.

Hector was expecting my arrival and he strode out of the open garage bay to meet me wiping grease from his hands with a rag. He was shorter than me but significantly wider through the chest and biceps. He wore oil-stained brown chinos and an equally-begrimed white tanktop undershirt. Black and gray tattoos covered every inch of exposed skin from his jawline down to his knuckles.

As I stood meekly aside, Hector pocketed his shop

cloth and walked slowly around the car sizing up the damage. Once he had made a complete circuit, he stopped directly in front of me and grinned, showing a whole row of gold bottom teeth.

"She was pretty fuckin' pissed off, eh, *ese?*" I had heard Jordan's phone conversation with Hector and at no point had he said that a *woman* had damaged the car. He had simply stated that a friend needed some repairs done right away.

"Yeah, super pissed." I agreed.

"So… Jonesy says you need to get street legal fast and cheap?"

I nodded. Hector hooked a thumb through a belt loop and scratched the back of his head with his other hand.

"No way I'm gettin' factory parts for *el sueco* here, but I can fix ya up with shit I have lyin' around and have you on the road by tonight if you don't need her pretty. I got time and I sort of owe Jonesy a favor." He looked at the car in silence for a few seconds, making mental calculations, then held out a hand with a dollar sign tattooed on the palm. "Say four-fiddy?"

I counted out four hundred and fifty dollars, severely decreasing my bankroll. I handed the stack of bills to Hector along with the keys and he pocketed both.

I said, "If I can use your phone, I'll call a cab. Officer Jones said I could wait at his place until you were finished."

Hector put a hand on my back and started walking toward the building, pulling me along with him, saying, "Forget that. I got a loaner you can use."

We walked through the main workshop, past stacks and racks of car parts and several elaborately-pinstriped vintage autos in various stages of disassembly. Hector lifted a key ring off of a hook on the black-painted rear wall, opened a door, and gently pushed me through, following me into a back alley.

A handful of less-fancy vehicles were parked along a chain link fence behind the building. Hector asked me, "Can you drive stick?" and handed me the key.

I had driven a non-automatic-shift car exactly once and it hadn't been pretty, but I understood the general principle and I wasn't about to look weak in front of this man, so I of course said, "Sure."

Hector patted the roof of a big, brown behemoth with chrome letters spelling out *F O R D* across its nose and *Custom 500* on its flank. The car had dents and rust and no hubcaps.

"I'll call when your little *carrito* is done," he said. "Drive safe."

We shook hands and Hector disappeared back into the garage. I opened the massive door of the steel beast and grunted in surprise as I dropped down into the shockingly low seat. I pulled the door closed, sealing me into the cockpit with a sound like a submarine hatch sealing shut. My ears popped.

I inserted the key and started the engine. In sharp contrast to the car's rough exterior, the engine purred like a sleepy lion. I pumped the gas a couple of times and the purr amplified into a deep, menacing growl that rocked the car gently from side to side, swaying the fuzzy dice hanging from the rearview mirror.

A black shifter knob the size of a billiard ball sat atop an angled rod protruding from a segmented rubber cone on the vast floorboard. I examined the diagram engraved on its surface. Pressing in the clutch pedal with my left foot and the brake with my right, I wrestled the car into gear, eased off the brakes, and started rolling forward. There was nothing in front of me, so I went for it, accelerating out of the alley and into traffic.

The ride back to the Jones home felt like the chase scene from *Bullitt*. Hector's rough and ready Custom 500 powered up and down the San Francisco streets with a vengeance, bouncing over the lips of hills with bumpers scraping asphalt and leaning vertiginously through turns.

The sound of honking horns followed me the entire way as I survived near miss after near miss navigating through traffic. When I pulled up to the curb in front of Jordan's building and managed to shove the car into first with a sound like grinding coffee beans and set the brake, he came down the steps to meet me, laughing and shaking his head.

"How'd that go?" he asked as I exited the vehicle, "I see you're not driving the little blue punching bag anymore."

I explained that Hector had promised to have the Volvo ready to roll by nightfall and asked again if I could make some calls while I waited. I said that they'd be long distance and that I'd give him a few bucks for the trouble. Jordan waived off my offer of money and held his front door open for me.

As we climbed the stairs, the smell of cooking meat made my stomach growl. I hadn't had anything to eat since breakfast that morning and now it was mid-afternoon. The entrance to Jordan and Rachel's apartment was between the living room and the kitchen. As I walked through, Rachel was to my right, transferring a hamburger patty from a frying pan onto a plated and be-ketchuped bun on the counter beside the stove.

"I thought you could use something to eat," she told me, setting the plate on the table and dumping a pile of barbeque-flavored potato chips from their bag onto the space beside the burger.

I thanked her and sat down in front of the food. While Rachel poured me a glass of diet cola over ice, Jordan lifted a telephone from a counter dividing the kitchen from the living room and placed it beside me on the table, its cord trailing behind. I asked if he had a pen and some paper I could use and he laid both beside the phone.

As I ate the delicious hamburger, I phoned my apartment. The call was answered by Louis, the drummer for a band called Library Voice. I asked him to read me Rudy's number, which I had scrawled on the kitchen wall beside the phone inside of a heart.

I wrote down the digits as he read them out to me, then we exchanged a few pleasantries while I finished eating (including the news that my bedroom had been taken over by invaders in my absence). We both said, "Later," and I depressed the phone's cradle button long enough to disconnect and get a fresh dial tone.

I punched in the number for Rudy's house. I listened to the phone ringing down the line four hundred miles away in Glendale.

I was super nervous to speak to Rudy, but I didn't know who else to call. He clearly understood what was happening with Girl better than I did. As far as I could tell, he hadn't called the police. I had to put aside everything Girl had told me about him and try to give him the benefit of the doubt for now.

The phone rang once… twice… three times… four… Then there was a click and I heard *Girl's voice!*

"Hello?" she said.

I freaked. "GIRL?!?" I began, "How are you—"

"KEE-HEE-GHEE-HICK-HEEE! Gotcha! Abbey and Rudy can't come to the phone right now! Start talkin' at the beep!"

BEEEEEP!

I took a deep, calming breath and started speaking. "Mr. Zamora? Are you there? Please pick up the phone. It's me, Guy... I mean John Mann. But... You know... Not really. My name's actually Guy. Girl... I mean Abbey... She's like...gone. We're in San Francis—"

"Hello? Hello?" Rudy had heard me through the answering machine and picked up the phone. "John? Or... You said... Guy?"

"Yeah. Sorry. My real name's Guy Larsen." Jordan and Rachel had retreated to the living room to give me some privacy. I slouched down in my chair and faced the wall. I lowered my voice and plunged in headfirst. "It was Gir —Abbey's idea to do the whole babysitter thing. I don't really have kids. I'm just...like...a kid myself, I guess. I'm nineteen. Anyway, Abbey and me... We met in a bar and... like...she kinda convinced me you were...like...a bad guy or whatever...like you molested her and shit, and..."

He interrupted, speaking excitedly, "I understand. This isn't the first time Abbey's done something extreme. She's never quite gone *this* far and she's never sucked somebody else into one of her shit shows—at least as far as I know—but I get that she was using you." He paused to catch his breath. "So. Where is she now?"

"I don't exactly know," I started to explain. "We were driving to Portland to find her mother..."

"In my car?" He interjected.

"Yeah. In your car. Again, I'm really sorry about everything. She really did tell me some horrible things about you."

"Before I picked up it sounded like you were saying San Francisco?"

"Yeah. That's where we are now. Or at least I am. She saw the thing in the newspaper about you and then found out I heard your phone messages and she didn't take it well. She...kinda flipped out. And...like... She left. I don't know where she is now. Probably on a bus to Portland?"

Rudy didn't reply for a while. I could hear him breathing. When he spoke again, it was to say, "So that asshole from The Times actually printed the story. Motherfucker." Rudy heaved a heavy sigh and continued. "I got a call two days after you sent me to the hospital. Some reporter who said he was verifying some facts. I told him I didn't want him to write about what happened and he said he didn't actually need my permission. Such a jerk. What did it say in the paper?"

"It was in that 'weird news' section. They said you, like, got drunk and lost control of the nail gun. They printed your name and everything. Even said you were an associate producer at Orion."

"Heh." He gave a bitter chuckle. "Dickhead gave me a promotion. Big of him."

"Mr. Zamora? Rudy? I don't really know what to do next. I was thinking about driving North following the bus route and see if I can find Gir—Abbey along the way."

"Good," he agreed, "Smart. I'll join you. You can tell me what she said about me and I can fill you in on some truth. Do you have any photographs of her?"

I thought about my collection of Polaroids—Girl and I completely naked in our lounge chairs with her legs open wide; the two of us facing each other during the marriage ceremony with my half-boner between us; the group shots of Girl and me surrounded by our wedding party of nude senior citizens. "Um…no." I said.

"Okay, I'll bring a couple of school pictures we can show people along the way. I'll bring her meds, too. I found them in the bathroom so I take it she's been off 'em this whole time?"

I didn't know what he was talking about and I told him so. "Um… Meds? What kind of meds?"

"Oh, shit… Let's see… Lithium, antipsychotic, antianxiety, mood stabilizer… It's a whole cocktail situation. Been keeping her pretty functional for a few years now, at least when I can get her to take 'em. She's just like her mother, though—convinces herself that she's better off without 'em and then, well—welcome to Hell, Mr. Larsen! When those two get *together* off their meds? It's no damn picnic, let me tell you."

"Wait…what?!?" My chest was getting that tight feeling it got when the world I *thought* I knew shifted sideways with the sound of a needle scudding across the surface of a record.

I forced a few slow, deep breaths and asked, "Abbey and her mother… They *know* each other?"

"Oh, sure!" Rudy confirmed, "The court gave me sole custody, but Abbey and Lily are like big, dysfunctional magnets always being drawn together. Listen—Guy? We can talk about all this in person. Can you meet me at the airport? There's a commuter flight that leaves every couple of hours that I can get on through work. If I hurry, I can be at SFO in…" I heard paper rustling as he consulted some sort of schedule. "…about four hours, give or take."

As I drove down the 101 freeway toward San Francisco International, I thought back on the last couple of hours.

I had talked on the phone with Rudy for a while longer as I told him about the situation with his car and explained that I wouldn't have a way to drive to the airport for a little while. He told me that he'd wait in a specific airport lounge for me and said to just get there when I could. He explained how to find it and I wrote down his directions on the paper Jordan had given me, which turned out to be the back of a pad of parking ticket blanks.

I guess Rachel could tell that I was feeling pretty overwhelmed when I got off the phone, because she suggested that I lay down and close my eyes while I was waiting for Hector to work his magic on the Volvo.

She ushered me into a small, windowless guest room at the back of the apartment which might have been a walk-in closet at one point in the building's history. From the framed prints of fairy tail heroines, I guessed that the space usually hosted a visiting granddaughter. I fell asleep as soon as my head hit the little, pink pillow on the tiny bed.

When Officer Jones woke me with a shake of my shoulder, it felt like I had only been sleeping for a few minutes, but when I stood up and followed him down the hall into the kitchen, the sky outside the windows was dark.

Jordan told me that Hector had called to say that my car was ready and I thanked him and Rachel again for their hospitality. Rachel insisted that I take a paper bag of leftovers from the supper I had slept through, they both wished me luck and told me to drive carefully, and I left.

The ride back to Rollerz was even more action-packed than my first time behind the wheel of the muscle car due to the darkness of the hour, but I made it in one piece, retracing my route and eventually rolling into the alley behind the garage. I parked, grabbed my doggie bag, and exited the boat of a car on wobbly sea legs, glad to be back on solid ground.

Hector met me at the back door and walked me through the shop to the front parking lot, where I got my first look at what he had done to Rudy's little blue Volvo.

Hector had clearly stated that the repairs wouldn't be made with factory parts, but I was ill-prepared for the hybrid monstrosity that greeted me. The previously rectangular taillights were gone, along with the boxy blue fenders which had housed them. Now, the rear of the car sported a pair of white 1960s-era tailfins with cone-shaped lights protruding from round chrome settings. A strip of sanded steel showed where the new additions had been welded into the existing body.

The doors had also been replaced. Girl had smashed the glass in each of the four-door's side windows. Rather than replace only the glass—which, I supposed, would have been impossible without access to another Volvo for parts—Hector had swapped out the doors entirely.

Rudy's car was now a two-door. A single long door from some mid-century American sedan stretched from front to back on each side. Here, too, bare metal welds showed where the car had been modified in order to receive the replacement hinges and latches. The new doors were pink with big kidney-shaped chrome rearview mirrors jutting out on silver stems like a mollusc's eyestalks.

"Ready to roll, *ese!*" Hector flashed his golden grin and handed me the keyring, now containing an additional key which unlocked the new doors. "I topped off your fluids and tightened a few things up under the hood while I was at it."

I dropped the sack of food, backed away, and began laughing. At first I was just chuckling and shaking my head at the absurd appearance of the car. Gradually, though, my chuckles amplified into full-blown hysteria.

I couldn't. Stop. Laughing.

The events of the day had finally broken my brain. First I'm knocked unconscious, then I find out that the person I'd been closer to than anybody I'd ever met—and who I *married*—isn't who I thought she was *at all* and that she's been lying to me non-stop as long as I've known her. Now I'm getting ready to meet my *murder victim,* driving a tri-colored clown car!

I was gulping and choking, rendered helpless with laughter.

I forced myself to stop laughing long enough to catch my breath. I doubled over with one hand on my knee and the other against the front wall of Hector's garage. When I looked up, I saw that I was leaning on the Rollerz graffiti mural, my hand on the oversized boob of a chola in *Día de los Muertos* facepaint and the guffaws started up again.

I fell backward, my ass against the wall, and slid down until I was sitting with my head on my knees. I needed to get my shit together before I could drive to meet Rudy. I reached into my pocket and pulled out the baggie of joints. There were five left. They were a little bent, but perfectly serviceable. I extracted one from the ziploc and pulled my fingers along its length, straightening and smoothing it. I put it in my mouth, looked up at Hector and asked, "Do you mind?"

Hector walked over and sat down beside me on the concrete with his back against the wall. He produced a silver Zippo with a Mexican flag enameled on one side and snapped a flame in front of my face.

"Not if you share."

I lit up and we sat and smoked in silence, passing and puffing until all that was left was a roach too small to hold, which Hector placed on his tongue and swallowed. I was feeling much better, my fevered brain soothed by the calming influence of the THC.

I asked Hector how to get to the airport from where we were. He stood and disappeared through the garage door, returning a moment later with a Thomas Guide map book which he opened on the Volvo's hood. I got up and joined him, watching as he traced the route with a finger.

I retrieved my supper from the ground and jotted

turn-by-turn directions on the bag with a black Sharpie Hector pulled out of his back pocket. I handed the marker back, opened the oversized door of the undersized car, and sat behind the wheel. I had to twist to the left and reach behind me to access the handle and close the door. Still turned sideways, I cranked the window down and looked up at Hector. I thanked him, told him that he was an automotive madman (this elicited another gleaming smile), and pulled out into traffic.

The car looked ridiculous, but it ran great. It was punchier up hills, it shifted smooth as silk, and the brakes were tight and responsive.

As I turned south onto the 101, I dumped the paper bag out on the passenger seat. There were two pork chops in waxed paper, a square of cornbread wrapped in a napkin, and a banana.

I was pretty high and munchy as hell. I picked up a chop and ripped off the paper with my teeth, speeding through the night. I felt in control for the first time all day. I was ready to face whatever messed-up adventure fate had in store for me.

Gripping the meat in my mouth to free up my right hand, I turned on the radio and twiddled the dial to KOME, cranked the volume way, way up, and sped on down the freeway with the music blasting, a crazy, determined grin on my face, and pork grease dripping down my chin.

CHAPTER 18

I made excellent time, arriving at the airport in under thirty minutes. I parked in the short-term garage and followed the Eastern Airlines signs. As I approached the terminal, I saw my reflection in the glass doors. I had removed my sunglasses to drive, but facing my bruised and battered face looking back at me, I once again donned the faux Ray-Bans before pushing through into the bustling concourse.

I pulled Rudy's instructions from the back pocket of my (his) jeans. They said to look for a door labeled *Frequent Flyers* located between Bay Area News and Peet's Coffee just past the Eastern ticketing counter.

I found the door and opened it. I stepped through into a smoke-filled, wood-paneled lounge that looked like it belonged in a golf course clubhouse. As the door closed behind me, the din of the airport—a mix of crowd noises and loudspeaker announcements and ringing telephones —was instantly muted, replaced by the subdued playing of a live pianist at a baby grand in one corner.

Businessmen and businesswomen in suits—mostly on their own, but a few of them in clusters—drank and smoked at small round tables and along the well-appointed bar which extended the length of the right-hand wall. The bar was tended by a red-headed woman who sported a white shirt, a black vest, and a narrow blue and white necktie patterned with little Eastern Airlines logos.

I spotted Rudy sitting at the far end of the bar, facing my direction. He was wearing a black nylon bomber jacket with an embroidered "Orion" on the breast and a baseball cap that said "Caddyshack" on the front. He was the only other person in the lounge not wearing a suit and the only other one wearing sunglasses.

I approached him and sat on the adjacent stool. The bartender came over and asked to see my membership card. Rudy said, "He's my guest," which seemed to appease her because she asked me what I was drinking. I ordered a Budweiser and she moved away to fetch it.

Rudy and I sat and looked at each other in silence through our shades. The bartender brought my beer, which seemed to break the tension. I drained half of the bottle in one thirsty series of gulps.

Rudy took a sip from the glass of amber liquid in front of him, then said, "Let's see what she did to you."

I set my sunglasses on the bar and Rudy let out a

long, low whistle of appreciation before stating, "I'll see you and raise you," and removing his hat and glasses.

Rudy looked like hammered shit. A mottled strip of bruises surrounded his eyes like a raccoon mask, dark purple closer to his swollen nose and fading to a deathly greenish-yellow around the edges. A puckered bindi of a scab dominated his forehead with a tightly-spaced row of similarly clotted punctures across the stubbly, recently-shaved left side of his head. The ear on that side was cauliflowered like a boxer's and was a deep maroon color.

His lips, on the other hand, actually looked better than I would have expected after their duct tape decortication; merely reddened and cracked like he'd just returned from a ski trip.

I looked down and away, ashamed that I had caused this man so much trauma. The bravado I had felt driving on the freeway, music blasting and buzzing on weed, evaporated completely with my first sight of Rudy's damaged face.

I took another swig of beer, swallowed, and mumbled, "I'm...just...so sorry."

He put one hand on my shoulder and raised his drink with the other. "Survivors!" he declared.

I clanked the base of my bottle against the bottom edge of his glass and returned the toast, meeting his direct gaze with a sidelong glance.

"Survivors."

Just then the bartender came back to our end of the bar and saw our naked faces for the first time. She put a hand to her throat like she was clutching an invisible string of pearls.

"Holy shit! Which one of you won the fight?" she gasped.

We looked at her and then at each other.

Rudy said, "At this point I'd call it a draw."

He and I laughed.

The bartender barked a short laugh of her own which expressed more nervous surprise than humor and said, "Let me buy you gentlemen another round. You look like you could use it."

She reached beneath the bar and grabbed the bourbon bottle from the well. As she replenished Rudy's glass with a generous pour, I said, "I'll have the same." She added a second glass to the bar and dispensed three fingers for me.

I never would have predicted it, but with our nervousness about meeting each other blunted by the whiskey, Rudy and I started to develop a comfortable rapport. As we talked it became clear that both of us had had the experience of simultaneously loving Girl and being victimized by her; Rudy for much longer than I, of course, on both extremes of that spectrum.

As I began thinking of him as something of a friend, I felt like I owed this man an explanation of exactly *how* I had come to be complicit in his attempted murder.

"I really need to tell you what Gir—Abbey said about you…" I began.

Rudy interrupted me, "Why do you keep calling her 'Grabby'? You did that on the phone, too."

"Oh, yeah!" I laughed, "Sorry about that. Abbey sort of…I don't know…rebranded herself? As long as I've known her, she's been 'Girl.' I keep catching myself because I assumed you didn't know her by that nickname. It's what everybody in the scene calls her, though. In, like, the punk clubs and stuff. That's where she *really* spends her time when she tells you she's at, like, friends' houses and shit. I don't think she actually *has* many friends her own age."

"'Girl,' huh?" Rudy thought about this as he took a drink. "So…like that wresting lady that calls herself 'Woman,' right?"

I nodded and made an affirmative grunt with my mouth full of liquor. It turns out Rudy was pretty perceptive.

"I get it," he said, "She was pretty obsessed with Woman for a few days after I took her to see that show. You know, if you're used to calling Abbey 'Girl,' go ahead. That's fine. It kind of suits her, actually."

He suddenly turned to me as a realization hit him. "Hey! Shit! Girl and Guy! I bet she *loves* that!"

"Yeah," I agreed, "She made a really big deal about

it when we met. Like we were brought together by fate or whatever. I guess I fell for it pretty hard. Honestly, I wasn't like...a killer or whatever before Girl."

I explained my new worldview which had developed regarding *My life B.G.* and *My life A.G.*

He nodded while he digested that for a moment then downed the rest of his drink, pulled out his wallet, and tossed some bills on the bar.

"I absolutely want to hear all about how she talked you into trying to kill me," he said, standing and picking up a small, black overnight bag from the next barstool, "but we really should get on the road."

We exited the lounge and made our way through the airport terminal and into the short-term parking garage. As Rudy and I walked between vehicles toward the section where I had left his car, I thought I should prepare him a little. After all, I didn't know how strong his emotional connection to his Volvo was and he was, like, *old.* I didn't want him to have a heart attack or something when he saw the monster that Hector had wrought.

"So...your car..." I began, "Girl broke the taillights and some windows and, like, mirrors and stuff..."

"Oh. Wow. Okay. Good thing you didn't get pulled over driving it," he replied, sounding decidedly unconcerned.

"Yeah...about that..." I continued, "I couldn't exactly *drive* it without, like, at least fixing the taillights. And

I couldn't exactly find a Volvo dealership on such short notice..."

We turned left past a concrete pillar with *5A* stenciled on the side and approached the car. We were facing the rectangular front grille with its aggressively masculine logo and diagonal chrome slash. So far, so normal.

"There she is!" Rudy said with a smile, "She doesn't look so ba—"

He rounded the fender and the car's profile came into view, with its giant pink doors and white tailfins. He stopped in his tracks and his bag fell from his grasp.

"Soooo..." he sighed, "Your life A.G."

"Totally." I confirmed.

Rudy and I discussed what our next move should be. We decided to drive back into the city and show Girl's picture around the Greyhound station to see if anybody remembered her. We knew that she was heading to Portland and Lily. If she *did* take the bus, we figured that with the bus stopping to take on and disgorge passengers in a half-dozen towns between San Francisco and northern Oregon, we'd be able to overtake her and rein her in before anybody else got hurt.

Rudy said he was pretty tired from rushing around and catching the flight north, so I drove first. It occurred to me that it was going to be nice having somebody to share the driving duties during the next leg of the adventure (as Girl would call it).

As we pulled onto the freeway I asked, "So do you want to hear Girl's version of her origin story? Maybe let me know if there's *any* truth in it at all?"

Rudy said, "Absolutely. Shoot."

I started at the beginning, with Rudy the student teacher impregnating the impressionable middle-schooler and her parents' attempts to keep Rudy away from their daughter as she carried her own daughter to term. As I recounted the tale, I glanced to my right and saw Rudy with his head bowed, massaging his temples with the thumb and middle finger of his left hand.

I continued, "Then, the night Lily gave birth…"

Rudy cut in, still looking down and rubbing his head, "…I dramatically stole the baby from the hospital during a raging storm while everybody was busy with accident victims!"

I swerved the car in surprise. I got it back under control and exclaimed, "Then it's *true?!*"

"No, of course not!" Rudy shook his head, chuckling humorlessly. "It was in a screenplay I brought home. Part of my job is reading scripts and estimating budgets for location shoots, props, sets and whatnot. Abbey's always reading them."

My chest had tightened when I thought for a

moment that trusting Rudy had been just as much of a mistake as trusting Girl was turning out to be. I breathed a deep sigh of relief.

I went on to relate what Girl had said about her relationship with her father—how Rudy had fled with her to Southern California, how he had named her by choosing the first name in the baby names book, the years of treating her like she was his wife.

I recounted the purported sexual abuse starting after the trip to the circus on her thirteenth birthday and her subsequent decision to enlist the help of her new boyfriend to end her father's life.

"Speaking of which," Rudy interjected, "There was another screenplay I brought home that involved a wife drugging her abusive husband, tying him to a chair in their garage, and shooting him execution style to make it look like a mob hit."

"Wow," I said.

"Yeah, wow," Rudy agreed. "I'm really glad I don't own an actual gun."

"She told me that you owed, like, some gambling debts or something to some shady dudes and that the police would assume that they were responsible for... what happened."

"So how did she knock me out? Slip something into my drink?"

"The enchiladas. Sleeping pills like her friend

attempted suicide with last year."

Rudy was silent for a quarter mile before he quietly spoke again.

"It wasn't a friend who tried to kill herself. It was Abbey. Maybe I should fill in some details about...what did you call it? Her origin story."

CHAPTER 19

When Rudy and I arrived at the Greyhound station after stopping for directions and a bathroom break at a gas station near the freeway offramp, it was eleven o'clock Sunday night. We asked the man at the ticketing window if there was anyone on duty who had been working earlier that day—say, late morning or early afternoon?

He looked at us suspiciously from behind his protective glass. To be fair, we were both wearing sunglasses. Inside. At night. We looked sketchy as hell.

A large Black woman with an air of authority appeared behind the ticket seller and gently moved him aside with a hand on his shoulder.

"May I help you gentlemen?" she asked, firmly but not unkindly, her voice rendered metallic by a louvered screen fitted into the round opening in the barrier.

Rudy reached into an inside pocket of his bomber jacket and pulled out a small leather wallet which he flipped open casually, revealing a San Francisco Police Department badge.

The gold, seven-pointed star exactly filled a purpose-made inset in the top half of the leather holder. Below the fold, the case held a photo ID card inside of a clear plastic sleeve.

Rudy also produced a school photo of Abigail Zamora. While continuing to hold the badge at eye level, he slid the photo underneath the pass-through slot at the bottom of the cashier's window.

"We're looking for this young woman. We believe that she may have hopped a bus to Portland earlier today. Any information you can share will go a long way toward saving a life."

I could see where Girl got her flair for manipulation.

The woman behind the glass wore an ID card on a Greyhound-branded lanyard around her neck identifying her as Mrs. Baxter. Her expression softened as she picked up the picture and examined it. Girl's hair in the photo was shoulder-length and dark brown. She wore a white headband decorated with silk roses and an embroidered peasant blouse. With her full eyebrows, she looked like a young Frida Kahlo.

"Oh, the poor dear. I hope she's not in too much trouble," Mrs. Baxter said almost to herself. She looked back up at Rudy. "Gloria will be starting her shift at five-thirty. She's the only ticketing agent who works both

Sunday and Monday this week. I think some of the maintenance staff who come in around then might have been here, too, but their schedules are handled by an off-site office, so I couldn't say for sure."

Rudy folded the badge back inside its leather case and returned it to his pocket. When Mrs. Baxter slid the photo back toward us, Rudy held up a palm.

"You keep that. Show it around for me when the shift changes. I'll talk to—Gloria was it?"

Mrs. Baxter nodded as she took the picture back and leaned it up against the side of a coffee cup full of pens and pencils.

"I'll speak with Gloria and anyone else who might have anything useful for me in a few hours," Rudy continued. "In the meantime, we'll be around if you need us. Thank you for your assistance."

We turned away from the window and walked across the spacious station, past a sparse population of travelers dozing on benches.

"That's a pretty realistic badge," I commented when we were out of Mrs. Baxter's earshot.

"I got a friend in props. He worked on *Streets of San Francisco.*" Rudy pulled the wallet back out and handed it to me. "He gave me this for my birthday a couple years back 'cuz he knew I was a fan. It's the one Michael Douglas used on the TV show. I thought it might come in handy so I grabbed it on my way out of the house."

I looked at the laminated card below the gold star. Across the top in white letters against a blue background was the word POLICE. Beneath this, a young Michael Douglas stared earnestly at the camera. The text to the right of the photograph identified the bearer as "Keller, Stephen D." and listed his title as "Inspector."

With Rudy's dark hair and narrow features it was a plausible enough likeness as long as you didn't examine it too closely. The shiny badge and the shock horror of Rudy's battered face would keep most people from even looking at the ID photo.

We looked around us at where we'd be spending the next several hours. The long, open space was dotted with reasonably comfortable-looking padded benches upholstered in blue and orange vinyl. On one end of the station was a shuttered lunch counter beside a half-dozen square tables with chairs upended on their tops. A sign on a pole said it opened at seven a.m. On the opposite end of the depot was a cluster of vending machines, beyond which were the doors to the bus loading area.

I got coffee and packaged pastries for us from the machines while Rudy located a schedule of routes between San Francisco and Portland on a wooden rack of brochures near the ticket windows.

It turned out that there were two separate buses with daily departures to points north. One went to Sacramento then followed Interstate 5 straight through

Oregon and on to Seattle with minimal stops. The other took a longer, more scenic journey, following Route 101 along the Northern California coast, serving multiple towns along the way, before cutting inland and continuing to make frequent stops all the way to Portland.

The former was a more direct route, but only left twice a day during the week and only once on Sundays. The latter took longer, but departed several times daily, including weekends. Girl could have taken either bus.

We resigned ourselves to sitting around until we could talk to Gloria on the off chance that she remembered which bus Girl had boarded.

While we waited, sipping hideous coffee and nibbling stale honey buns, Rudy continued Girl's *genuine* origin story, which he had begun on the drive from the airport.

According to Rudy's version of events, Lily really did get pregnant when she was still in school in Portland, but unlike in Girl's account, Lily wasn't fourteen. She was seventeen. And it wasn't Rudy who got her preggers.

Rudy hadn't even *met* Lily at this point! Lily had been sleeping around for a few years and was either unwilling or unable to identify the baby's father.

True to Girl's story, religious leanings contributed

to the decision to go forward with the birth. It was also religion that brought Rudy into the picture. He was working his way through business college doing office work for the Catholic church which was attended by Lily's parents, Danny and…wait for it…*Abigail!*

Girl wasn't named at random from a book. She was named after her grandmother.

At the request of Lily's parents, Rudy and Lily were introduced by the church's priest. Baby Abigail was eleven months old at this point.

After only a handful of dates it was decided that Rudy was a good influence on Lily and that the young unwed mother should marry him. Rudy faced a lot of pressure to wed Lily, including—but not limited to—Danny and Abigail Senior offering to pay for Rudy's schooling if they got hitched.

Rudy's parents were dead and from the age of thirteen he'd been raised by his aging grandmother under near-poverty conditions. The financial assistance was impossible to resist. There was a hasty, unglamorous wedding. Rudy got his degree and a job in construction estimating. Lily and Abbey moved into his modest apartment.

Once she was married off, Lily's parents basically washed their hands of her. She had been a difficult child and an even more problematic teenager, developing an intense attraction to drugs and unsavory older men. She also suffered from mental illness, but that wouldn't be understood and addressed until several years into her marriage to Rudy. As far as Lily's parents were concerned, Lily was simply a bad egg.

During the first year of the marriage, a school friend of Rudy's headed south and landed a job in the film industry. One thing led to another and Rudy ended up joining him, relocating to LA with his young family.

The temptations of the big city were too much for Lily to resist. It was the start of the 1980s and cocaine was everywhere. Lily cared little for a life of motherhood; she wanted to party and she had no reservations about trading sex for drugs.

Rudy tried everything to keep the marriage together. At one point he convinced Lily to check into a rehab facility that they could barely afford. While there, she underwent psychiatric evaluation and was diagnosed as having bipolar syndrome. She was prescribed medication to help control its symptoms, but her commitment to their use was sporadic.

After a couple more difficult years—during which Lily ping-ponged between trying to be a good parent and indulging in wild, reckless bouts of drug abuse—she and Rudy were divorced.

Despite not being Abbey's biological father, Rudy was awarded sole custody. A record of petty drug possession charges and a history of neglectful behavior meant that Lily was only allowed to spend time with her daughter if the visits were closely supervised. Rather than have "some social worker cunt up my ass," as she put it, Lily simply didn't bother. She disappeared from Rudy and Abbey's lives for several years.

Abbey was six at this point and was already beginning to show early signs that she might share her mother's mood disorder. Her bad behavior in school got her in constant trouble. Complicating things for Rudy, Abbey idolized her free-spirited mother and resented her father's attempts at rule-setting. The divorce proceedings had revealed to Abbey that Rudy wasn't her "real" dad, making his role as a single parent to an already rebellious child that much harder.

When Girl was seven and a half, Rudy got a job advancement which enabled him to buy a house in Glendale, away from the center of Los Angeles. His daughter was now in a better school district with fewer destructive influences. His insurance coverage improved, affording him the opportunity to get Abbey professional help dealing with her mental instability.

For a few years, things seemed to be looking up.

Lily, in the meantime, had reinvented herself. She adopted a more exotic-sounding variation on her maiden name of Flores and became Lillian La Fleur. A lack of inhibitions both on casting couches and in front of the camera landed her roles in a string of low-low budget horror exploitation films. She used her C-list celebrity status and—Rudy speculated—some cozying up to the judge in his chambers to get the supervision requirement removed from her parental visitation agreement.

She re-entered Girl's life like a tornado enters a trailer park. Lily would do things like showing up on a Saturday morning when father-daughter plans had already been made, waving a sheaf of legal papers in Rudy's face and screaming at him, "I have the right to take my little girl to the movies if I fuckin' want to!"

This pattern persisted for a couple more years, with Lily being a consistently inconsistent presence who brought nothing but sporadic chaos into young Abbey's life.

During one unannounced outing, Lily got it in her head that if she introduced her estranged parents to their now twelve-year-old granddaughter, it would be a path to reconciliation and—if she played her cards right—a hand-out. She bundled Girl into her beat-up AMC Pacer and headed for Oregon.

As soon as she crossed state lines, Lily had committed felony kidnapping.

Four days later, after a number of phone calls reassuring Rudy that Abbey was safe and giving him time to arrange a flight to Portland, Danny and Abigail Flores turned their daughter in to the police.

Lily was arrested while exiting the Zoppé Family

Circus' touring big top, where she had taken her daughter for her thirteenth birthday. Girl spent the evening sitting beside a social worker in the precinct house until Rudy arrived to pick her up. She did *not* take it well.

"Detectives?" a gentle voice woke me.

Rudy and I had fallen asleep on one of the bus station benches. His head was against the wall and mine was on his shoulder. Mrs. Baxter was standing in front of us along with a 30-something woman with smooth skin so dark that it had bluish shadows. The new woman was looking at us with obvious concern through thick-lensed cat's eye glasses.

"Gloria's ready to talk to y'all now," said Mrs. Baxter by way of introduction.

Rudy stood up and I followed suit. We took turns shaking Gloria's hand.

"Thank you so much for your time, Gloria. Please forgive our appearance," Rudy said smoothly as Mrs. Baxter left us to our business. "We've been through the ringer on this case."

He gestured with one upturned palm toward another bench which was facing ours. Gloria took a seat. We sat facing her. I noticed for the first time that Gloria was holding the school photo Rudy had provided.

"Mrs. Baxter says you officers need to know if this

girl got on a bus yesterday?" Gloria had a distinctive, high-pitched, almost childish voice that reminded me of Billy Holiday. I detected a very faint accent; perhaps Nigerian.

"Yes," Rudy replied, "any information you can give us would be extremely helpful. Do you remember her?"

"That's just the thing..." Gloria tilted her head down and looked studiously at the photo in her hands, then her eyes turned up to us, peering apologetically over her glasses. "I don't remember any pretty little Mexican girls *by themselves* getting tickets yesterday. There *was* a kid who looked just like this, but she was with her mom and daddy. And three brothers."

I spoke up. "Actually... She didn't look very much like that picture yesterday."

After a moment of deliberation, I reached into my pocket and slid out the stack of Polaroids.

"She looked more like..."

I tilted the pictures away from Rudy's view and shuffled through them until I found the most modest shot from our visit to the naturist resort. It only showed our naked bodies from the waist up. I was embracing Girl from behind, leaning down to kiss her smiling cheek. She was wearing heavy eyeliner and black lipstick. I had a hand on each of her breasts, covering them. I handed the photo to Gloria and pocketed the rest.

"...like this."

Gloria's eyes widened. She compared the photos side by side, looking between the prim and proper schoolgirl in her one hand and the naked punk rocker with the bleached buzzcut and pink forelock in her other.

"Oh, yes," she confirmed, handing the photos to Rudy. "*Her* I remember! She had been crying. Her makeup was all running down her cheeks. She dropped a fistful of money on my counter and said something like, 'Gimme a ticket on your next bus to Portland.' I tried to explain that if she waited a couple of hours, she could catch the Sacramento Express and get there quicker, but she started yelling at me, 'I can't wait that long! I need to get out of this f-ing town!' only... You know... She didn't say f-ing."

"So she got on the one that makes all the stops?" I asked. Rudy was currently distracted by the Polaroid in his hand.

"Yeah, the Coastal Chief."

"What time was that?"

"The bus departed at two forty-five p.m."

We thanked Gloria and asked her to pass on our gratitude to Mrs. Baxter as well.

We visited the men's room before heading to the car, entering adjoining stalls to do our business. From the other side of the partition, Rudy said, "You told me you didn't have any photos of Abbey."

I cleared my throat. "Well, I didn't—you know... I

didn't think you'd wanna see your daughter naked."

"Is she naked in *all* of those pix you have?"

"Kinda, yeah. We sort of spent a couple days in a nudist camp."

There was a several-second pause while the only sound was the splashing of our simultaneous streams before Rudy said, "Your life A.G."

"My life A.G.," I agreed.

Back in the car, I got behind the wheel out of habit. Rudy settled into the passenger seat. Before we pulled out of the parking lot, we discussed our plan of action. Rudy unfolded the brochure listing the towns the bus routes serviced along with departure times.

The long route which Girl had taken took nearly nineteen hours to get to Portland with all of its stops, compared to the more direct route which still took twelve. Following the shorter route in a car, we figured we could cover the same distance in a little over ten hours.

We should be able to intercept Girl's bus, we calculated, somewhere around Eugene, Oregon.

"Do you have a map?" Rudy asked.

"There's one in the glove compartment," I answered.

Rudy opened the glove box and a stack of envelopes tumbled into his lap. They were the wedding cards that Girl and I had received from the residents of Turtle Terrace. On top of the stack was the marriage license.

Rudy lifted it from between his feet, read it, and held it up facing me, his eyebrows raised quizzically above the tops of his sunglasses.

"Can I call you *Daddy?*" I smirked.

CHAPTER 20

We took turns driving. We took turns telling stories. While Rudy took the wheel on the way to Sacramento and points north, I told him how Girl and I had met. I described the gas station heist. I recounted our time amongst the naked denizens of Turtle Terrace.

When I got to the part of my story where Girl elicited sympathy from Dale and Tony with her tale of feuding families, Rudy shook his head and muttered under his breath, "Goddamn *Rosa and Julian*."

"What was that?" I asked.

"*Rosa and Julian*. It was another screenplay I brought home to work on. A gender-swapped Romeo and Juliet set in the Texas oilfields. In the 1870s a white guy steals his Mexican business partner's idea for a new, improved drilling rig and patents it as his own. One family gets rich and the other ends up working for them. A hundred years later, two of their descendants—Rosa and Julian—fall in love and get secretly married."

"That sounds about right," I agreed.

We swapped driving duties at a rest area with a view of Mount Shasta. While I drove, Rudy told me about Girl's suicide attempt the previous year and the first time she had caused him bodily harm—both of which stories involved Abbey's relationship with her mother.

When Lily was taken into custody on Girl's thirteenth birthday, Girl blamed Rudy. While Lily was detained in Portland, where the arrest was made, Rudy collected his daughter and they boarded a plane home to Southern California.

Halfway through the two-and-a-half hour flight, Girl stabbed Rudy in the neck with the fork from her in-flight meal and started screaming that she was being kidnapped.

The fork didn't hit any major blood vessels, lodging in the trapezius muscle above Rudy's collarbone. A nurse practitioner who was seated a few rows behind them tended to the injury. Girl was taken to the rear of the airplane and chaperoned for the remainder of the journey by a flight attendant and another passenger—an elderly woman who identified herself as a retired teacher.

Upon arrival at LAX, Rudy and his daughter were met at the gate by a male and female pair of airport security officers and confined to a holding room until, after an examination of documents which Rudy produced from a carry-on briefcase and a series of phone calls to the Portland police—as well as a call to Girl's psychiatrist—they were finally allowed to proceed home to their house in Glendale.

Girl spent the next several months in a state of depression during which she barely spoke to her father other than to occasionally explode in fits of anger. She would accuse him of abusing her by keeping her away from her mother and tell him that she wished he was dead so she could live with Lily.

It was during this period that Girl began adopting a rebellious fashion sensibility featuring short, spiked, candy-colored hair and strategically-ripped clothing. Rudy tried to impose limits on what he viewed as inappropriately mature makeup and too-short skirts, but it was an uphill battle.

Lily, meanwhile, had been sentenced to 70 months in the Oregon Women's Correctional Center in Salem for one count of second-degree kidnapping and one count of custodial interference.

After 32 months, Lily's remorseful attitude during parole hearings saw her transferred to a halfway house euphemistically named the Liberty Rose Hotel in Portland's Sellwood neighborhood. There, she would continue to have her movements strictly supervised while she was allowed to earn cash by working at a nearby grocery store. She had a strict curfew and all drug and alcohol use was strictly forbidden as a condition of what basically amounted to house arrest.

A couple of months into her stint at Liberty Rose, Rudy and Abbey received a red envelope in the mail containing a letter from Lily. In the letter, she expressed her sorrow for being a source of trouble and promised to entirely stay out of their lives from that day forward.

Girl did not take this well.

On Christmas morning, Rudy opened Abbey's bedroom door to wake her up to open presents. He found his daughter unconscious on the floor in a puddle of vomit. Beside her were an empty package of sleeping tablets. On the front of her white flannel nightshirt she had written in lipstick the words "MeRRy XMaS".

Girl's psychiatrist recommended—and Rudy agreed to—a three-week inpatient treatment program for suicidal youths with treatable mental illnesses.

Girl emerged freshly medicated and therapized, allegedly ready to be a model student as well as an engaged and considerate daughter. Before long, she started telling Rudy about new friends she had made at school, sometimes even sleeping over at their houses on weekend nights.

For a whole year, Abbey seemed to be getting better and better. She and Rudy started going to movies and professional wrestling shows together. She started to enjoy cooking, often making dinner for her father. And what do you know—she even started babysitting!

We continued up Interstate 5 as it carried us farther north. As soon as we passed the "Welcome to Oregon" sign (It's "The Beaver State!" You really *do* learn something new every day!), it started raining. It was only a light drizzle and didn't last long, but the featureless pearl-gray sky would continue to spit on our windshield every few miles to remind us not to get too comfortable.

Accustomed as we were to California weather, Oregon's caught us off guard. It was too overcast to see clearly in sunglasses but without them the unbroken ashen cloud cover created a near-blinding glare. We resigned ourselves to squinting like Clint Eastwood.

An hour beyond the border, we drove through the city of Grants Pass. It was there that the bus Girl was riding connected with the I-5 heading toward Portland. Rudy and I discussed stopping at the Grants Pass Greyhound depot and asking around, but we decided that our time would be better spent pushing ahead. According to the timetable, the Coastal Chief had already made its Grants Pass stop.

There were several smaller towns due to be serviced along the route, so if we kept up our pace without stopping, we should pass Girl's bus and arrive in Eugene ahead of her. Our plan was to meet her bus when it arrived and convince Girl to let us drive her the rest of the way to Portland where we could all talk to Lily together.

Twenty miles beyond Grants Pass, Rudy and I were both feeling the call of nature and the fuel gauge was dipping below an eighth of a tank. According to the exit sign, the next town was called Wolf Creek. We pulled off the freeway and into a heavily-wooded area with little evidence of civilization. Oregon, I had noticed, was much, much greener than even the greenest parts of Northern California.

Between the uneven forested terrain and the ramshackle buildings scattered amidst the foliage on either side of the road, it felt like we had taken a wrong turn into hillbilly country. We rolled slowly past a peeling billboard that reassured us that we *were* in the village of Wolf Creek, but we had yet to find a gas station—or any other business which might have a working restroom —among the clusters of boarded-up storefronts tucked between trees along the community's ostensible main drag.

We were getting ready to pull over to relieve ourselves on the side of the road and then head back toward the freeway when we rounded a dense thicket and spotted a Shell logo on a pole in front of a building which appeared, from the miscellany of signage scattered across its patchwork facade, to be a combination filling station, convenience store, bar, and restaurant.

There were two antiquated pumps, one of which thankfully had *DIESEL* stenciled in white across its greasy green belly. Stopping alongside, I saw that a sheet of notebook paper had been taped next to the nozzle with the words, *PAY INSIDE B4 GASSNG!!!* written in red marker.

We left the Volvo/Cadillac amalgam, which Rudy had christened "Frankencar," and walked into the equally hybrid establishment. A spring-loaded, wood-framed screen slammed behind us like a gunshot, making us freeze in place just inside the door.

We had become accustomed to the diffuse midday brightness and we were unable to venture deeper until our eyes adjusted to the darkness within. There were no lights lit inside the building other than a dim red neon sign which flickered unsteadily in one distant corner, advertising a brand of beer I'd never heard of.

I thought that perhaps the place was closed for business, the door left unlocked out of some sort of misplaced country-living faith in humanity. As my pupils dilated, though, I began to make out the shapes of bodies sitting motionless in the gloom. Flannel shirts and trucker caps framed white faces which stared silently in our direction. It felt like we'd stumbled into a nest of redneck vampires.

To our right was a cluster of tables around which sat pale locals with plates of pale food in front of them. To our left, along a counter cluttered with point-of-purchase displays for spark plugs and Slim Jims and a jar of pickled eggs, sat a row of individuals gripping coffee cups and beer bottles.

"Restroom?" I ventured tentatively.

The human-shaped shadow behind the counter lifted an arm and pointed wordlessly toward an even darker hallway at the rear of the room. We walked slowly between the ranks of diners, their heads swiveling as one to track our passage.

Nobody spoke.

The men's room was vile. Under a flickering, buzzing fluorescent tube, a single stall with no door contained a deeply stained toilet with no seat. Located between the stall partition and a sink with no handles on the faucet was a urinal covered in a schoolbus-yellow patina. On the floor in front of it was a worn impression in the linoleum. This was full of urine.

The hellish stink in the room short-circuited my olfactory sense and bored directly into my brain's pain center like two pencils stabbed eraser-deep into my sinus cavity. I breathed through my mouth as I straddled the puddle and used the urinal while Rudy entered the stall. No conversation was exchanged while we pissed. When we finished, we looked at the useless sink then at each other. We both shrugged.

Back in the main room I approached the counter to pay for our gas. At this distance I could see that the proprietor was a white woman of advanced years with a permanent scowl and a smoker's complexion.

As I was pulling out cash, I heard Rudy say, "Guy. Look." I turned to see him standing in the open door and pointing over his head to a metal sign which stuck out perpendicular to the outside wall above the entrance. It was a faded blue rectangle with a running greyhound on its surface.

"Does the bus to Portland stop here?" I asked the woman.

She scowled even deeper and muttered, "Yeah. So?"

Rudy walked over to us and pulled out his badge along with the Polaroid of Girl with my hands on her tits. "Has the Coastal Chief stopped here in the last couple hours?" he asked. "We're looking for this girl."

The storekeeper eyeballed the ID card. "That's Michael Douglas," she sneered. She looked through us to the dimly-lit dining area. "Tom? We got a troublemaker over here pretendin' to be a San Francisco cop."

I heard a chair scrape the floor as someone pushed away from their table. Turning, I saw an obese plaid flannel torso rising up from a chair on two denim toothpicks. I looked up into a face that featured a white walrus mustache and yellow-lensed aviator shooting glasses.

Tom took a step toward us and declared, "I spent forty years on the force. I ain't gonna sit by and watch some pantywaist city boys impersonating officers o' the law! Phillis, get Sheriff Billy on the line!"

Rudy and I didn't wait around while Phyllis phoned Sheriff Billy. After a cartoonish bit of choreography that consisted of looking in unison first at each other then at Tom then at each other again and then at the door, we took off running.

When we reached the car, I did a cop-show slide across the hood, landing on my knees in the gravel and scrambling to open the driver side. Meanwhile, Rudy got in the passenger side, slammed and locked the oversized door, and started slapping the dashboard saying, "Go! Go! Go!"

I got the engine started and we sped away, negotiating Wolf Creek's twisty country roads at top speed before eventually shooting down the entrance ramp back onto the Freeway.

We drove in clenched silence for several miles before one of us—I'm not sure who—started chuckling. Soon we were both laughing out loud and whooping like we were the Dukes of Hazzard escaping the long arm of Rosco P. Coltrane.

Rudy turned on the radio and static-muffled music started playing. Some adjusting of the tuning knob and the song resolved into "Eastbound and Down"—the theme from *Smokey and the Bandit*.

Jerry Reed's voice blasted from the speakers, warning us that Smokey was hot on our tail. We sped along, singing along with the chorus, each of us spontaneously changing the lyrics to "northbound and down" and grinning like mad.

When Girl and I were on the road, she was constantly framing everything as a grand adventure. Despite this, I could never shake the anxious feeling that we were living on borrowed time. When she and I were together, I was rarely able to simply enjoy the moment and take things as they came. I was always worrying about what bad thing might happen next.

This felt different. Easy. Purposeful.

Driving with Rudy felt like I was on a road trip vacation with, if not a father figure exactly, at least an older male role model of some sort. I had felt a similar sense of masculine comfort while smoking a cigar with Tony outside his RV. I was starting to realize how little of this sort of paternal camaraderie I had experienced growing up and how much I viscerally craved it.

I was raised primarily by my mother. I had a half-brother who was so much older that we never had a chance to truly bond; he lived on the other side of the country. My father, while sincerely well-meaning, was himself the product of an upbringing which ill-prepared him for parenthood. When my folks split before I had finished junior high, I basically never saw him again.

I relaxed into my seat and watched the verdant landscape whip past the windows, my foot heavy on the gas. The only radio stations we could pick up featured either country-western or preaching, so we listened to good ol' boys twang on about guns and trucks and cheatin' gals as we raced northward.

Just past the town of Myrtle Creek, I was snapped out of my reverie by the sight of a big silver and white vehicle up ahead. As we gained on it, the running dog decal on the back window of the bus came into view.

I reached over and turned off the music. I eased off the accelerator to match the bus' speed. I swerved into the left-most lane, pulled up alongside, and feathered the pedal, keeping parallel with the big motor coach while Rudy rolled down his window and leaned out, looking up and trying to spot his daughter.

Our car moved gradually down the left side of the bus as Rudy peered closely at each tinted window for signs of Girl's bleached-blonde buzzcut with its pink shock lock.

We slowly made our way to the front of the bus without any luck. Rudy pulled in his head and sat back down, facing forward.

"I'm gonna do the other side," I said, and punched the gas, speeding ahead of the bus.

We were the only two things on the road as far as I could see either in front of us or behind. There were three lanes total. I turned sharply, cutting across the middle lane in front of the bus and continuing into the right.

I slowed, again mirroring the speed of the Greyhound. I rolled my window down and Rudy unbuckled his seatbelt. He squeezed between the front seats into the back of the car. Once there, he again leaned out and craned his neck upward to get a view of the bus windows.

As I gradually reduced speed, sliding backward in relation to the right side of the bus, I saw the driver give me a dirty look as I eased past his door. Once again we made our way along the towering vehicle, the shiny silver side panel the only thing visible to me.

We covered a third of the bus… Half…

When we were almost to the end, Rudy was suddenly beside me, squirming back into the passenger seat. "She's there! I saw her!"

"Did she see you?" I asked. "Our plan to head her off in Eugene's gonna work better if she isn't expecting us."

"I can't say for sure. I think we made quite a stir among the passengers. A lot of them were pressing up against the windows on our second pass. Probably trying to get a look at the weird-ass car. Abbey was way in the back and all slumped down. I could just see her eyes. She was kinda hiding and peeking over at us. She wouldn't have recognized the car the way it looks now and I pulled back in as soon as I saw her, so maybe we can still surprise her."

I backed off and crossed over to the fast lane once again, away from Girl's side of the bus. As I sped ahead, we both tried to hide our identities as much as possible; Rudy by pulling down his baseball cap and averting his face, me by tugging up my hood. The bus receded into a speck in my rearview.

I should have stopped for gas. There were plenty of opportunities; I kept seeing signs with little pictures of pumps on them before freeway exits. But I was only an hour away from Eugene! And I was driving a fuel-efficient diesel! And the little light next to the gauge only came on a little while ago!

Like they always say: Hindsight is twenty-twenty. Well they can go fuck themselves.

Just beyond the Yoncalla exit (Yes, of *course* it had a little gas pump picture. You can go fuck yourself, too.), the engine started making sounds like a fat man with a hunk of beef lodged in his throat. Soon thereafter it cut out altogether, the RPM and MPH needles drooping impotently, leaving the car in an ever-slowing coast down a low hill we had just crested.

I muscled the now-unpowered steering wheel to the

right and came to a stop on the gravel shoulder.

Rudy and I both exited and leaned against the pink and chrome door. I fished out the Djarums and held them toward Rudy. He fingered one of the two remaining clove cigarettes from the crumpled pack and I pulled out the other with my lips. As I wadded the empty container and shoved it back in the pocket of my hoodie, Rudy produced a disposable lighter and lit us both.

"Well, shit," Rudy said.

"Well, shit," I agreed.

We stood and smoked without talking. After a few minutes, Rudy broke the silence. Looking at the black cigarette he was holding by its gold filter between two fingers, he said, "I've never tried one of these. They're kind of intense." He did a thing with his mouth like a cat who ate peanut butter. "My tongue is numb."

I expelled a smoky little breath of a laugh through my nose and nodded. We settled back into silence.

It started to drizzle. A few cars went by, their tires shushing on the damp tarmac. I pushed upright away from the car door and took a step closer to the pavement. I could hear another car coming over the rise a couple of hundred yards back. As it appeared, I leaned forward and stuck out my thumb.

SSSHHHUUUSSSHHH

A brown Jeep Wagoneer sped past without slowing.

I put my hands in my pockets and waited, hood up

and shoulders hunched against the pissing Oregon mist. Rudy had his cap low and his collar up, the nylon of his black bomber jacket glistening.

After a while the rain stopped. The sky still showed no traces of blue, but the haze brightened and the day warmed somewhat so I lowered my hood.

A larger vehicle hove into view—an eighteen-wheeler. Once again I stuck out my right thumb. This time I increased the urgency by also waving my left arm above my head, fingers splayed.

SSSHHHRRROOOWRRRSSSHHH

I turned to follow the truck's passage, my open palm becoming a middle finger directed at its receding hulk.

I felt a hand on my shoulder. "My turn," Rudy said, and we swapped places.

Rudy and I traded off every few cars. A dozen more ignored our attempts to flag down assistance, including a white stretch limo, a silver DeLorean, and a vintage Ford Falcon with day-glo skeletons painted all over it driven by a guy with a mohawk.

As the skeleton car passed, I heard "Viva la Revolution" by The Addicts blasting from the open windows and I was annoyed that the driver didn't recognize me as a fellow punk—or at least stop to help another weirdo car. I watched him drive away, admiring the bad-ass paint job, and saw a second person pop up in the previously empty passenger seat.

"I think that guy was getting head on the highway!" I told Rudy.

We were both getting discouraged and we were looking at the map to figure out how long it would take to walk to the closest gas station when something—a sixth sense or a familiar engine rumble—made us both look up from the map to see the Greyhound reach the top of the hill heading our way.

"Oh, screw this!" Rudy exclaimed and stepped into the path of the bus with his prop police star held up authoritatively and the other hand palm out like Superman preparing to stop a train.

The bus' brakes hissed and squawked and clunked and the bus swerved to the side, stopping behind the Volvo with a mighty wheeze, the left wheels still in the roadway.

Rudy strode across of the nose of the bus and pounded on the door with the side of his fist. It opened with a hydraulic swish and he stepped inside. I scrambled to follow him and caught up as he was showing the driver Girl's picture.

The driver was a slim white guy of about sixty. He wore a military-style jacket in cadet gray with two blue stripes on each wrist and a shield-shaped patch on the upper sleeve that said, "SAFETY—26 YEARS." On his silver-haired head sat a captain's hat which matched the uniform. The front of the hat featured a heavy-looking brass medallion with the familiar running dog logo.

"I dunno. I mighta seen her," the driver was saying in a Louisiana drawl, pushing his hat further back on his head with one finger under the bill. "Folks come 'n' go. I make a awful lotta stops. You can go on back see if'n she's aboard."

Rudy accepted the driver's invitation with a nod and strode down the aisle toward the back of the bus where he'd seen Girl peeking over the windowsill earlier. I followed, glancing left and right at the other passengers. They were a true cross-section of Americana.

An elderly Black couple held hands and watched us guardedly as we moved past them. A big-haired metal rocker in shades and spandex dozed with his head on a folded leather jacket against the window, a guitar case taking up the adjacent seat. A Mexican family dressed like the migrant workers they probably were filled three consecutive rows on one side, the half-dozen children sitting passively, hands folded in laps as the father scowled at our presence and the mother crossed herself.

We reached the rear of the cabin and looked around. Girl was not there. Rudy took a few steps back toward the center of the bus and rotated slowly, addressing the passengers, badge raised in one hand, the polaroid in the other.

"We're looking for a teenage girl, five feet tall with short bleached blonde hair with a longer pink piece in front. She was last seen wearing..." He faltered, unsure how to continue and gestured toward me with the photo.

"Um...probably a denim jacket?" I filled in. "She might have been carrying a little plaid suitcase?" I wasn't as good at sounding commanding as Rudy was.

A few rows from the back on the left side sat a woman in her mid-thirties with mousy light-brown hair under a floral headscarf which was tied at the back of her neck. Her eyebrows and eyelashes were a lighter shade and a spray of faded freckles decorated her nose and upper cheekbones. She wore no makeup.

The woman put her hand on the shoulder of the forty-something man sitting in the seat in front of her and said, "Mitch? Wasn't Jeanie talking to her?"

The man lifted his head grudgingly from his *Sports Illustrated* magazine and looked over his right shoulder. He grunted, "Jeanette! Where's that freaky broad you were sittin' with?"

Rudy and I turned toward the direction Mitch was looking.

From the last—apparently empty—seat on the right came a small, high-pitched voice: "You mean Maria?"

A little girl popped up and draped herself over the seatback in front of her, her chest against the headrest and her arms hanging down. She must have been kneeling on the rear-most seat cushion. She had red hair and freckles and was clearly the daughter of the headscarf woman. "She got off back when we stopped to let the penguins out," she said shyly.

"Jeanette!" the mother exclaimed, embarrassment coloring her cheeks. To Rudy and me she explained, "There was a group of Catholic sisters who got off the bus in Roseburg." She turned back toward her daughter. "It's not nice to call them penguins, sweetie. We call them *nuns.*"

"But that's what Maria called them!" protested Jeanie.

Rudy addressed her directly. "So, this girl—Maria?" He looked at me quizzically and I gave him a little nod of confirmation. He looked back at the kid. "When Maria got off, did she say anything to you?"

"Yeah, she saw you driving around the bus and said you guys were looking for her and that she'd be fucked if you found her, so—"

"JEANETTE!" both parents shouted in unison.

"Well it's what she said!" Jeanie shrugged dismissively, elbows bent and palms up.

"Then what happened?" Rudy asked the girl.

"She got all fidgety and pulled her little bag out from under the seat and hugged it until the bus stopped in a big parking lot with a restaurant and stores and stuff. When the pen— when the *nuns* got out, Maria said, 'Catch ya later, kid! Stay cool!' and ran off the bus.

"I watched her out the window. A man came out

of the restaurant and was getting into a car with, like, pictures all over it. Maria went up to him and I saw her pull a bunch of money out and hand it to him then they both got in the car and drove away while we were still sitting there. The bus driver was outside smoking. My daddy was, too." Jeanie bunched up her face to make it clear that she did not like smoking and certainly didn't approve of her father's habit.

I spoke up. "This car with the pictures on it... Were they pictures of, like, skeletons? Did the driver have hair like this?" I spread my fingers above my head, mimicking a mohawk.

Jeanie nodded excitedly, grinning ear-to-ear and mirroring my hand gesture. "Yeah! And the sides were all bald!"

The bus driver turned out to be a really nice guy. He always carried a couple of army surplus five-gallon jerry cans filled with diesel fuel in the storage compartment underneath the bus. He generously emptied one of these into Frankencar's tank, waving off our offer of cash with a jovial, "Jes' bein' a good Christian, officers!"

We now had enough fuel to get us the rest of the way. Rudy drove, hurtling north at top speed. We were going to drive straight through to Portland, hopefully arriving at Lily's halfway house before dark.

We blew by the signs indicating exits for the city of Eugene. We no longer needed to stop at the Greyhound station there since Girl had disembarked and caught a ride with the driver of the skeleton-covered art car. Since the little girl on the bus saw cash exchange hands, we were working on the assumption that Girl had bribed him to take her all the way to Portland.

I spied a cluster of matching brick buildings in the distance as we rushed by, reminding me that this was a university town, but other than that Eugene was just a blur of trees.

Onward north we continued, Rudy manning the wheel while I kept us entertained by surfing the constantly-shifting radio landscape—college alternative blending into oldies which morphed into southern rock near the state capital of Salem. We sang along to all of the music, sometimes making up our own (usually off-color) lyrics. Now that we were gassed up and rolling again, we were both in high spirits.

As we were passing through Wilsonville, the mileage signs on the highway informed us that we would hit Portland in a mere seventeen miles. We stopped at a truck stop to pee, grab a bite to eat, and find a map which would help us navigate our way to the Liberty Rose Hotel. While Rudy shopped for maps inside, I used the pay phone by the parking lot to call information and get the hotel's address, which I jotted on the back of one of the wedding gift envelopes.

I hung up as Rudy stepped out through the swinging glass door carrying a bag full of chips and beef jerky and holding a folded roadmap aloft victoriously. The map's cover featured a photograph of a bridge arching across a river underneath the words, "City of PORTLAND and vicinity." Below the photo was a graphic of a red rose and the words, "City of Roses."

I started Frankencar and pulled back onto the interstate while Rudy consulted the street index on the back of the map to locate the coordinates of Tacoma Street. He then flipped the map over and used the letters and numbers in the margins to pinpoint our destination.

A short time later, Rudy turned down the radio (We had both been singing along to Midnight Oil's "Blue Sky Mine" with our mouths full, changing the chorus to "Who's gonna SHAVE ME?") and pointed to the upcoming exit sign.

"Get off here," he said, "Terwilliger."

"Terwilliger? I hardly know 'er!" I wisecracked, changing lanes onto the ramp toward Terwilliger Boulevard.

The map showed that The Liberty Rose Hotel was at the far end of a bridge—one of many spans which connected Portland's east and west sides across the Willamette River. Just off the freeway, I followed a sign with a right-pointing arrow and the words "Sellwood

Bridge." This led me to a matching sign at the next intersection, this one pointing to the left. I took the turn and the bridge came into view in the distance on the far side of a cemetery.

What I saw down the lane in the next block made me slam on my brakes. Next to the cemetery gate sat the skeleton car, empty. Its nose was wrapped around the thick concrete base of an old-timey lamp post and the inside of the windshield was covered in blood.

CHAPTER 21

We parked across the street from the accident scene just as a tow truck was backing up to the gaudily-painted Ford Falcon's rear bumper. The car's owner climbed down from the truck's passenger seat. He had blood covering the lower half of his face and all down the front of his shirt.

While the tow operator got busy coupling the back of the skeletonmobile to his truck, the mohawked owner of the crashed vehicle paced angrily back and forth in a grassy patch beside the road, hands in the pockets of his stud-covered leather jacket, shooting paincd looks at his car's crumpled front end.

Rudy and I crossed the street on foot to confront the man. As was becoming habit, we approached with Rudy in the lead, police badge and polaroid prominently presented.

The guy didn't see us right away. He was focused on his vehicle, repeatedly shaking his head as if to deny the reality of the damage. Rudy got the punk's attention by clearing his throat and saying, "Excuse me, son."

The man stopped pacing and spun to face us. His nose was obviously broken, bulging unnaturally and split across the center. Quickly-crusting blood had dowsed his lips, his chin, and the front of his white Dead Kennedys T-shirt. Both eyes were in the early stages of blackening. Rudy and I gave each other a look that said we recognized Girl's handiwork.

Up close, it was clear that the car's owner was closer to Rudy's age than to mine. He might even have been *older* than Rudy's thirty-seven years. The skin of his cheeks was rough and pockmarked with ancient acne scars and the stubble on the not-very-recently shaved sides of his head was sprinkled with gray. Vertical lines creased the space between his eyebrows as he scowled at the badge.

"What the fuck you want?" He asked indignantly in a high-pitched, nasal Brooklyn accent which took me by surprise.

His eyes flicked down to the photograph in Rudy's hand and his expression changed like a fist unclenching. His eyebrows shot up and his eyes and mouth opened comically wide. Without warning, the man's hand shot out and snatched the picture. He alternated between looking at it and holding it out to show it to us, back and forth, back and forth, trembling with fury as he shouted animatedly in his adenoidal dialect.

"It's that crazy bitch! The crazy fuckin' bitch what crashed Lisa! You gawta arrest the crazy cunt! She almost got me killed! And look at Lisa! She's fucked!"

Rudy reached over and gently retrieved the polaroid from the man's shaking hand. "Lisa?" he asked.

The man ran a hand down his face and took a deep, shuddery breath to calm himself. "Sorry, officer," he said more quietly (In his voice it sounded like "AWfissuh"), "That's my car's name. Bone-a Lisa."

He shrugged one shoulder and cracked a half-hearted smile, showing a missing front tooth. I wondered if that, too, was a result of his run-in with Girl.

The tow truck driver pushed a lever and Lisa's tail was hoisted into the air. The winch continued to pull the Falcon toward the truck and into towing position. As the car's grille came away from the lamp post, the front bumper fell to the ground with a rattle and clank.

"Awww, man!" Lisa's owner moaned and sat heavily onto the top of the concrete pole's wide base. He reached down and lifted the chrome bumper vertical, leaning it against his chest and wrapping his arms around it, his head hanging down.

Rudy squatted, bringing his face lower than the man's and looked up into his eyes. "I know this is a difficult time for you, mister...?"

"Hanover. Dirk Hanover."

"Mr. Hanover, I really need to find this girl. I know

she approached you when the bus she was riding stopped outside the restaurant in Roseburg. Could you please tell us what happened after that?"

"Yeah, sure," Dirk said apathetically. "She come up to me with a fistful o' dollars and said she needed a ride to Portland. I said I was goin' that way and she shoved the money in my hand and got in." He lifted his head slightly and pointed his busted nose at Frankencar across the street. "When we saw you guys hitchin' next to the highway I said 'bitchin' car' and started to slow down, but she slid onto the floor next to her suitcase and said,"—his voice shifted even higher as he imitated Girl's manic exclamation—"NO! DON'T STOP! THEY'RE LOOKING FOR ME!"

His voice returned to normal. "That was the only time she talked the whole ride except to hand me a red envelope with an address on it and tell me that was where she needed to go. I know the area. I seen the sign on the front o' the building before. So I says okay I'll getcha there and after that she just sits starin' out the window til we pull offa the freeway."

"What happened then?" I asked. "How did you crash the car?"

Dirk sat up straighter and looked at me for the first time. "*I* didn't crash the damn car! That crazy bitch did!" He was shouting again. Once more, he took a deep breath, closing his eyes for a moment.

When he had regained his cool, he continued, "Listen. I felt bad for the kid. She looked like she was goin' through some shit and I wanted to cheer her up so when we was gettin' close I started flirtin' wit' her a little. I says, like, 'Yer hotel's right across the bridge there but maybe we can have some fun before I drop you off. You could come over ta my place and party. I gots booze. I gots weed. I gots porn. Maybe I make ya smile. Maybe you make me smile.' Then I kinda put my hand on her tit. I was just *teasin'!*

"Anyway, she grabs the wheel and steers Lisa straight inta that post! Crazy little bitch! She coulda killed us both! I hit my face on the steerin' wheel an' I'm out like a fuckin' light! When I comes to, she's gone!"

We thanked Dirk for his help and wished him luck getting Lisa repaired. He asked if we would make "that crazy bitch" pay him for the damages. Rudy lied and said we'd make sure that happened. He asked the man for a phone number where we could reach him and Hanover produced a folded piece of paper from the pocket of his leather jacket.

He held the paper out and said, "That's my number on the bottom there."

I took the paper and opened it. It was a photocopy of a hand-written announcement that The Drizzling Shits were looking for a new bassist. Below a drawing of a skeleton playing a guitar while sitting on a toilet (clearly executed by the same artist who had customized Lisa), were the words *Contact Dirk Diarrhea* and a phone number.

In the pervasive Portland humidity, the paper felt distinctly softer than I was used to paper feeling in Los Angeles. It was almost like cloth.

Just as this observation occurred to me, translucent circles began appearing on the flyer as fat raindrops spattered down onto it's surface. I re-folded the sheet and tucked it into the pocket of my hoodie before it could become saturated.

We ran back to Frankencar through the suddenly torrential downpour and continued our drive to the Liberty Rose with Rudy behind the wheel. I glanced back for one last look at the crash site and saw Dirk tenderly sliding Lisa's bumper into her open rear window, seemingly oblivious to the deluge which was plastering his mohawk down against the side of his head. I faced forward again.

Rudy drove us onto the Sellwood Bridge, an antique concrete structure just wide enough for a single lane of traffic in each direction. The precipitation was already inches deep on the roadway and oncoming cars splashed a curtain of water onto the low, narrow sidewalk which ran along one side. A waist-high railing of cracked cement was the only thing preventing a pedestrian from being swept off into the river.

Halfway across, the Liberty Rose Hotel came into view on the far side of the bridge. It was an unassuming three-level beige rectangle with a row of square windows on each floor. It looked exactly like what it was—an institutional warehouse for offenders trapped in the purgatory between incarceration and freedom.

We reached the building as lights were coming on along the length of the bridge, casting a row of illuminated circles in the gathering dusk. Rudy stopped the car at the curb.

"Do you suppose Abbey is in there talking to her mom?" he asked, nodding his head toward the double doors on the front of the building.

Before I could respond, we got our answer. One of the doors opened and a tall, muscular woman in a security guard uniform emerged and stomped down the four low steps to the paving-stone pathway leading to the sidewalk. She was carrying Girl facing forward, her thick arms wrapped around Girl's torso.

Girl's fists punched empty air and her feet kicked ineffectually at nothing. Her face was scrunched up and her mouth was working. With the car windows shut and the rain loud against the roof, I could only imagine the obscenities Girl was screaming.

I looked toward the hotel and saw a thin woman hugging her own midsection as she stood in the open doorway watching the drama. She was wearing a knee-length maroon skirt with a matching vest over a striped shirt. She had a nametag over her breast and white shoes on her feet. Her long, dark hair was tied up in a bun on the back of her head. This had to be Lily, dressed for a shift at the grocery store.

I turned my attention back to Girl, who had stopped struggling and was standing where the guard had set her down. Her arms hung limply at her side and her head was bowed. The woman who had so forcibly escorted her off of the property now had a hand on Girl's shoulder and looked like she was speaking gently to her as they were both pelted by raindrops.

Girl hadn't spotted Rudy and me. I watched as she brushed the big woman's hand off dismissively and walked away toward the road, showing no concern that she was getting soaked. She didn't look up as she passed our car, trudging through the downpour back the way we had just come.

The sound of the rain surged in volume like the applause of an enthusiastic audience as Rudy opened the driver's side door and stepped out, calling after her, "Abbey!" just as a crack of thunder clapped, drowning out his shout.

Girl kept walking.

I exited the vehicle as well, intending to go after her. A voice, just loud enough to be heard above the torrent, made me pause and turn back.

"Rudy!"

It was Lily. She was running toward us, her sensible cashier shoes splashing through puddles. Beyond her I saw the security guard re-enter the building, closing the door.

"Lily!" Rudy spun around to face his ex-wife. "What happened?"

Lily didn't slow down until she collided with Rudy, her palms flat against his chest. She looked up into his eyes. I realized that she was just as short as her daughter. The resemblance didn't end there. Her eyebrows, her lips, her facial expression; she was the very image of Girl. Also just like Girl, Lily spoke in an unbroken, breathless rush.

"Oh, Rudy! I'm so sorry! Abbey showed up out of nowhere and she was talking nonsense like she and I were supposed to run away together or something and I told her that I couldn't do that. That I had to stay here until my sentence was up and the last time we ran away together I got in trouble and messed everything up for everybody. I said that she was better off without me and that I would just drag her down. She freaked out! She started yelling that nobody loved her. That she had done terrible things to you so you wouldn't want her back and that her husband had lied to her— *Husband?* What was she talking about? She's only fifteen! Then she started picking things up and smashing them! Ashtrays, coffee cups—she threw a potted plant through a window! A *closed* window! Then Juniper—that's the house security guard—she busted through the door and grabbed Abbey and tossed her out on the street! Then I saw you and— OH MY GOD!"

Lily pulled away and pointed toward the bridge, her other hand flying to cover her mouth, eyes wide with the shock of what she'd seen.

Rudy and I turned to look and saw Girl far off in the distance. She had made it to the middle of the bridge. Illuminated by a streetlight like a spotlit performer on a stage, she was climbing up to stand on the low concrete railing beside the footpath, one hand on the lamppost for support.

"She's gonna jump!" Lily screamed and took off running.

Rudy and I followed, dodging a few passing cars as we crossed the street to where the sidewalk transitioned onto the bridge's walkway.

Sprinting onto the bridge, I was hit with a rush of vertigo as the ground to my right fell further away with each hurried step, ultimately being replaced by the rushing, rain-swollen waters of the Willamette a hundred feet below.

I tore my gaze away from the maelstrom underneath my feet and looked forward. Lily had already reached Girl's location and had now actually *joined* her on top of the moss-dappled barrier, one arm hugging the pole for dear life and the other reaching toward Girl.

Before Rudy and I made it to the pair of women, Girl appeared to be climbing down. Maybe Lily had said something to make her daughter change her mind about ending it all. As we approached them, however, and stood panting in the pool of illumination, I saw that Girl had stepped down to the *outside* of the handrail. The walkway had no outside ledge. Her feet were between the handrail's concrete supports.

She now clung to the wet railing, which came up to her chest, by only her fingertips. Her arms were extended straight out as she leaned back, nothing behind her but the long drop into the fast-moving current far below.

Girl's shock of pink hair was washed flat against her face by the rain, concealing her right eye. Her visible eye was unblinking. Expressionless. The raindrops pulling her eyeliner into black streaks down her face made it impossible to tell whether she was shedding actual tears, but from the vacant way she was staring I feared she had mentally checked out.

Lily was sobbing; begging, "Abbey, NO! NO, NO, NO! Don't do this! Please!"

Lily stepped shakily down, joining Girl on her precarious perch outside the safety of the guardrail. Keeping one arm wrapped tightly around the streetlight pole, Lily embraced Girl with the other arm, pressing her daughter against the outside of the bridge.

Rudy and I stepped forward at the same time, each of us grabbing one of Girl's shoulders, holding her in place. Still clinging to Girl's shoulder with one hand, I placed the other on her cheek. She just stared past me.

I couldn't tell if my love for her was entirely selfless or the most selfish thing in the world, but at that moment I knew that without her in it my life had no meaning. I had to try to reach her through the black depression in which she was mired.

I pressed my own cheek to the other side of her face, positioning my lips so that I could talk directly into her ear over the sound of the storm.

"Come on, Maria," I said, my lips brushing her skin, "Don't make me live without you. I'm your knight in shining armor, right? Let me make it all better. Remember what we said 'I do' to? Through the good times and the bad, right? You and me against the world. Fuck the rest of 'em. I know shit looks hella bad right now but together we can figure it out. Please. Let me love you."

I pulled back and swiped the hair away, meeting her gaze. She blinked rapidly several times. Her eyes focused on mine. Her lower lip started trembling and she looked around, taking in her surroundings.

"Daddy?" she said, peering at Rudy, "Do you hate me?"

"No, princess," he answered, "I could never. I love you."

She turned toward Lily, who still clung to the post with white knuckles, a look of terror on her face.

"Mommy? You're not gonna leave me, are you?"

"I won't, Abigail. I promise I won't. I'm sorry I said those things." Lily forced her mouth into a smile, but her eyes still looked scared. "Let's just get off this stupid bridge, ok?"

I had a quick glance about. Cars had stopped in both directions to watch the scene being played out under the streetlight. Off beyond the end of the bridge, I saw flashing lights approaching. Somebody had called the police. I heard the sound of a helicopter nearby.

I took a step back and reached a hand out to Girl. "Yeah. Come on. Let's get off this stupid bridge."

Girl reached forward and took my hand. I held it tighter than I'd ever held anything before.

With Rudy guiding her by her elbow and Lily pressing a supporting palm to her back, Girl swung a leg up and over the railing.

What happened next happened so incredibly fast that nothing could be done to stop it. Still, it happened in slow motion...

Out of the corner of my eye I saw movement. When I looked toward the motion I saw Lily's fingers sliding across the surface of the lamppost. As I watched helplessly, her grip slipped from the wet metal and her arm began windmilling.

As she fell away, she made a startled little squeak.

Her other hand must have clutched Girl's jacket in an instinctive effort to save herself, because Girl was immediately yanked back. Rudy lost hold of her elbow. Her knee caught on the railing, but it was not enough to hold her.

Girl flipped backward off of the bridge.

I was jerked forward by Girl's hand in mine. My belly hit the rail and I was looking down into Girl's face.

Girl whimpered, "Guy?" as our rain-slicked hands were pulled apart.

I watched helplessly as Lily and Girl disappeared, flailing, into the dark water below.

CHAPTER 22

The search for Girl and her mother lasted all night. Rudy and I sat on an old flower-print couch in the waiting-room-like lobby of the Liberty Rose Hotel, recounting the events of the last few days again and again; to the uniformed officers who were first on the scene, then to a couple of detectives in rumpled suits, then to Lily's parole officer, and finally to a sleepy junior agent from the Portland branch of the FBI who left once she was satisfied that—despite the original kidnapping charges against Lily—no interstate crime had been committed.

The already-cramped space became more and more crowded as law enforcement personnel arrived and curious residents of the building wandered in. Chatter from police radios provided a constant background noise of updates from ground, air, and water-based attempts to locate the fallen women.

Just before dawn, word came in that a helicopter

team had spotted two bodies on Stevens Point, a sandy outcrop a few miles downriver from the Sellwood Bridge, adjacent to Willamette Park.

Rudy and I were on our feet instantly. We followed a cluster of cops to a squad car idling outside, where the rain had stopped for now. We all leaned into the open doors and listened to the car's radio as an officer on the scene gave us a moment-to-moment account of the riverside happenings.

"Chopper circling. Spotlight shows two women halfway in the water. They're tangled in debris against a wooden piling..."

There was a full minute of radio silence, then:

"Paramedics onsite. Victims being examined..."

More silence. The small crowd which had gathered around the police cruiser held their collective breath. Eventually one of the cops pushed the button on the radio's handset and asked, "Sharky? What's happening now?" It seemed they knew each other.

"Sorry, Al. It's pretty intense here. Okay, let's see... The guys performed CPR for a while on both of 'em. One of 'em is on a backboard now. It looks like one of them is still hanging onto the other's... Oh, shit. They just covered the one on the ground with a blanket. Face and all. Okay, they got the hand to let go. Backboard one's on a gurney. They're loading her into the rig. Hang on. I'm gonna go talk to them..."

Al said, "Roger" and we all listened anxiously. Without thinking, I reached over and took Rudy by the hand. He squeezed back and held on.

After a few minutes, Sharky came back on the air. He sounded more subdued; reverent.

"One of them didn't make it. The coroner's on the way. The other one is still unresponsive but they hear a heartbeat and they pumped a bunch of water out of her lungs. She's breathing but just barely. They're taking her to OHSU Trauma. They're both just so…little."

The two officers exchanged thank-yous and goodbyes and Sharky signed off. Al turned to Rudy and me.

"Get in your car and follow me. I'll take you to her."

OHSU, I was to learn later, was Oregon Health and Sciences University, the preeminent medical school in Oregon and one of the best in the country. The connected hospital included one of the top-tier trauma centers around.

As we made a U-turn and followed our police escort back across the Sellwood Bridge, though, I didn't know any of this. I turned and looked to the right as Rudy drove us past the spot where Girl was snatched away from me.

"Is she dead?" I whispered.

"One of them is," Rudy responded.

We drove in silence after that, speeding through traffic that pulled aside to let us through—the white sedan with the blue and gold stripe and the words *PORTLAND POLICE* across each side, lights flashing and siren screaming, followed by the absurd blue and pink Frankencar with the white tailfins.

At one point we took an uphill turn and wound our way between university and hospital buildings until we arrived at a set of doors with the word *EMERGENCY* above them and parked behind the cop car in a spot that was probably not intended for visitor parking. Al and his partner got out of their vehicle and waved for us to accompany them. They walked in with the confidence that comes with familiarity and approached the desk.

Al spoke to the nurse on duty, gesturing toward Rudy and me each in turn. There was some head shaking and then some nodding. Officer Al looked our way and said, "Follow us."

Through pairs of double doors and down twisty corridors we hurried along behind the two uniformed policemen. Their utility belts undulated hypnotically with every rapid step. When we stopped, we were facing a glass partition.

On the other side, a crowd surrounded a bed. I craned my neck one way and then the other, trying to see beyond the green scrubs and white lab coats to the horizontal figure which was the focus of all their attention. I caught a glimpse of bare toes, quickly obscured by a piece of equipment being rolled into place.

I saw a tiny hand being gently lifted onto a little platform where IV tubes were inserted into veins.

Then a figure in a paper gown took a step to one side and I spotted it; between a rubber-gloved hand holding an oxygen mask in place and the gray box of a cardiac monitor—a glimpse of pink hair!

This was *Girl* being tended to! She was alive!

When I was a kid I loved joke books. I'd check them out of the library and memorize puns, one-liners, and riddles. Some of my favorites were the totally absurd ones. For instance:

A carrot and his wife are crossing the street when a car hits him. In the hospital later, a doctor tells her, "He'll survive, but he'll be a vegetable for the rest of his life."

That joke kept running through my mind as I tried to process the information Rudy and I were receiving. We were sitting in a too-bright waiting room as the sun shone blindingly through white venetian blinds onto lemon-yellow walls and furniture upholstered in lime-green vinyl. A white-haired doctor in sky-blue shirtsleeves and a wide paisley tie sat on the edge of a blonde-wood coffee table, looking sincerely at Rudy.

"Your daughter's vitals are stabilized," the doctor was explaining. "Her respiration is shallow but steady and cardiac activity is strong. The EEG shows no abnormal brain activity. She's quite simply unresponsive."

"So when you used the word 'comatose'..." Rudy trailed off, the request for clarification hanging in the air.

"No pain reaction, pupils not responding to light, we've administered IV stimulants but she has not yet regained consciousness."

"So is she...like...a vegetable?" I asked quietly.

"We don't believe at this point that Abbey is in a vegetative state."

The doctor was answering my question, but he was still looking at Rudy.

"As I said, Mr. Zamora, EEG readings—the strength of the brain's electrical signals—those appear normal. She's being moved over to our neurology department right now. They can perform a CT scan which will give us a clearer look at whether Abbey sustained any catastrophic brain injuries, but for now I urge you to remain optimistic. It's entirely possible that at some point soon she'll simply wake up."

Girl did *not* simply wake up.

Rudy and I sat in the overly cheery waiting room for a solid twenty-four hours, eating vending machine food and receiving sporadic updates on Girl's unchanging condition. We took turns napping on a padded bench in a corner beside a mural depicting frollicking squirrels hiding acorns and pinecones among polka-dotted mushrooms with smiling faces.

At one point one of the plain-clothes police detectives who we had met in the lobby of the Liberty Rose the previous night came in and talked to us about Lily. Somebody would need to make an official identification of the body, we were told. Rudy said that he'd contact Lily's parents and that somebody would be at the Medical Examiner's office the following day to take care of it.

When he left, Rudy turned to me and said, "I guess we're going to be in town awhile. You okay with that?"

"Yeah," I answered, "Girl and I were pretty much running away with no real long-term plan of action. I basically walked away from my job. I'm sure they've given it to somebody else by now."

Rudy nodded slowly, thinking. "Okay, cool. I cashed in my vacation time and said I'd be gone at least a week but I have people to cover for me if it takes longer. My department has a lot of redundancy. Lets get out of here and grab a room."

OHSU Hospital and the medical school which birthed it occupied the top of Marquam Hill, an area of steep, narrow streets south of downtown Portland whose rolling heights reminded me a lot of San Francisco. Back in Frankencar I drove, winding my way down to the flat, park-littered neighborhoods alongside the river. As I followed signs directing us toward the city center, Rudy kept an eye out for suitable lodgings.

We eventually pulled into the parking lot of a generic-looking motel called Happy House Motor Inn whose sign advertised weekly rates. Inside the lobby, we were greeted with boisterous enthusiasm by a bearded and smiling Indian gentleman.

"Welcome to Happy House! Welcome! Welcome! I am Ranjy! Ranjy Patel! Are you needing some rooms?"

Rudy and I had discussed our respective money situations and decided that we should save some cash by sharing a room. I informed Mr. Patel of this fact and his smile widened. He wiggled his bushy eyebrows up and down.

"We have a room with a king-sized bed—very romantic!"

"Two doubles are fine," Rudy said firmly, jerking a thumb in my direction. "He's my nephew."

"Of course! Of course! Your *nephew!*" Mr. Patel didn't wink, but you could tell he wanted to.

We paid for one night with the option to expand that to a week at a lower daily rate later if need be. Ranjy grabbed a room key from the rack behind him, but instead of simply handing the key to one of us, he lifted a hinged portion of the desk and came through the opening.

"This way, this way," he said and walked back out the door where we had come in. We followed him down the covered walkway which ran along the front of the long, low building of rooms. He was wearing a knee-length turquoise kurta over yellow linen pants. Brown leather sandals the color of his skin exposed the gnarliest set of toenails I had ever seen.

We reached our door and Ranjy Patel unlocked and opened it, presented Rudy the key with both hands, and said, "I hope you have a happy stay in my Happy House."

We got settled into the room which would be our base of operations for however long it took to take care of things in Portland. I walked back to where we had left the car in front of the motel office and re-parked it in front of our door. I got our bags from the trunk and took them inside.

The bathroom door was closed and I heard the shower running. While Rudy was freshening up, I did what I always did in a new space; I looked for music. I had always been that way. Music was a friend that made me feel at home. I fell asleep to music. Music made the world feel less scary.

On the nightstand between the two beds was a clock radio. I switched it on and fingered the little tuning wheel, guiding the radio's red indicator to the left of the dial. I heard snippets of Journey and Kenny Loggins and Alabama as I explored Portland's airwaves, making my way down to the low numbers which alternative radio generally inhabited.

In one of those moments of synchronicity that felt like the universe kicking me in the nuts, when I found the local college station they were playing "Girlfriend in a Coma" by The Smiths.

I'd been holding so many feelings inside, just trying to keep moving forward, but Morrissey's sweet voice warbling a weird-ass song about exactly what I was going through finally crumbled the dam I had piled up against my tears. I fell back onto the bed and started crying; heaving, gulping sobs exploding uncontrollably from my throat.

Rudy opened the bathroom door to see what was wrong. Tears running in rivulets down my face, I pointed at the radio and hiccupped, "Suh-sometimes he wants to st-st-strangle her, but ruh-really, he'd huh-huh-hate anything to happen to…WAAAAAA!"

As the song continued to play, Rudy came over and sat beside me on the bed. I felt the comforting weight of his arm across my shoulders as I continued to wail and Morrissey continued to sing about whispering his last goodbyes.

By the time the song's final chord faded, we were both weeping.

Lily's parents, Danny and Abigail Flores, lived outside of Portland proper in a suburb called Beaverton. Rudy didn't want to give them the news about their daughter over the phone, so after I took my turn in the shower and changed into some slightly less road-grody clothes, we got back in the car and headed out with Rudy driving and me navigating.

We drove through Portland's shockingly clean downtown and into a tunnel that took us to the highway connecting with points west.

We soon found ourselves amidst dense, green wilderness. I found out later that this was Forest Park, one the largest wooded areas within city limits in the whole country. It was hard to believe that we were still in a major metropolitan area as we drove between the old-growth trees. I wouldn't have been surprised to spot a bigfoot dashing across the roadway.

Danny Flores was a paunchy man in his late fifties. He had a neatly-trimmed white mustache and receding iron-gray hair. His high forehead and big square glasses gave him a wise, owlish appearance. He was mowing his front yard when we arrived. He turned off the lawnmower's engine and turned, scowling suspiciously at the crazy-looking car that had just pulled into his driveway.

When Rudy stepped out, the older man's expression instantly changed to one of unabashed joy. He smiled broadly, showing a row of straight, white teeth, and called out, "Rudy! My boy! What are you doing here?"

Arms outstretched, Danny reached Rudy in three long strides and gathered him into a loving embrace.

Rudy hugged back and they stood like that for a few seconds, clearly enjoying the moment. When they separated, Danny kept his hands on Rudy's shoulders and examined his ex-son-in-law's injured face. "What happened to you?" he asked.

"Carpentry accident. Listen, Danny, I have some news. It's not good. Is Abigail home?"

Danny said that she was and invited us in. Danny shook my hand as Rudy introduced me (simply as Guy —he didn't want to distract from the unpleasant task at hand by taking time right then to explain my relationship to the family). Danny looked at me, taking in the bruises on my face, and then turned back to Rudy.

"He a carpenter, too?" Danny asked as we walked toward the front door. Rudy chose to interpret the question as rhetorical.

The Flores house was modest and homey. A delicious smell told me we were arriving unannounced close to dinnertime. We entered into a vestibule featuring a small shrine to Our Lady of Guadalupe. As we walked through the entryway, three cats greeted us with ankle rubs and loud purring.

We found Abigail the elder standing at the stove,

lifting sizzling chili rellenos from a huge, cast iron skillet onto a serving platter. The genetics on the maternal side of this family tree were strong. Like her daughter and granddaughter, Abigail was barely five feet tall with lusty eyebrows and full lips.

"Who did I hear you talking to outside?" she asked, turning off the stove. Looking toward us, she spotted Rudy and called out, "Rodolfo!" She hugged Rudy, then slapped him playfully on his chest.

"Why didn't you tell us you were coming to town?" she chided lovingly. "I would have made something special!"

Danny stepped over to his wife and put an arm around her waist.

"I don't think it's a social call, *mi hermosa*. Rudy has something important to tell us."

Abigail's smile faded. She picked up a roll of aluminum foil and covered the tray of food. She placed it in the oven to keep warm and untied her apron, dropping it on the counter. Crooking a finger at us, she said, "Come," and walked out of the kitchen.

We followed Abigail through a cozy living room with two well-used recliners facing a console television and into a front sitting room that looked like nobody ever sat in it. A matching floral-print sofa, loveseat, and wing back chair surrounded a coffee table with a spotless wax finish which reflected the big picture window. To one side was a fireplace, the mantel covered with framed photos of Lily and Girl. A large crucifix hung on the wall above. It was a rustic wooden carving that looked a hundred years old.

Abigail and Danny sat on the love seat, his hand on her knee and hers on his. She gestured for Rudy and me to sit opposite them on the sofa.

A silent anticipation hung heavy over the group of us gathered there. The Flores couple looked at each other, a wordless communication passing between them. Then they looked toward us, their heads turning in unison.

As Rudy cleared his throat and inhaled, about to talk, Danny spoke first. "It's Lily, isn't it? She's gone, isn't she?"

Rudy closed his mouth and nodded, tight-lipped.

"Was it suicide?" asked Abigail, clutching the crucifix which hung on a delicate gold chain around her neck.

Rudy leaned forward, one hand reaching out as if to stop her thoughts before they could fully form. "No! No, Lily was trying to *stop* Abbey from…from taking her own life."

Rudy went on to tell Girl's grandparents how Girl had received a letter from Lily saying that Lily was going to stay out of their lives and how Girl had taken this news hard and decided to drive up to Portland to confront Lily about it. He told them that I was Girl's boyfriend and that

I had been doing the driving. He left out the part where I tried to kill him with a nail gun.

Rudy recounted the events of the rainy night on the bridge; how Girl had threatened to jump and how we had all convinced her that life was worth living because she was loved. By the time he got to the part where Lily's unfortunate fall had doomed both women, Danny and Abigail were leaning forward, holding hands, their cheeks wet with tears.

Danny told us that they had received a similar letter from Lily soon after she was remanded to the Liberty Rose halfway house. The letter had read like a suicide note, he said, and they had tried reaching out by telephone but Lily wouldn't take their calls.

They had been so long estranged from their daughter that they had not taken the extra step of driving across the river to check on Lily in person. Hearing the regret in the man's voice as the realization hit him that he would now never have a chance to repair the damaged relationship was absolutely heartbreaking.

When I explained that the police needed a relative to provide a definitive identification the following morning, I was surprised that Lily's parents immediately offered to be the ones to perform the task. It would be their final chance, Abigail explained, to take care of Lily as they had failed to do when she was alive.

Rudy and I left Mr. and Mrs. Flores to attend to their daughter's final needs while we looked after their granddaughter.

Back up the hill at OHSU Hospital, we were finally allowed to see Girl. The soft, steady sound of a heart monitor was the only noise in the room. Rudy and I perched on the edges of chairs on either side of her bed, each of us holding one limp hand. For some reason it surprised me how warm Girl felt. She looked so small and so very lifeless.

A rigid brace encircled her neck. Her head was wrapped in thick bandaging. From the chest down, she was covered by a thin blanket which bulged strangely around her pelvis and near her right ankle. Her mouth was open slightly and there was no movement beneath her eyelids.

A clear, flexible tube thick as a milkshake straw snaked out of her left nostril, held in place by a strip of white medical tape. Thinner tubes, secured with more tape, connected the backs of her hands to hanging bags of fluid. A cluster of wires extended from under the blanket, their visible ends plugged into the front of an electronic device on a pole near the headboard—the source of the quiet beeping.

After we had sat quietly with Girl for twenty minutes or so, we were ushered back into the waiting room we had spent so much time in earlier. Once again our senses were bombarded by the whimsical decor while we were briefed by the white-haired doctor.

The CT scan, he told us, showed a temporal lobe concussion and some spinal cord compression in Girl's neck. He could not predict when—if ever—she would regain consciousness.

Until such time as she did, she would need to be cared for in a hospital setting. She required regular tube feeding as well as intravenous fluids and antibiotics to stave off infection while she healed several broken bones including a minor skull fracture. If her comatose state persisted, physical therapy would be necessary to prevent muscle atrophy.

A helpful patient advocate named Linda gave Rudy referrals to a couple of long-term coma facilities back in Southern California. For now, though, Girl would be driven by ambulance to Portland International Airport, where an Air Medical Services plane fitted with a mobile intensive care unit would fly her south.

Until a permanent care home was engaged, she would be housed at the same Glendale hospital where Rudy had the nails pulled out of his skull.

Girl's transport arrangements were handled with surprising efficiency. She would be flying in three days' time.

It was already after dark when we left the hospital. Rudy and I booked another night at Happy House in order to take care of one additional piece of business; I called Dirk Hanover (AKA Dirk Diarrhea) from the hotel room and arranged to meet him that night at a downtown club called The Satyricon, where his band was playing a gig.

While we drank beer and ate delivery pizza in the motel room, resting and waiting for a reasonable time to head out to the show, Rudy and I chatted and got to know each other better. As the college radio station played an eclectic mix of reggae, new wave, and goth (At one point "Happy House" by Siouxsie and the Banshees came on and I held a middle finger up to the gods), Rudy told me how he and Lily's parents had bonded through the years of dealing with their daughter's struggles with addiction. I, in turn, regaled Rudy with more tales of my adventures on the road with his daughter.

"You know," he said at one point, "your story is pretty wild. If you ever really *did* want to write a screenplay..." He held his beer bottle up in a toast, took a swig, and concluded, "Just sayin'."

We piled into Frankencar at nine-thirty. Between the two of us, my beer buzz was the less pronounced, so I drove us north along the river to Portland's Old Town, a section of the city developed in the late nineteenth century, where we found The Satyricon. The club occupied the bottom floor of a once-fancy victorian-era building on a once-fancy street that featured old brickwork sidewalks.

A marquee above the door advertised the bands playing that night, including Dirk's Drizzling Shits. Also on the bill: The Wipers, Poison Idea, and Dead Moon.

Loud music surrounded us as we opened the door and stepped into a compact bar and seating space covered on every surface with graffiti. I paid the skinhead girl at the door a five dollar cover charge for each of us while Rudy went over to the bar and got us two bottles of Pabst Blue Ribbon.

Leaving the barroom, we passed through an opening into the performance area and joined the small cluster of spectators in front of the stage. The Drizzling Shits were already rocking out, but they were the bottom-billed act and it was quite early, so there wasn't much of a crowd yet. Even so, the small combo was putting on an energetic performance for the modest turnout.

Dirk's band was still *sans* bass; they were currently a three-piece. Dirk was on the mic, growling and screaming about something (I think I made out the words "Pope," "cunt," and "pancakes" in the repeating chorus). A tall Black girl in a fringed blue suede vest and silver hot pants with her hair in lemon-yellow Zulu knots punished a sticker-covered guitar. A skinny shirtless white boy on drums completed the trio, his shoulder-length straight black hair hiding his face as he pounded the skins, head-down and aggressive.

I caught Dirk's eye and he held up three fingers.

Sure enough, three songs later the band finished their set to tepid applause. Nobody called for an encore.

Dirk gave his bandmates an "I'll catch up to you" wave and jumped down off the front of the low stage as they began packing their equipment. He came up to Rudy and me, wiping sweat from his face with a bandana, and said, "Hey. What'd you wanna talk to me about?"

Rudy put on his authoritative police voice and said, "Come outside with us for a moment, please, Mr. Hanover." He strode toward a side door without looking back.

Dirk looked pleadingly at me. I extended a hand in Rudy's direction and said, "Let's go."

Dirk and I came through the exit a few seconds behind Rudy. When we stepped out onto the sidewalk, the Volvo was parked at the curb. Rudy was leaning against one big pink door, holding out the vehicle's keys between his thumb and forefinger.

"She's for you, Dirk. Her name's Frankencar. We're not cops. That girl who crashed Bone-a Lisa is my daughter and she doesn't have any money to pay you. I figured this was the least I could do."

Dirk's battered face broke into a child-like grin, showing his missing tooth.

CHAPTER 23

Back in Los Angeles, Rudy and I soon fell into a routine where we traded off sitting at Girl's bedside at Glendale Adventist Hospital during visiting hours on alternating days.

Rudy had stepped back into his job at Orion Pictures, where his seniority allowed him to organize his hours around spending time with his daughter.

For my part, I got in touch with Edwin, the shroomhead movie projectionist. He trained me to run the machines then sponsored my application to join his union. As a member of *IATSE*—The International Alliance of Theatrical Stage Employees, Moving Picture Technicians, Artists, and Allied Crafts—I enjoyed a significantly higher salary than I'd ever had, a solid benefits package, and a flexible schedule.

Facilitated by a letter of recommendation from the priest at Danny and Abigail Zamora's church, Rudy secured a spot for Girl at a facility in Burbank, the cost of which would be partially underwritten by The Catholic Charities. The institution, called Saint Dymphna's Care Home, housed stroke victims, patients with advanced forms of dementia, and sufferers of other conditions which required round-the-clock nursing.

They had limited space, so Girl was placed on a waiting list. Rudy was told that a spot would be opening soon. In the meantime, we continued to sit our daily vigil at the hospital.

A bed at Saint Dymphna's became available a few weeks later. On the day Girl was to be transferred, Rudy and I met at Glendale Adventist and supervised the process as the tiny, motionless young woman we both dearly loved was gently lifted onto a gurney and wheeled through hallways and out to a waiting ambulance.

Rudy had recently gotten a promotion at work which included the use of a shiny new company car to replace the Volvo he had gifted to Dirk Diarrhea. With the increase in my income, I, too, had my own set of wheels for the first time in my life (albeit a more modest, ten-year-old beater). In our respective vehicles, we followed the ambulance to Girl's new home.

As part of the intake procedure at Saint D (as the staff there called it), Girl was given a thorough physical assessment by the home's on-call doctor, including an evaluation of how well her injuries were mending and a complete blood work-up.

A few days later, the doctor called Rudy and asked if they could speak in person. Rudy in turn called me and we met at the doctor's office which was located in a nearby cluster of buildings housing a collection of medical practices including a cardiologist, an ophthalmologist, and a women's clinic.

The doctor, a young Haitian with a French accent, was named Dr. Baptiste. He smiled welcomingly as he motioned for us to sit in a pair of gray metal chairs across from his gray metal desk.

"Thank you for coming in. I could 'ave spoken over the telephone, but we 'ave something to discuss which is, I think, better addressed face-to-face." He opened the folder in front of him and rotated it to face Rudy and me.

"As a matter of routine, we run a comprehensive blood panel when a new patient arrives at Saint D." Dr. Baptiste pointed with the tip of a gold ballpoint pen to several spots on the printout in front of us. "As you can see, Abigail's kidney function is normal, 'er white and red cell count is fine, she tests negative for all venereal diseases... But there is one test which came back positive."

He pronounced this with drawn-out gravity: *Poe-ZEE-teeeeeve.*

I looked at the line item he was indicating with his pen.

hCG: Positive for pregnancy.

Dr. Baptiste sat back and allowed silence to sit heavily in the room as Rudy and I digested the information.

Girl was pregnant.

Girl. Was *pregnant.*

Girl was in a *coma.* And *she was pregnant.*

The facts kept slipping through my brain's fingers like a wet bar of soap. Every time I thought I had a grasp on the situation, the words would just repeat meaninglessly in my head as I hyperventilated and the world went white around the edges.

Girl. Pregnant.

I heard muffled voices like distant thunder, but they held no meaning.

Pregnant. Girl.

"Guy? Did you hear me?" Rudy's voice cut through the fog, echoey and muted like it was on the other side of a wall.

"Girl's pregnant," I mumbled.

Rudy was gently slapping my cheek. His face was inches from mine, locking eyes. "Guy. Did you hear what I said? We have to make some choices here. Together. This is *your* baby we're talking about."

"There is still time," Dr. Baptiste interjected, bringing me back from my fugue state. I blinked rapidly several times and looked around at the utilitarian little office, my gaze finally landing on the doctor's kind face.

"No decision needs to be made today," he said. "Take the week. Talk about it between yourselves. Discuss Abigail's condition with family and clergy. At the end of the day, we want to do what is best for everyone."

Back at Rudy's Glendale house, we spent the evening eating take-away burritos and drinking straight whiskey from collectible jelly jar glasses featuring characters from Archie comics. We were sitting side by side on a maroon sectional couch in the sunken living room.

The radio in the big entertainment console across from us was tuned to KROQ. The DJ, Rodney Bingenheimer—AKA Rodney on the ROQ—was playing "Institutionalized" by Suicidal Tendencies.

Rudy and I had gotten quite close during the month or so that we'd known each other. Shared trauma will do that. We were spending the evening getting buzzed on Jack Daniels while mulling over the options facing us regarding Girl's newly-discovered condition.

Obviously, the primary question was whether to allow the pregnancy to continue. From a purely emotional standpoint, I didn't know whether I was ready to be a single father or not. I was making better money now, but I wasn't even twenty years old. I still felt like a kid myself! I just wanted to have fun!

On the other hand, if Girl was able to make *her*

feelings known, neither of us doubted that she would wholeheartedly embrace the idea of having a baby with me. It would appeal to all of her overly-romantic ideals. Additionally, I missed Girl terribly; Rudy made it clear that he did as well. Even though she was still alive, his daughter wasn't currently *living* among us. The idea of having a part of her back, vital and awake, was undoubtedly appealing.

Then we talked about Danny and Abigail Flores. They had just lost their daughter and granddaughter in one shattering event. Depriving them of a great-grandchild seemed very unfair. Also, they were devout Catholics. If Rudy, on whose shoulders the decision ultimately fell as the guardian of a minor, directed the staff of Saint D to abort the pregnancy, it would absolutely destroy the loving relationship he had built with the Floreses.

But there were also medical issues to consider. Could a coma patient even carry a baby to term? And if she did, what would that baby's delivery look like?

Dr. Baptiste, anticipating that we would have questions, had made himself available to discuss whatever we needed, even outside of office hours.

Rudy reached over beside the sofa and picked up an avocado green telephone which he placed, cord trailing from the wall, next to the liquor bottle on the coffee table in front of us. He dialed the beeper number printed on the business card Dr. Baptiste had provided before we left his office and punched in his own phone number when prompted.

Rudy replaced the receiver in the cradle and we both stared at the phone, waiting for the callback. Rodney was playing "Los Angeles" by the band X.

As Exine Cervenka was singing about finding it hart to say goodbye to her best friend, the phone rang. I stood up, crossed to the stereo, turned the volume knob down until it clicked off, then returned to the couch.

As I sat next to him, Rudy shifted closer to me until our legs were touching and angled the receiver so that it was pointing upward between his ear and mine.

From the earpiece, I heard, "You paged me?" in Dr. Baptiste's melodic accent. He pronounced "paged" with two syllables—*pay-jed*.

"Thank you for calling us back at such an inconvenient hour, Doctor," Rudy said.

"Not at all," the doctor replied, "I'm glad you took me up on my offer to 'elp."

For the next half hour, Rudy and I asked about every aspect of caring for a pregnant coma patient before, during, and after the birth. Dr. Baptiste was the picture of calm confidence as he answered every one of our questions.

We learned that, since Girl was in excellent health (other than the fact of her unconsciousness), there was no reason not to assume that the pregnancy would progress just as successfully as if she was awake. Maybe even better, since she was essentially in a forced state of bedrest. The biggest change to Girl's care would be a modification of her tube feeding regimen to increase certain nutrients and raise the fat content.

When we asked how the actual birth would be carried out, I was surprised to learn that it would probably *not* be a cesarean section.

"While it is certainly rare, there 'ave been several cases of women in Abigail's condition delivering naturally. Labor is a largely automatic process. We will monitor the baby's growth and administer drugs to induce if things don't 'appen on their own and of course we will be prepared to intervene with a C-section if necessary, but as I said—she is a 'ealthy girl."

When we ended the call, Rudy and I looked at each other.

"We're really going to do this, aren't we?" I asked.

"I think we really are." he replied.

He poured us each another stiff drink and we toasted.

"Here's to you, grandpa," I said.

"Back at ya, daddy," Rudy said.

I spent the night in Girl's bedroom, too drunk to drive home. As I lay there smelling Girl's smell on her pillow, I thought about the fact that nobody had mentioned that the baby might not be mine.

For the next nine months time seemed to have no meaning. The hours I wasn't working I spent sitting beside Girl, holding her hand and talking into her impassive face about memories and plans for the future. Sometimes it felt like the days dragged on forever. The weeks, however, seemed to pass in the blink of an eye.

The long days and short weeks turned into months marked by the size of Girl's belly. Before I knew it, I was feeling little kicks against my palm as I talked as much to the baby as I did to Girl. The three of us already felt like a family to me.

Dr. Baptiste had introduced Rudy and me to a middle-aged nun, a former hippy named Sister Gianna who was a trained midwife. The two of them would be monitoring Girl and her unborn child throughout the pregnancy, he explained, and would both be present at the birth.

Sister Gianna had assisted with another comatose birth a couple of years earlier (that patient's car had been T-boned by a truck when she was four months pregnant and the coma medically induced) and so had a pretty clear idea of what to expect in Girl's case.

With my increased income, I had rented an attic apartment over a house in the Los Feliz neighborhood, halfway between my old place in Hollywood and Rudy's Glendale home. It was easily affordable and only a short drive to Saint D in Burbank to the north.

I arrived home one night at eleven-thirty after screening a double feature of *Police Academy 3* and the Mexican action movie *Rosa de la Frontera* in a grindhouse cinema in Boyle Heights. My apartment had its own entrance from the outside of the house, accessed by a steep set of exterior stairs which had clearly been added to the building without the involvement of an architect. As I stood on the rickety landing and unlocked my door, I could see the blinking light on my answering machine through the window.

Entering the apartment, I pushed the "play" button and Rudy's metallic voice came through the little speaker.

"It's go time, *amigo*. Baptiste just called. Abbey's water broke and he's talking about centimeters of cervix dilation and shit. See you at Saint D."

Beep.

I grabbed a slice of leftover pizza from the fridge and dashed back out the door, taking bites as I scurried down the shaky steps to the ground. My old Datsun 210 was parked at the curb. I got in and gunned it toward the freeway.

Twelve minutes later, I pulled into the circular driveway in front of Saint Dymphna's. As I crashed through the front door I was met by Celia, a staff member who I had gotten to know well over the last year.

"They're waiting for you," she said. "Abbey's doing great."

Celia turned and quick-stepped away and I followed her through the hallways to Girl's room.

Inside, the scene was surprisingly calm. Rudy was there, sitting out of the way in a chair near the door. He stood up as I entered and gave me a hug.

Turning my attention to the bed, I saw Sister Gianna, a set of gray scrubs replacing her usual habit and a tie-died cloth surgical cap covering her hair. She was sitting on a low stool at the foot of the bed.

Girl's feet were elevated in stirrups which had been fitted into receiving sockets in the bed frame. Her lower body had been draped in a sheet. The fabric tented between her spread knees blocked my view of her face. A light on a stand had been wheeled into place, illuminating the area where all the action would be happening.

Dr. Baptiste was standing off to one side in a white gown, his arms folded. In the corner behind him I saw a surgical cart, its bulky contents concealed beneath a cloth. Beside it was a pole holding several IV bags of liquid and an oxygen tank fitted with a regulator and mask.

When the doctor saw me, he walked over, peeling off one rubber glove, and shook my hand.

"I'm glad you could make it, Guy," he said in his reassuring tone. "You will soon be meeting your bébé."

"Soon" in this case was somewhat of an exaggeration. For the next three hours we waited while very little happened. Dr. Baptiste stepped out of the room occasionally, presumably to check in on other residents of Saint D or make phone calls. Rudy remained in his seat next to the door, chitchatting with the sister and me while purposefully avoiding looking at his daughter's exposed crotch.

On a low, wheeled table next to the bed sat a bulky gray box. Wires trailing from inputs across its bottom edge disappeared under the sheet. A narrow band of paper scrolled continuously from an opening on the front of the device, pooling in loose folds into a wire basket below. Squiggly lines undulated along this paper's surface. Sister Gianna kept a close eye on these markings, calling out the duration of labor contractions and the time elapsed between them.

"Twenty seconds. Thirteen minutes apart."

More waiting. Smalltalk about the weather and last week's episode of *Knots Landing*.

"Thirty-five seconds. Eight minutes apart."

This continued until, just as the doctor was returning to the room from one of his excursions, Sister Gianna sat up straighter and announced, "Ninety seconds. Three minutes apart."

She stood and started gathering towels into a stack on the end of the bed. She pulled on a pair of rubber gloves and extracted a set of birthing forceps from their sterile paper wrapper.

"It won't be long now, everyone," Doctor Baptiste said to the room at large. He rolled a second low stool up next to the one the sister was sitting on and turned to address me directly. "Sit 'ere, papa. You can cut the umbilical cord."

Sister Gianna held out a paper gown so that I could slide my arms into it. Once it was covering my front, she handed me a pair of rubber gloves, which I donned while she unwrapped another instrument and laid it on the mattress near me. It was a pair of angled scissors with curved blades.

Watching a baby being expressed head-first into the world is amazing. I had seen a video of the procedure in high school health class, but nothing could have prepared me for experiencing it in person.

This particular birth was especially surreal for a couple of reasons: Firstly, it was *my* kid! I was becoming a father! Secondly, the baby was emerging in near silence. No screaming mother. No birthing coach urging her to push or to breathe. Just the wet sounds of the slimy head sliding out of the birth canal.

As the baby's cranium came into view covered in thick black hair, I worried to myself, not for the first time,

"I hope it's mine."

The rest of the head emerged and Sister Gianna took hold of it, gently rotating as tiny shoulders appeared. Then, abruptly—with a gush of fluids that explained all the towels—she was cradling an entire newborn human in her gloved hands. The forceps had not been required.

She shifted the baby's weight onto one forearm with practiced efficiency, freeing the other hand to deal with the umbilical cord. She produced two spring-loaded plastic clamps from somewhere and clipped them onto the cord, a couple of inches apart. She held the isolated segment toward me and I used the scissors I had been given to sever the cord between the clamps with a gristly crunch.

Sister Gianna then grabbed a clean towel, wrapped it around my baby girl and placed her into my arms so that she could deal with the placenta.

Any doubts I had concerning my paternity were instantly dispelled as I looked at my daughter. She had my ears, with the weird little notch on the tops. She had my dimpled chin. And, right before her face crumpled into her first angry cry, I saw my own blue eyes looking back at me.

I stood and carried my squalling bundle across the room to meet her grandfather. Rudy raised himself from his chair, looking dazed and happy. Dr. Baptiste joined us, our heads all bowed to admire the new arrival.

As we stood there, murmuring comforting words into the bawling little face, a high-pitched, scratchy voice cut through the noise.

"What the *FUCK* is going on?"

It was Girl! She was awake!

Dr. Baptiste sprung into action, stepping quickly to the head of the bed and talking soothingly to Girl, "It's okay, Abbey. You're okay."

I turned to watch as Dr. Baptiste pulled the shockingly long feeding tube from Girl's nose while she cried and coughed violently.

"Try to lie still, Abbey," he was saying calmly, "I know this is scary, but you're okay, I promise." He turned to Rudy. "Papa? Come talk to Abbey."

Girl was whimpering—a heart-wrenching keen of pain and confusion. "Everything *huuuuurts!*" she whined.

Girl started shaking her head and tried to pull her knees to her chest. The doctor moved down to gently hold her legs in place in the stirrups, keeping her still while Sister Gianna finished cleaning up after the expulsion of the placenta. Rudy moved to Girl's side and took her hand.

"It's okay, Princess. I've got you. You're alright." I could see tears on Rudy's cheeks.

Girl was crying louder now, but she had stopped thrashing.

"Daddy? What's happening?" Her voice was rough and raw-sounding from disuse and from the abrasive feeding tube. "Where's Mommy? Is she in trouble?" she asked plaintively.

"Mommy's not here, Princess." Rudy was holding Girl's hand and smoothing her forehead with his other palm. "There's somebody else here you'll be happy to see, though."

Rudy beckoned me to join him with a sideways nod of his head. I stepped around the foot of the bed still holding the baby, whose crying was starting to subside to little hitching gasps.

"Hey, beautiful!" I said to Girl, "It's good to see you back."

Girl stopped crying and looked at me blankly. She blinked. Her gorgeous eyebrows pulled together in a scowl of concentration. She looked back at Rudy.

"Daddy? Who's this guy? Why is there a baby here?"

"Girl?" I implored, confused, "It's me!"

She looked back at me. "*Me* who? I've never seen you before. What the fuck is all of this?" I could tell she was starting to panic again, looking around with wide eyes.

Dr. Baptiste weighed in. "It's not unusual to be... Let us say... *Disoriented* after the sort of trauma Abbey 'as experienced." He stepped to the opposite side of the bed and squatted down so that he could address Girl at eye level. He took her hand in his.

"Abbey?" He said, getting her attention. "What is the last thing you remember?"

She knit her brows again, thinking, then looked the doctor in the eye. "I was at the circus with my mother," she said, "Today's my birthday. I'm thirteen."

CHAPTER 24

35 YEARS LATER

"Ladies and gentlemen, please welcome to the Nuart stage the screenwriter of *Origin Story*, Guy Larsen!"

I flinch slightly as loudspeakers on the side walls blast Killing Joke singing about living in the eighties.

I take a deep breath and walk down the aisle from the rear of the cinema. The audience around me applauds politely, the quiet patter of the clapping mostly drowned out by the music.

The Nuart Theater in Los Angeles often hosts question and answer sessions with celebrities to accompany their showings of classic, cult, foreign, and generally older films, but writers are never the most popular guests. Crowds favor those with a more active role in bringing a story to the screen. I'm sure the attendees of tonight's feature would prefer a chance to hear from the movie's controversial director or the woman he cast as the star of the show, Lily Larsen. My daughter.

In the moments after her birth jolted her mother out of the coma, I envisioned myself raising the baby with Girl. I pictured bringing into reality the domestic bliss we imagined in that San Francisco hotel room over Sunday comics and French toast.

Once it became clear that Girl's head injury had erased three years of her memories, however, my plans for a shared future were dashed against the rocks. Just like Girl's skull had been.

In the days following her awakening, Girl refused to have anything to do with me or her daughter. Rudy tried to reason with her. He explained what had happened. He told her who I was. He broke the news of her mother's death. He described how we struggled to make the right decision regarding her pregnancy.

"We didn't know if you'd ever wake up," he told her. "We thought that if you could have spoken… we thought you would have *wanted* to…"

"Well, you were *WRONG!*" she had interrupted him. "I don't know who that dude is and I certainly *don't* remember *fucking* him! It's like I got pregnant from being raped in my sleep and you forced me to *keep* the stupid thing! I don't! Want! His! Baby!"

I was devastated.

Girl was angry with Rudy and she absolutely *hated* me. She blamed both of us for Lily's death and for forcing her to have a baby when she was only (as far as she was concerned) thirteen years old.

To complicate matters, even though Girl was out of the coma, she was far from out of the woods. Her fall from the bridge and subsequent battering as she washed ashore downriver had left her with physical and cognitive impairments in addition to the amnesia.

Her face drooped on one side like a stroke victim. She had no grip strength and both feet pointed down limply when she lifted them. She could only walk with the help of leg braces and a pair of canes that had built-in wrist supports.

She had difficulty identifying everyday objects, referring to an apple as a "big berry" and a window as a "glass hole." She was going to need nearly constant care and assistance with everyday activities—and she adamantly refused to live with Rudy or me.

Danny and Abigail Flores stepped up. They were eager to redeem themselves after the way they had abandoned their daughter during her difficult years. They welcomed Girl into their Beaverton, Oregon home, ready to pay for the necessary physical and speech therapy along with anything else their granddaughter needed. They dedicated themselves to helping Girl regain whatever function was possible.

Meanwhile, I moved into Girl's old room in Rudy's house in Glendale so that we could provide a loving home for the baby that Girl had abandoned. We made the decision to name her after her grandmother, just as Rudy had named his daughter after hers. She was christened Lily.

I had gotten my marriage to Girl annulled once it was clear that we weren't going to have any kind of relationship. Because of this and since it simplified certain paperwork moving forward, the baby was given the last name of Zamora.

From the beginning of her life, I told little Lily about her mother and our brief time together. I wanted her to grow up knowing that she was born out of love.

I left out the more transgressive parts of our story, but when Lily was around two years old I began writing about my relationship with Girl in full detail—drugs, crimes, and all. I thought that maybe I could get Girl to read it at some point, perhaps jump-starting her memory or maybe simply inspiring her to let me—or at least Lily—into her life.

As my written account of what Rudy liked to call our "grand love story" expanded to book length, my newfound enthusiasm for writing inspired me to enroll in community college. I thought I might pursue a career in journalism.

A creative writing professor offered to take a look at my manuscript, tentatively titled *New Wave Romance*. He, in turn, shared it with his partner, who was a reader for a literary agent. One thing led to another and a little over a year later my book—now titled *Origin Story*—got a tiny initial print run through a small independent publisher in Albuquerque.

Rather than calling it a memoir, the decision was made to release the book as a novel with the words "This is a true story" centered on the page between the dedication and the start of the first chapter.

A modest promotional tour followed. After a signing appearance at Powell's Books in Portland, I jumped in my rental car and drove to the Flores home, determined to present Girl with her own copy of the book.

I wrote a note on the flyleaf: *"Maria, I hope you'll let the words on these pages serve as your memory of our time together. Yours forever, —Monty"*

Despite Girl's deliberate estrangement from us and Lily, Danny and Abigail had been providing Rudy and me with regular updates through the years. She could walk without assistance now, we were told, although she still had a noticeable limp. Her speech was still a little slurred, apparently, but cognitively she was more or less normal.

Abigail had home-schooled Girl at first, but now she was enrolled in Beaverton High—albeit in a grade that reflected the age she perceived herself to be. Her diminutive stature helped her to fit in with classmates who were all several years younger than Girl actually was.

From what Danny had told me in a recent conversation, it sounded like Girl was doing well in school. The rebelliousness she had previously exhibited —so clearly exacerbated by her bipolar disorder—was nowhere near as evident as before her brain was scrambled by the mighty Willamette River. She was still on psych meds, but her Portland psychologist had reduced them all to the minimum dosages.

As I rang the Flores' doorbell, I was extremely nervous. It had been almost four years since I'd had any direct contact with Girl and the last time I saw her she basically accused me of rape.

The door opened and there she was. She was so beautiful. Her hair was a jaw-length bob. It was a rich, natural brown with honey-colored highlights framing her face. She was wearing an Ace of Base T-shirt and a teal denim skirt with black leggings underneath.

She stared at me blankly. "Can I help you?" she asked.

I should have known that she wouldn't recognize me. Since she'd seen me last, I had grown a pretentious little beard and long sideburns. I had on a Wu-Tang Clan snapback cap and a plain white tee under a black linen suit jacket and faded blue jeans. I was trying to look like an author.

"Hi, Abbey," I began. I knew from her grandparents that she had no memory of ever calling herself "Girl."

"Do I know—?" she started to ask, a look of wide-eyed innocence on her face. Then, all at once her expression changed. Her luxurious eyebrows dropped into a scowl. Her nose wrinkled and her lower teeth showed above a protruding lower lip. "Oh, it's you! That *Guy* guy! What do *you* want?"

"I just came to give you this." I held the book out facing her. The dust jacket featured the title all in caps, *ORIGIN STORY*, the words stacked one atop the other in a tall serif font, taking up the top two thirds of the cover, white against a sunset gradient. The bottom third had "A Novel by Guy Larsen" in red against a black background. Protruding from the top of this black bar were the silhouettes of a man and a woman on opposite sides of the title. The man was looking back over his shoulder and reaching toward the woman with one outstretched arm as she walked away from him. It was about as generic as a 1990s book cover could get.

She folded her arms and scowled harder. "I don't want it. I don't want *anything* from you."

"But I *wrote* it for you!" I pleaded. "Please? Just read it?"

"No." She slammed the door in my face.

I laid the book on the mat and walked away.

I flew back to Los Angeles. I tried to forget about Girl just like she had forgotten me. I made a concerted effort to stop pining for a future that would never exist.

I threw myself into my writing. I wrote band reviews for the *L.A. Weekly*. I helped a friend who was trying to break into comedy craft his stand-up routine. This led to a gig in the writers' room for a late-night talk show, crafting lame monologue jokes about Bill Clinton and Tonya Harding.

At a club opening in Santa Monica I ran into my old roommate, Sue, whose car I used to borrow and who's panty-smuggled hash I used to smoke. She was a pediatric nurse now. We dated. We got married. We spent a year or so trying to be a happy couple, but Girl was just too big of a presence in my life still. I was co-parenting Girl's daughter along with her father and constantly talking about the reports I was receiving from her grandparents.

When Sue found my stash of nude photos of Girl from our wedding at Termite Terrace, it was the last straw. We had an amicable divorce and went our separate ways.

A little while later, Lily started showing an enthusiasm and talent for performing. She appeared in a couple of school plays and, this being Los Angeles, her teacher encouraged Rudy and me to enroll her in a workshop for child actors. Within a couple of years she had appeared in a number of television commercials and had a small speaking part in a romantic comedy as a Girl Scout who convinces the male lead to buy a box of cookies for the female love interest, setting up the "meet cute."

Capitalizing on his showbiz contacts, Rudy started working as Lily's manager. On his advice, Lily Zamora took my last name, becoming the more lyrical (and less ethnic) Lily Larsen. She shot a couple of TV pilots and one of them got picked up.

If you watched The Disney Channel around the turn of the millennium you no doubt saw her play the plucky best friend of a girl who was secretly a time traveler from the future, getting in wacky misadventures while trying to prevent catastrophic events.

I reach the front of the theater and climb the four wooden steps to the stage where the young woman who introduced me stands clapping and smiling in my direction. Her name is Luella. She's a hip millennial with choppy black bangs and horn-rimmed glasses, wearing ripped jeans and a promotional T-shirt for the *Origin Story* movie. It features the two lead actors in profile, their foreheads touching. They're each blowing a gum bubble and the two pink blobs are squishing together to form a heart. Above their heads the title is scrawled in punky teal handwriting against a black and white checkerboard background. The whole thing is so nineteen-eighties it's sick-making.

Luella is the theater's assistant manager as well as the host for my Q&A. I had first met her earlier in the evening when I arrived at the Nuart. When she unlocked the door and let me in, the smell—popcorn butter with notes of bleach, dust, and sweaty moviegoers—hit me with a wave of nostalgia. I had been an usher at the theater before I worked at the Pussycat and later I had run the projection booth. It had not changed a bit.

Luella introduced me around to the theater staff and briefed me on how the evening would go; she would say a few words before the screening and then, after the closing credits rolled and the lights came up, I would be introduced. Luella would conduct a brief interview to get the conversation started, then I would take questions from audience members who would have a microphone held for them by another Nuart employee.

In the meantime, I was told, I could have whatever snacks I liked on the house. For the next forty-five minutes before the theater opened I stood in the lobby eating Red Vines and making smalltalk with the handful of star-struck employees who had surrounded me. I might be a third-rate celebrity to the general public but to these film fans I was a brush with greatness they would post about on social media. I had to admit the attention felt pretty good.

"I read somewhere that you actually worked here back in the day?" a dapper, bow-tie-sporting young man named Glen asked, touching my arm and gazing at me flirtatiously. I confirmed that I had and that got me started name-dropping eighties celebs who I had met either as guest speakers ("John Waters was a super sweet guy!") or customers ("Daryl Hannah and Jackson Browne came in once *totally* wasted.") while my circle of admirers chuckled adoringly.

A 20-something with four piercings in her nose and both arms completely sleeved in tattoos requested a selfie. We stood in front of a framed poster for *Origin Story* displaying the same graphic that was on Luella's shirt. I saw myself smiling back from the phone screen in her outstretched hand, a lanky, gray-haired Gen X-er in a flannel shirt; the least hip-looking person in the room. When did I get so old and boring?

Eventually the doors were opened and the line of people that had formed outside filed in. I took a seat in the back row of the auditorium and watched as it filled nearly to capacity. *Origin Story* was a popular movie and it had only become more well-regarded in the fifteen or so years since its initial release. It was the feature film debut of a director who had gone on to win consistent accolades for his later body of work.

When Rudy first approached me about adapting my book into a screenplay all those years ago, the iPhone was new, the US was about to elect our first Black president, and Pluto was apparently no longer a planet.

For me, though, one of the most significant events of the late Noughties went unnoticed by most: The pro wrestling personality who performed under the ring name Woman—the inspiration for Girl's nickname—was killed by her wrestler husband in a shocking murder/suicide. For me, this tragic event felt like the universe telling me to forget about Girl once and for all.

I tried. Believe me, I tried.

Rudy, meanwhile, had relinquished his role as Lily's manager to a larger talent agency and accepted an associate producer position at a medium-sized film production company. In this capacity, he had been tasked with finding the right vehicle to showcase the talents of a young upstart director named Clarence Harvey.

Harvey was making waves at festivals around the world with his short films. These shorts, set in underground music clubs and gang-dominated East L.A. neighborhoods, were dramatizations of actual events. His work was funny, violent, street-smart, and romantic—a potent and oh-so-commercial mix that quickly got Hollywood's attention. Harvey was suddenly the industry darling. Every studio in town, it seemed, wanted to throw money into his first feature-length project.

Enter Rudy and *Origin Story*. Rudy got a copy of the book into the hands of Harvey's management team and Harvey read it. And he loved it. The mix of 1980s punk nostalgia, violent crime, and tragic romance, all based on a true story, was exactly what the young director was looking for.

I didn't want anything to do with the project. I was determined to put my time with Girl behind me. For the better part of twenty years I had been torturing myself—hopelessly devoted to a long-lost love I couldn't have.

Nevertheless, Rudy convinced me to take a first pass at the screenplay by invoking the almighty dollar. The film rights to the novel had never been optioned during its short publishing run, so they were still in my hands. Penning the script myself would earn me a double payday, as both the rights holder and the screenwriter.

Everybody involved was thrilled with my work. The production was greenlit. There was just one major obstacle: the ending.

The director, Clarence Harvey, was known for gritty and subversive stories. He loved my dark, depressing finale where the young woman woke from her coma during childbirth only to have no memory of her whirlwind romance and the man who had up to that point been the love of her life. Fade to black. Silent credit roll. Not a dry eye in the house.

The money people, however, said no way. The movie needed to end with a heartwarming reunion; the freshly revived mother who we all thought permanently lost embracing her newborn daughter and her loving man. Happily. Ever. After. Upbeat music over the credits.

Harvey almost pulled out, which would have resulted in the whole project being scrapped. His participation was rescued when the production company negotiated two key factors: Harvey could include (brief) full frontal nudity (male and female) *and* he would have control over the casting of the film.

For the part of Guy, Harvey chose the lead singer of a little-known British post-punk band who had a reputation for whipping his dick out during concerts and who had never acted before. In the role of Girl, Harvey had only one actress in mind: the *real* Girl's own daughter, Lily Larsen.

Since her run on The Disney Channel, Lily had been trying to shake her wholesome child-star image. She auditioned for movie roles but the only things she was offered were the less-pretty comic relief best friend parts—exactly the kind of character she had played for two seasons on *Borrowed Time.* She simply didn't have the height, figure or looks that Hollywood wanted in a leading lady.

She tried her hand at music, recording an EDM album, but it only got to number one hundred eighty-seven on the dance charts and her label gave her no support. Rudy and I put up our own money to shoot a video for the single, but nobody wanted to see Lily Larsen, plucky girl next door, lip syncing on a rooftop surrounded by shirtless male backup dancers.

Giving Lily the part of Girl in *Origin Story* was a genius, career-revitalizing piece of stunt casting. Although the public thought of Lily as an adolescent because of her TV persona and she could still easily pass for mid-teens, she would be nearly twenty-one by the time filming began. This meant that the nudity required for the role wouldn't be breaking any laws even while her squeaky clean image was being definitively shattered.

The advance publicity for the movie had sparked renewed interest in the novel and so a second printing was ordered, this time in paperback. The cover featured a photo of Lily from one of her hair and makeup tests for the film. Except for having my blue eyes, Lily already looked remarkably like her mother. With her hair cut and bleached and wearing brown contact lenses, she matched my written description of Girl in the book to a tee.

I walk to center stage and shake hands with Luella, acknowledging a few straggling bits of applause with a wave as the music is faded out. Two office chairs sit in front of a red velvet curtain. A wireless microphone has been placed on each. A low table between them holds a glass of water.

A resounding *boom* thumps from the speakers as I pick up the microphone. I don't see any stands, so I guess I'll be holding it while I talk.

I sit in one chair and Luella takes her place in the other. I look out toward the rows of seats. The house lights are up but spotlights on the ceiling prevent me from getting a good view of the audience. I shade my eyes with a hand and scan the faces peering back at me to see what kind of viewers this movie still attracts in the twenty-twenties.

The crowd is an eclectic collection of L.A. film buffs. I see a number of hipster beards and couple of porkpie hats. There are the Beverly Hills types; men in expensive jackets over retro tees, women with designer handbags on their laps and chunky necklaces. I spot a few aging punk rockers, their sleeveless shirts showing off leathery tattoos. At one end of the front row, a fifty-ish Mexican-looking woman with bright red lipstick is slumped low in her seat wearing sunglasses and a floppy-brimmed hat like a movie star who doesn't want to be recognized. I'm sure she's someone, but I can't place her. The rest of the front row is taken up by a group of Asian teens dressed like characters from the film, their meticulous cosplay impressively precise.

"Thank you for joining us tonight, Mr. Larsen,"

Luella says into her microphone. Her amplified voice pulls my attention away from my people-watching.

I turn to face her. I hold the mic to my mouth. "Guy. Please." Feedback drowns me out. I pull my hand away from my face slightly and repeat, "Guy."

"Guy. Gotcha. So, Guy, before I open up questions to the audience, why don't you tell us a little bit about the...well...origin..." (polite chuckle from the attendees) "...of *Origin Story*. I understand it's inspired by your actual experiences?" She looks at me with a wide-eyed stage smile, playing to the back of the house. She's very good at this.

I'm nowhere near as comfortable with public speaking as my host is.

"Yeah, that's true," I say, forgetting to talk into the microphone. Luella nods toward it and I put it back to my lips. "Yeah, I mean...um... Some...um...liberties were certainly taken for, like, dramatic purposes, but yeah. I'm the 'Guy' in the movie, more or less. And 'Girl' is... was... is..." I falter, "Um...a real person."

"And, in case any of you didn't realize this," Luella looks at the audience and gestures toward me, "Lily Larsen, the star of the movie, is actually Guy Larsen's *daughter!*"

A gentle murmur travels through the room as the few people who haven't made this connection catch on.

"Yup," I confirm, "I'm Lily's dad."

"And that of course means that Ms Larsen's mother..." Luella pauses for effect, "Is Girl! She was playing her *own mother!*"

Again, the audience members not old enough to have had all of these facts drummed into them *ad nauseam* during the film's initial release mutter their surprise.

Luella turns back to me. "Are you still in touch with Girl?"

"No, I'm afraid not," I say. "I... I actually have no idea where she is now."

A few weeks after Girl's graduation from Beaverton High School, Danny Flores died in his sleep from a pulmonary embolism. It was not long after my divorce from Sue and I had moved back in with Rudy temporarily while I looked for a new place of my own. When Abigail phoned with the news, I took the call.

Rudy immediately booked a flight to Portland for the three of us—Rudy, Lily, and me—to attend the funeral, lend Abigail emotional support, and help get Danny's affairs in order.

We arrived at the Flores home on a Friday afternoon. The funeral was going to be the following day at the Flores' church.

I parked our rental car in the driveway and we

walked to the door, Lily holding my hand. I was nervous to see Girl. Abigail hadn't said how she was reacting to her grandfather's death, but I hoped that it might be the impetus for her opening her heart to, if not me, at least her daughter.

Lily was six years old and she'd still never met her mother. Danny and Abigail, however, had visited us in Glendale when Lily was four and she'd been speaking to them on the phone since she was old enough to talk. She called them "Tata" and "Tita."

Before we could ring the bell, the door opened and Abigail stepped out crying. She pulled the three of us into a hug.

"Oh, niños! She's gone! Abbey is gone!" She sobbed.

Rudy put his hands on Abigail's shoulders and held her at arm's length. "What do you mean, she's gone?" he asked with a tinge of panic in his voice. It was the same wording she had used to inform us of her husband's passing: *Danny is gone.* With Girl's past history, I was picturing suicide and I was sure Rudy was too.

"Last night I told *Abesita* that you three were coming. She said a very unkind profanity to me and stomped away to her room and slammed the door."

As she spoke, Abigail motioned for us to follow and we trailed her inside. We all took seats in the immaculate front sitting room where we had gathered the last time a family member had died. Abigail sat on the loveseat where she and Danny had received the news of her daughter's fall from the Sellwood Bridge. Rudy and I took our familiar spots on the sofa. Lily sat on my lap.

Abigail resumed her story.

"A few of the ladies from the church came by last night with food. I made Abbey a plate and spoke to her through the door, but she didn't answer. I left the plate on the floor outside her room and told her to eat something and she'd feel better. The women stayed and we talked on the patio until after dark. When I went to bed the plate was still in the hallway. It was still there this morning, so I knocked and opened her door. Her bed was empty. I called her name through the whole house but she wasn't here."

Abigail stood and took a few steps out of the room, grabbing something from around the corner, then continued speaking. "On the kitchen table I found this." She dropped what she had retrieved onto the coffee table between us.

It was the copy of *Origin Story* I had placed on Girl's doormat a few years ago. It no longer looked new. It had clearly been read and read again. The dust jacket was worn around the margins. The book's edges were smudged with fingerprints. There were points marked with dog-eared pages throughout.

On the novel's cover was a Post-it note on which Girl had written, *"I can't. I'm sorry. Don't hate me. —A"*

We soon discovered that Danny's car was gone. We alerted the police, but we were informed that this didn't qualify as a missing person case, even though Girl was technically missing. Girl was an adult; if she wanted to leave, there was nothing we could do to stop her. The only way we could get any help from the police at all was to report the car as stolen.

We did so and it was located a few days later in the long-term parking lot at Portland International Airport with a different car's license plates on it.

It was pre-9/11. Relatively anonymous air travel was still possible. A passport wasn't even necessary for an American citizen to visit Canada. More importantly, Americans didn't need a passport to get into Mexico, either, and Girl had become fluent in Spanish since she'd been living with her grandparents.

Rudy and I paid a private detective agency for two months of investigative work. They discovered that Girl had withdrawn the contents of her college savings account the day she disappeared, but other than that they came up completely empty-handed.

Girl was gone.

Luella asks me about *Origin Story's* critical reception. We discuss the fact that the film was completely snubbed at the Oscars and the Golden Globes, but that it received two BAFTA nominations in the UK: Best Actor in a Leading Role for Stuart Carter-Jones, the English rocker who played Guy, and Best Adapted Screenplay for yours truly. Neither of us won.

The only accolade the movie *did* receive was Best Kiss at the MTV Movie Awards for the nude wedding kiss which included a (prosthetic) semi-erect penis silhouetted against the setting sun. Lily and Stuart accepted the award and as they reenacted the kiss for the live audience (fully clothed this time), Charlie Sheen held a black censorship bar in front of Stuart's crotch.

My telling of this story gets a nice round of laughter in the theater.

Luella announces that it's now time for the Nuart audience to ask any questions they might have for me. I ask if the stage lights can be lowered a little so I can see who's speaking. Luella looks up at the projection booth and makes a throat-cutting gesture. The spotlights in the ceiling dim and then go completely dark.

The assembled moviegoers, previously only visible as vague shadows, suddenly seem very bright and very close.

"Oh! Hi there!" I say, eliciting more laughter.

"Raise your hand if you have a question and Glen will bring you the microphone," Luella tells the crowd.

One of the cosplayers in the front row puts up a hand. Glen jogs down the aisle and drops theatrically to one knee in front of her, the elbow of his mic hand propped on his thigh and his other hand on his hip. He shoots a toothy grin in my direction and I give him a little thumbs up.

The young woman, wearing a duplicate of Girl's mother's grocery store uniform from the bridge scene, leans forward and asks, "How did you feel about seeing your daughter nude? My dad would lose his shit!"

"Yeah, that was weird at first, but—you know... It's just acting, right? Besides, I wasn't on set when they were shooting any of those scenes. *That* would have felt... I mean... Just—no." I shake my head, covering my eyes, and the audience chuckles. "I didn't even view dailies of that stuff. By the time I saw the finished movie, I was, like, emotionally invested in the character she was playing, so it didn't really feel like *her,* exactly, if that makes sense...?"

The girl smiles. "Yeah, sick. Thanks."

Glen stands and scans the room for raised hands, trotting back up the aisle to the rear of the auditorium for the next question which has to do with Lily LaFleur and whether Lily Larsen would consider doing a remake of one of her grandmother's films.

As the evening progresses I get more and more comfortable answering what turn out to be pretty interesting queries on a wide variety of topics—from the songs chosen for the soundtrack to the decision to change the ending from the book.

Glen bounces around holding the microphone for one person then another. I'm at my most charming and funny and the audience seems to like me, laughing at the right places and occasionally applauding politely following an anecdote.

After about forty-five minutes of back and forth, Luella breaks in to inform the room, "Okay, folks. We have time for one more question."

The mysterious Mexican movie star in the front row holds her hand up and Glen makes his way over, sitting in the empty seat beside her and holding the mic in her direction.

The woman removes her hat, revealing ebony hair with white strands throughout. One piece in the front is dyed pink. She removes her oversized sunglasses. Her eyebrows are lush and full. Her dark brown eyes gaze into my soul.

"Are you still in love with Girl?" the woman asks. Her voice is at once immediately familiar and wholly new. She's acquired a slight accent since last we spoke.

I look deep into her eyes. Eyes that I haven't seen in so many years. Eyes that are looking at me with a softness I never thought I'd experience again.

I stare so long that the audience starts to get uncomfortable. Somebody coughs.

I pull myself together and, my eyes still locked with

hers, I play to the crowd, saying, "Of course. You never get over your first attempted murder."

The audience laughs.

Luella laughs.

The woman who asked the question is trying *not* to laugh, but then the corners of her mouth pull up and her full lips part, showing the gap between her front teeth. She lets go of decades-old resentment and gives in to the moment.

"KEE-HEE-GHEE-EE-H-KEE-GH-HEE-HICK-KEE!!"

Acknowledgements

A lot of the places, people, and events in this book were based *very* loosely on real-world counterparts. I want to thank everybody who made the 1980s as radical, righteous, and sometimes grody as they were.

Thank you, also, to all of my early readers, including Karla, Natalie, Tom, Paul, and especially to my editor Jordan. Each of you had a big hand in shaping this book.

My biggest thanks, though, are reserved for you —the reader who took a chance on an unknown author, dropped your money, and spent some precious time allowing me tell you a story. I love you like Guy loves Girl.

ABOUT THE AUTHOR

Marky Watson

Marky Watson has written music reviews for free weeklies as well as scripting animated children's television and sketch comedy. This is his debut novel.

An accomplished visual artist and actor, Marky lives in Tucson, Arizona with his wife and an indeterminate number of cats.